First Edition.

Published May of 2024
by Indies United Publishing House

Edited by Jennie Rosenblum – www.jenniereads.com
Cover design by Vila Design – www.viladesign.net

ISBN: 978-1-64456-684-8 [Hardcover]
ISBN: 978-1-64456-685-5 [Paperback]
ISBN: 978-1-64456-686-2 [Mobi]
ISBN: 978-1-64456-687-9 [ePub]

Library of Congress Control Number: 2023949423

Join Author Robert J. Emery online at:
http://www.robertjemeryauthor.com

INDIES UNITED PUBLISHING HOUSE, LLC
P.O. BOX 3071
QUINCY, IL 62305-3071
IndiesUnited.net

Megastar

A Novel by
R.J. Eastwood

The phenomenal rise of singer Addison Stone led to fame and fortune.
It was everything one man could have hoped for in a lifetime…
except for the woman he loved.

"What we call the beginning is often the end. And to make an end is to make a beginning. The end is where we start from."

T.E. Lawrence, a British essayist,
playwright, literary, and social critic poet.

The year is wherever your imagination takes you.

Chapter 1

The Dolby Theater, Hollywood, California

There is not an empty seat in the house. The auditorium is packed with the whose-who of the entertainment industry for the annual *Entertainer of the Year Awards*. The stage is bare except for a blue curtain backdrop, a large elevated television screen, and a podium, on which sits a gold statuette of a male figure with its hands outstretched in a welcoming manner.

A man dressed in a tuxedo enters from stage right and approaches the podium. The applause is polite but reserved; few outside the music business know who he is.

"Good evening, ladies and gentlemen. My name is Jonathan James." He speaks with the remnants of a British accent. "Since I have spent much of my adult life with tonight's honoree, I have the honor of presenting the Outstanding Entertainer Award in the music category. Over the years, there have been endless stories about this gentleman. I caution you not to believe everything you read or hear because much of it remains unconfirmed myth spread by—" James pauses—he's thinking. "Hmm, come to think of it, every last bit is true."

The audience roars with laughter.

"Before I get myself into trouble, let us watch the life and times of an extraordinary entertainer revered as one of our time's greatest singers and entertainers."

The theater goes dark. The elevated television screen comes alive. A handsome young man is making his public singing debut before a packed live audience on the hit TV series *Sing America Sing,* followed by a montage of his phenomenal rise to fame and fortune.

The video ends, the house lights come on, and the audience responds with thunderous applause.

"Ladies and gentlemen, I am pleased to present the Outstanding Musical Entertainer Award to my dear friend and boss, Addison Jordon Stone."

The audience is on their feet with applause, hoots, hollers, and whistles as a frail-looking Addison Stone is rolled to the podium in a wheelchair. James helps him to his feet. The two men briefly hug.

Addison places his hands on each side of the podium to steady himself. James hands Addison the gold statuette.

"Boss, you couldn't have done it without me."

Addison turns to the audience, "You see what I've had to contend with all these years? Pure English arrogance."

More laughter and applause.

Addison raises the award above his head. "Quite a handsome fellow he is." He sets the award on the podium, reaches into his jacket pocket, retrieves his notes, and begins his acceptance speech.

Honolulu, Hawaii

Two days later, Addison and JJ, as Addison calls him, were

back home at Addison's Honolulu waterfront estate.

Thirty-seven-year-old Addison, looking older than his years, was guided in his wheelchair by JJ across the living room's rich Brazilian cherry wood floor. JJ, an Englishman by birth, has been a fixture at Addison's side for eighteen years. He is fit and trim, six feet tall, with an angular, square-jawed face, light brown hair, and eyes.

Addison's complexion is a pale gray; dark circles cast shadows below his eyes. His once thick, wavy, dark brown hair has thinned and turned flour-white around his temples.

A full-grown Golden Retriever followed a few steps behind, a present from an anonymous fan when the dog was just a puppy. Addison named the pup *Windy* after the calm Hawaiian Pacific Ocean breezes.

As they passed the floor-to-ceiling stone fireplace, Addison eyed the mantle. He smiled pridefully at the *Outstanding Entertainer of the Year Award* statuette prominently displayed in the middle of the mantle and surrounded on either side by other awards he has received over the years.

"Looks good there, JJ."

"Yes, sir, it certainly does."

"Thank goodness for makeup," Addison sighed, "or I would have looked like they brought me back from the grave just for the awards ceremony."

They exited the French doors to the large patio overlooking Addison's estate on the North West Coast of Honolulu. It is a cloudless, sun-splashed morning. A gentle westerly breeze sways the fronds of the Palm trees that border either side of the velvety Shamrock-green lawn that rolls past the swimming pool to the white sandy beach of the azure Pacific Ocean.

JJ eased Addison into his rocking chair. Windy settles in his usual spot on the Koa wood deck to Addison's right.

"Might there be anything I can get you? Coffee, perhaps?"

"No thanks, JJ."

"You're due to take your medication in half an hour."

"Oh, yummy, I can hardly wait. Why do these doctors keep

feeding me all those pills when they know I'm bloody well near rocketing off the planet for good?"

"Don't say that, sir. The medications are to provide you more time."

"Mumbo jumbo bullshit, JJ. More time for what?"

JJ grinned. "If you require anything, I'll be inside."

Addison snickered. "Lurking like you always do if I choke while sucking my thumb."

JJ chuckled low. "You're trying to get a rise out of me. I never lurk."

"I've seen you peeking out the shutters over there. That's lurking."

JJ raised an eyebrow. "Will that be all?"

"How long have we been together?"

"Eighteen years, sir."

"It took forever to get you to stop calling me sir or Mr. Stone. Now, we need to work on your wardrobe."

"I beg your pardon?"

"All these years, black suit, tie, shoes, and socks. You look like the Grim Reaper, for God's sake. Get yourself chinos or jeans, colorful shirts, and decent sneakers. If you haven't noticed, it's Hawaii."

"If you say so." JJ smiled, nodded, and began to leave. "I'll be in the study if you need me."

"And no more lurking, JJ."

"I promise, sir."

"May I remind you, *Sir JJ*, that a promise is only good if you keep it?"

"Yes, of course."

"Before you go, would you bring me the award? I want to sit here and hug it."

"Certainly, Mr. Stone."

When JJ was out of sight, Addison reached down and patted Windy. "You watch, Windy; JJ won't change how he dresses. I might as well be talking to myself like I'm doing now."

Windy looked at Addison as if he understood every word.

JJ returned with the Entertainer of the Year Award and placed it on the end table to Addison's left. "Be gentle with it, sir." He smiled and left.

Addison carefully lifted the golden statue, set it in his lap, covered it with his hands, and began to rock back and forth. The months of pernicious radiation, chemotherapy, and medications had taken their toll. He could no longer do the simplest things without JJ's assistance, which disturbed him terribly. But behind the timeworn, weathered face, it was still Addison Stone, the once-charismatic idol of millions. No entertainer was more revered and loved for his extraordinary and unique talent.

"Windy, Windy, how did we get from the floor of Chick's Diner to here?" Addison's head bobbed back, and he laughed. "How the hell, indeed? It's been a hell of a ride, I'll tell you, bumps and all, and there were plenty of those. When I'm gone, the name Addison Stone will be lost to history, and no one will remember how big a star I was."

Closing his eyes, Addison continued to rock and began humming a tune he knew well—*Your Love,* from the 1968 cult western *Once Upon a Time in the West.*

Chapter 2

The hamlet of Addison, Alabama, population 697, was a ten-minute drive down Route 278 to the 181,230-acre Willard B. Bankhead National Forest. The town prospered handsomely by catering to the needs of day trippers and campers seeking food and camping supplies before venturing into the prodigious Forest.

One dark, cloudy afternoon, a middle-aged couple and a young blond child moved into the small, two-bedroom furnished house next door to retired railroad engineer Ben Dickey. Ben was five feet seven in his stocking feet on a lean—some would say skinny—frame. His eyes matched a head of thinning brown hair.

Once settled in, the new family kept to themselves. They made no effort to befriend anyone, including Ben, whose house was fifteen feet away, leaving Ben to wonder why. He observed the man leaving before sunrise and returning after sunset several times. The woman, slightly plump with a round face and graying hair, left with the pretty young blond girl each morning, returned home alone, then left again in the afternoon, returning with the child. Ben assumed they were going to and from nearby Addison

Elementary.

On several occasions, Ben waved when he was outside and saw the man or the woman coming or going. He barely received a nod in return. He never saw the young girl playing in their yard.

One afternoon, as they returned home from school, Ben heard the woman loudly scolding the child but could not make out what she was saying. Ten minutes later, the woman left with her arms wrapped around two large pottery pieces. Minutes later, the child appeared at the door clutching a curly-haired blond doll tightly to her chest. She looked around to be sure the woman was gone, walked out, and sat on the lawn.

Ben watched her from his kitchen window. He was not sure, but he thought she might be crying. It concerned him enough that he decided to introduce himself. Outside his door, he observed the child for several moments before approaching her. He walked with a noticeable limp on his left side.

"Hi there."

The child did not look up or acknowledge Ben.

"I saw you sitting there and thought it was time I introduced myself."

The girl turned away and wiped at her eyes. "You're the man next door."

"Yeah. My name is Ben, Ben Dickey. What's yours?"

Without turning to him, the girl answered, "Lacy, Lacy Stone."

"Well, Lacy, it's nice to meet you. Welcome to the neighborhood. Who's your pretty friend?"

Lacy pulled the doll tightly to her chest. "Jane."

"Jane. I like that name."

"It's my middle name."

"I have a middle name, too. It's Randolph." Then, joking, he added, "Do I call you Lacy or Jane?"

Lacy turned to him and, with a straight face, said, "Do I call you Ben or Randolph?"

"Ha, good one. How old are you, Lacy?"

"Six going on seven. I'm in the first grade."

"Six is a great age."

"Is it better than seven?"

"You'll know soon enough, Lacy. I saw your mom leave a few minutes ago with some pottery pieces."

"Thelma makes them. The grocery store sells them for her."

"Hmm. And your dad? What does he do?"

"Wilbur got a job driving a truck for a delivery company in Cullum. That's why we moved here from Tennessee." Her gaze strayed again.

Ben took a step closer. "Don't mean to be nosy, but you looked like you might have been crying."

"You saw me crying?"

Ben shrugged his shoulders. "I thought I did."

Lacy took a deep breath, and her brow furrowed. "Thelma was on me again."

"Why?"

"My teacher told her I wouldn't participate in school activities with the other kids. Thelma threatened to ground me if I didn't."

Ben thought it odd that Lacy called her parents by their first names. "Hmm. Is there a reason you won't participate in school activities, Lacy?"

"I like being by myself. Is that such a big deal? Why can't people leave me alone? Why do I have to be like everyone else?"

Ben took another step closer. "Mind if I sit?"

Lacy shrugged again.

Ben sat on the grass next to her. There was an uncomfortable silence between them for several moments. Lacy's eyes teared up again, and she turned away.

"What's wrong, Lacy?"

"Nothing'."

"People don't cry for nothing. They're either happy or sad."

Lacy took a deep breath and exhaled slowly. "Thelma, Wilbur—" she paused and wiped at her eyes, "they're not my parents."

"Oh? Where are your parents?"

"They died when I was two. I have a picture of them in my room, but I don't remember them."

"I'm so very sorry, Lacy."

"Thelma told me they overdosed—that's the word she used—they overdosed from heroin."

Ben had no idea how to respond to that, so he didn't.

"You know what heroin is, Ben?"

"Yes, I do, Lacy. It can be very dangerous."

"Yeah." Lacy went silent for a few beats. "I'm the only one in my class without real parents. Some of the kids tease me about it."

"That's terrible, Lacy. Just ignore them."

"I try most of the time, but they really upset me."

"Who are Thema and Wilbur?"

"My father's parents. They adopted me after my parents died—I mean, *overdosed.* You have parents, Ben?"

"Mine are gone too, Lacy."

"How come you're the only one I see going in and out of your house? You live alone?"

"I do. My wife passed away from an illness when she was very young."

"Oh, sorry, Ben. You have kids?"

"I don't, Lacy."

Lacy's face splayed into a mischievous grin. "That makes you and me orphans."

Ben chuckled. "Well, ah, I guess you could say that."

Lacy laughed softly. "Ben and Lacy, next door orphans. You're always home, Ben. Don't you work?"

"I was a railroad engineer for many years, but I slipped and fell getting down from a locomotive, hurt my left hip pretty bad, and was forced to retire."

"What do retired people do all day?"

"Hmm, good question. I read books, watch TV, and sing in the Cullum Baptist Church choir. We rehearse on Saturdays and sing to the congregation on Sunday."

"Wow, a singer. Are you any good?"

Been smiled. "That's for others to decide."

Lacy turned pensive and looked away again.

"What is it, Lacy? What's bothering you?"

Lacy hesitated, looked at Ben briefly, then turned away and said softly, "Wilbur and Thema drink a lot and sometimes take drugs. When they do, they get into terrible arguments and threaten one another, and sometimes me too. Last week, I saw Wilbur slap Thelma. She cried and threatened to leave. When that stuff happens, it scares me. I lock myself in my room until they stop."

Ben found it surprising that Lacy was so open with someone she had just met. *Wow*, he thought, *this child must be hurting badly inside to share intimate details about what was going on in that house with someone she had just met. Let her know that you're aware.* "Yeah, Lacy, our houses are pretty close. I heard them arguing several times and wondered what was happening there."

"Oh, so you know?"

"Just that I hear them sometimes."

Lacy's eyes strayed, and she turned pensive again. Without turning to Ben, she said just above a whisper, "Ah, Ben, I know we just met, but you seem like a nice man."

"Thank you, Lacy. You seem nice, too."

"Am, Ben…you think maybe we could be friends?"

"Why not, Lacy? I'd like that very much." He extended his open right hand. "Let's shake on it."

With a broad smile, Lacy turned to Ben and shook his hand vigorously. "Can we keep our friendship a secret?"

"Ah, sure, if that's what you want, Lacy, no problem."

"Okay then, Ben, we're officially secret friends."

On that warm, sunny afternoon, the two orphans hit it off so well that Lacy began calling her new friend Uncle Ben. She needed someone to talk to, and Ben proved to be an excellent listener.

As the years passed and Ben and Lacy grew closer, he began to see how Wilbur and Thelma's drinking and drug use had severely affected Lacy emotionally. She was often withdrawn, sullen, and solitary. But Ben could do nothing about it but be there for her when she needed someone to listen.

One day, shortly after Lacy turned twelve, she and Ben sat on the lawn while Thelma was off delivering pottery pieces to the grocery store. Lacy rolled up her sleeve and showed Ben a bruise about the size of a tennis ball on the underside of her right arm below her elbow.

"How'd you get that, Lacy?"

"Thelma hit me with her hairbrush, and it's not the first time either."

"Why did she hit you?"

"I have no idea, Ben, but that happens when either or both are high on booze or drugs."

"Lacy, why didn't you tell me?"

"I don't want to start trouble by getting you involved."

Ben was outraged and considered reporting Thelma and Wilbur to Family Services. But he feared they would place Lacy in foster care, and he couldn't live with that, so he chose to do nothing. If it happened again, he vowed to step in. He'd cross that bridge if and when it became necessary.

"Lacy, promise me if either of them lays a hand on you again, you'll tell me."

"Yeah, okay, Ben."

On Lacy's seventeenth birthday, tragedy struck the Stone household. After imbibing one too many Bloody Marys at lunch, Wilbur lost control of his delivery truck, drove off the B. B. Comer Bridge in Scottsboro, crashed into the Tennessee River below, and was killed upon impact. There was no formal funeral, just a cremation attended by Thelma and Lacy, two of Wilbur's fellow truck drivers, and the funeral home staff.

Thelma cried; Lacy stood silent, displaying no emotion.

What little life insurance Wilbur had barely covered the cost of cremation. Thelma's pottery-making was hardly a thriving business; she had to find steady work. The grocery store owner mentioned the young day shift waitress at Chick Dempsey's Diner was leaving to attend college; Thelma applied for and got the job.

Thelma, already a bitter woman, became more so over being left to look after her granddaughter alone. She would often take out her anger and frustration on Lacy while on one of her frequent drinking binges, which only added to Lacy's mounting emotional scars.

Lacy graduated from high school when she was eighteen with the fifth-lowest academic score in her class. She was never popular; her classmates considered her odd and unapproachable. Despite her attractive features, her social life was nonexistent, nor did she care.

The day after Lacy's graduation, Thelma confronted her. "What are your plans now?"

Lacy retorted, "Are you serious, Thelma? I just graduated. I have no idea what I want to do."

"Well, it's either college or a job, and your grades won't get you into college. There's no money for that anyway, so you're left with one option: get a job because, dear granddaughter, we need the money."

"Get a job doing what?"

"Whatever; hit the pavement and start looking."

One month later, tragedy struck the Stone household yet again. Thelma, who suffered from an irregular heartbeat, had a massive heart attack and died on the floor of Chick's Diner. Because Lacy could not cover the cost of Thelma's cremation, Ben loaned her the funds. Lacy received a canister of Thelma's ashes. "Want them, Ben?"

"Me? Why would I want them?"

Lacy laughed. "That's what I thought." She promptly flushed

Thelma's ashes down the toilet.

In Alabama, a minor is younger than nineteen unless legally emancipated; Lacy was about to become a ward of the State. Ben was not about to let that happen. He retained an attorney in nearby Cullum and petitioned the State to become Lacy's legal guardian. He would assist her financially until she turned nineteen. The State granted Ben's request; he was officially Lacy's legal guardian.

Chick offered Lacy Thelma's job, which she accepted. With Ben's assistance, waitressing would keep her financially stable.

Chapter 3

One of life's unexpected turns was about to impact the rest of Lacy's.

Twenty-seven-year-old Johnny Paloma, a trained short-order cook, was traveling the backroads to Points East in his three-year-old black Dodge Charger with its shiny red leather seats. Passing through Addison, he stopped at Chicks for a quick lunch. As fate would have it, as Johnny entered the diner, he overhead Chick and the cook having a loud conversation in the kitchen.

"Jack, I don't have a replacement for you yet," Chick argued.

"You'll find one."

"But, Jack—"

"No buts, Chick. I'm 73, tired, and retiring. No more cooking for me except for my wife and me."

With no job lined up back East, a short stint in Addison would help to replenish his dwindling cash. Johnny quickly seized the moment. He introduced himself to Chick and told him he had overheard the conversation with the cook and was a trained short-order cook looking for work.

"My resume is in the car. Interested?"

"Ah, maybe. I'll take a look."

"Thanks, I'll be right back."

When Johnny returned, he handed Chick his resume. Chick looked it over and raised an eyebrow.

"Hmm, impressive, but you seemed to have moved around a lot."

"Yeah, I have. I decided if I didn't see the country when I was young, I might never."

"I'm happy for you, young man, but I don't need you leaving after a few months because you're itching to see more of the country."

Johnny lied through his teeth. "No, no, Mr. Dempsey. I've been looking for a place to settle. Before stopping here, I drove around this lovely little town and liked what I saw. I want to settle down, and Addison fits the bill."

Chick remained hesitant. "The question remains, for how long?"

"For as long as you'll have me," Johnny grinned. "I'll meet some pretty young lady here, get married, have kids, and happily spend the rest of my life here in lovely Addison."

Desperate to replace the retiring cook, Chick bought Johnny's story and hired him. He told Johnny about a small apartment nearby that was for rent. Johnny checked it out, liked it, moved in that day, and began working at Chick's the following morning.

In high school, Lacy had only dated two boys briefly. Her off-the-wall personality and stand-offish disposition—sometimes her arrogance—drove the boys away.

But this time, it was different for Lacy. Johnny Paloma was handsome, easy-going, and likable, and he considered himself a ladies' man. Lacy had blossomed into an enchanting young lady, which did not go unnoticed by Johnny. He wasted little time circling her like a wolf on the hunt. Lacy enjoyed the attention, and there was no denying Johnny's appeal, worldly ways, and charm. She was captivated by him.

When Lacy shared with Ben the attention Johnny was

showing her, his advice was swift and to the point.

"Lacy, stay the hell away from the Johnnys of this world. Chick told me he's a drifter and suspects he'll move on to greener pastures one day."

"Keep your britches on, Ben. I have no interest in him in *that* way. He amuses me, that's all."

"Yeah, well, don't be too amused. You're still underage and —"

"I got it, Ben; you made your point. Drop it already."

Ben was concerned that Lacy remained emotionally scarred from the childhood abuse she received from her grandparents. She was vulnerable, and the attention she received from Johnny Paloma could be a problem.

On Lacy's nineteenth birthday, Chick came out of the kitchen carrying a cake with nineteen glowing candles.

Lacy was speechless. Her hands went to her mouth. "Oh, my!

The noontime diners joined in singing *Happy Birthday*.

"Blow them out," Chick said.

Lacy blew out the candles, and Chick set the cake on a table.

"Cake for everyone," Johnny announced, then hugged Lacy.

That evening, Ben took Lacy to a fancy steakhouse in Cullum.

"Well, young lady, today you're legally an adult."

Lacy laughed. "Whatever the heck that means, Ben."

"Translation; welcome to the rat race." He removed a small box from his jacket and slid it across the table. "Happy birthday, kiddo. May you enjoy many more."

Inside the box was a whimsical gold charm bracelet boasting a stylish shoe, hearts, a wishbone, flower, lock, and key charms highlighted with shimmering crystals and cultured freshwater pearls.

"Oh, Ben, it's beautiful, thank you. I love you."

"I love you too, Lacy."

"You've been my savior, Ben. I can never thank you

enough."

"You're the daughter I never had, Lacy. There isn't anything I wouldn't do for you."

Lacy stood, went around the table, wrapped her arms around Ben's shoulders, and kissed him on the cheek.

The following day, Johnny approached Lacy. "Hey, birthday girl, how about I take you for a belated birthday dinner tonight? I know a great little Asian place in Cullum."

"Oh, I don't know, Johnny," Lacy answered shyly.

"Why not? It'll be fun. Come on, say yes."

Despite Ben's warning, Johnny was the charmer. Although hesitant at first, Lacy finally accepted.

Over dinner in Cullum that evening, Johnny entertained Lacy with stories of his expansive travels.

"One day, I hope to travel as you have, Johnny."

"There's a lot of this country to see, Lacy. Don't waste time; visit as many places as you can."

On their return trip home, Johnny unexpectedly took a detour into a wooded area a couple of miles outside Addison.

"Where're you going?" Lacy asked.

Johnny pulled over in a wooded area under tall trees and turned off the engine. He retrieved a zip lock bag from the glove compartment and held it up. "A little dessert to celebrate your birthday."

The white powder in the bag looked like the cocaine Lacy and Ben had found when cleaning a dresser drawer in Thelma's bedroom following her death.

Lacy's eyes grew big, and she shook her head. "No, thank you."

"Come on, Lacy, everybody does it."

"I'm not everybody."

Johnny shrugged and snorted a small amount of the powder. "Come on, just try a little."

"I said no."

But Johnny persisted. "A small amount, just so you know

what you're missing."

Despite her parents and grandparents' addiction, Lacy gave in, believing that a small amount would be safe and Johnny would stop badgering her. But what exactly was a small amount? Within a few minutes, the drug was in her bloodstream, and a pleasant euphoria and a sense of relaxation came over her like nothing she had experienced.

Johnny leaned close to Lacy and whispered in her ear. "There, you see, good stuff, just like I told you." He placed his hands on her shoulders, pulled her to him, and kissed her. Lacy drew back, but Johnny persisted and kissed her again. Lacy did not object this time, allowing her suppressed desires to take over. Minutes later, throwing caution to the wind, Lacy lost her innocence to Johnny Paloma in the backseat of his Dodge Charger on its shiny red leather seats.

The day came that would change Lacy's life forever; she missed her period. Panicked, she purchased a home pregnancy test that confirmed her worst fears; It struck her like a tornado. She cried for three nights before working up the courage to confront Johnny. He assured Lacy they would work it out together, whatever that meant.

When Lacy arrived for work two days later, Johnny Paloma and his black Dodge Charger with its shiny red leather seats were gone, most likely heading East for greener pastures, just as Ben had predicted.

Chick had no clue as to why Johnny left. "The SOB left without a bloody word other than a note hanging in the kitchen that he was leaving," Chick moaned. "What am I supposed to do now?"

That evening, Lacy cried as she broke the news to Ben. He was devastated. His love for Lacy was unconditional; Her troubles were his troubles, and her pain was his pain. Knowing the overwhelming challenges of raising a newborn alone, Ben suggested she consider an abortion.

"No, Ben, I would never forgive myself if I did. This is my

child; I will give it life!"

"Lacy, listen to me, please. It's not a walk in the park raising a child alone."

Wiping tears away, Lacy said, "I've made my decision, Ben, and there's no changing it. I'm going to see this through and give this child life."

Lacy spoke those words with such finality that Ben knew arguing with her further was fruitless. "Okay, Lacy, if that's your decision, I will support you."

"Thank you, Ben."

"You need to be under the care of an obstetrician. I'll arrange for you to visit one."

Lacy began crying again. Ben wrapped his arms around her and held her close. "We'll get through this together, sweetheart; we will."

Chapter 4

January 28th

It began to snow just before dawn, and an inch or so of loose white powder had accumulated.

Although her due date was approaching, Lacy continued to work even though Ben had begged her to stop. At 12:32, while serving lunch at one of the tables, Lacy experienced a sharp pain in her abdomen. It did not last long, and she brushed it off. Ten minutes later, carrying two plates of Chick's fried chicken to one of the tables, Lacy experienced a second pain; this one doubled her over. The plates slipped from her hands. Moaning loudly, she fell to the floor, barely missing pieces of chicken and broken dishes.

With the assistance of two lady customers, Lacy gave birth to a baby boy there on the floor of Chick's Diner, four feet away from where Thelma had died. An ambulance rushed mother and child through the snow-covered streets to Cullum Regional Hospital. When her doctor pronounced a healthy baby boy, Lacy was asked to list the baby's name. She looked lovingly at the pink bundle cradled in her arms, thought for a moment, and with a broad smile, said, "Addison—Addison Jordan Stone. His middle name was my Father's."

On the birth certificate, she listed the father as *Unknown*.

When Lacy and baby Addison came home, Ben had a surprise for her. He had set up a crib and a changing station in Thelma's bedroom.

"Ben, how can I thank you."

"Nothing but the best for little *Addy*."

"Addy," Lacy repeated with a smile. "I like that."

"Although, dear Lacy, he'll always wonder why you named him after his hometown."

"No. I bet Addy will embrace it as unique."

Ben chuckled. "We'll see about that."

By the time Addison was around four or five, Lacy's erratic mood swings began to affect him. One moment, she was happy-go-lucky; then, on the turn of a dime, she would descend into a dark space for no apparent reason, which confused Addison. He wasn't yet aware of his mother's turbulent past at the hands of her drug-addicted grandparents. A confused Addison would retreat to his room when Lacy was at her worst.

Addison began showing disturbing signs of shyness. Rarely did he smile or laugh. He would sit on the floor and stare at the television without reacting to what he was watching. It became apparent to Ben that Lacy's damaged personality was adversely affecting her son. When Lacy was in one of her darker periods, she would curse Addison and send him to his room for the slightest infraction.

To make matters worse, Addison began to stammer. It was just a word or two now and again, usually when he was upset about something, no matter how trivial. His reluctance to communicate with others plagued him with anxiety, frustration, and embarrassment.

It concerned Ms. Dunphy, Addison's homeroom teacher, enough to request Lacy come to school for a meeting.

"Thank you for coming, Ms. Stone."

"What has Addison done now, Ms. Murphy?"

"He's done nothing wrong, Ms. Stone."

"Then what?"

"Well, I'm concerned. Your son makes no effort to befriend the other children."

"We all have distinctive personalities, Ms. Dunphy. He'll grow out of it."

"Perhaps, but such behavior is not normal for his age."

"Yeah, well, it's how one defines normal, right?" Lacy said with a shrug.

After a slight pause, Dunphy said. "Have you considered having Addison tested for signs of attention-deficit/hyperactivity disorder or maybe autism?"

That angered Lacy. She gave Dunphy a stern look and popped to her feet. "What? My son is neither of those."

"I'm not suggesting that he is, Ms. Stone. However, it concerns me enough that I thought it best to bring it to your attention."

"Addison is here to get an education, and that's what he's doing. Look at his grades; they're all *A's*."

"Yes, Ms. Stone, his grades are wonderful. Autistic children, for example, often have special abilities. But by his own admission, he prefers being alone. As I said, that is not normal for his age."

"Please stop saying that, Ms. Dunphy. My son is not autistic or anything else!"

"I'm sorry; I didn't mean to upset you."

"Well, you have."

"I'm only looking out for Addison, and—"

Before Dunphy could finish, Lacy was up on her feet and out the door, slamming it behind her.

It was clear to Ben that Addison's core problem was his mother. Her disturbing mood swings continued to puzzle the young boy. Fueled by the abuse of her past, Lacy had drawn a veil of gauze between herself, her son, and reality.

Ben knew they both needed emotional repair, but from whom? If he could not save Lacy from her demons, he would try to keep them from becoming Addison's. Ben spoke with Lacy and convinced her that Addison had to make an effort to participate in activities in and out of school. Surprisingly, Lacy agreed, but nothing they suggested lit a spark in Addison. He had yet to experience the joy of life when one discovers all that the outside world has to offer.

Ben thought a computer would open up Addison's constrained views. Lacy adamantly disagreed.

"Not until he's twelve, Ben. There's too much damn trash on the Internet."

"Lacy, Addy's ten. Most kids his age already have a computer and a cellphone. They're already teaching these kids computer science."

Lacy scowled. "Did I stutter, Ben? Not until he's twelve."

"Hey, girl, don't get snarky with me."

"I'm not, Ben. I'm making it clear: no computer until he's twelve."

On Addison's twelfth birthday, as promised, Lacy and Ben gifted Addison with a new computer. When Addison removed the birthday wrapping and opened the box, his eyes lit up like a one-hundred-watt bulb.

"Wow! Thank you, Mom, thank you, Ben."

"The first time I catch you watching anything inappropriate, I'll take it away. And no Facebook page or email address until you're fifteen."

"Lacy, for God's sake—"

"Stay out of this, Ben."

From that day on, Addison began to spend his free time on his computer. His favorite site was YouTube for its interesting programs on almost any subject and endless music choices.

Although Addison wasn't into movies, while scanning YouTube for things to watch, he came across the 1972 John Wayne western titled *The Cowboys,* about a rancher forced to hire inexperienced boys as cowhands to get his herd to market on time. The drive is dangerous, and cattle rustlers, looking to steal the herd, trail Wayne and his young, inexperienced cowhands.

Addison enjoyed the film so much that he searched for other Western classics. He came across the 1968 epic Western *Once Upon a Time in the West,* directed by Italy's spaghetti western king Sergio Leone. The film became Addison's favorite for its realism, grittiness, and evocative music score, especially *Your Love,* the film's title song.

Addison was eighteen when he graduated high school. But, his years in school with others his age had not changed him. He remained a loner, was considered odd, and was mostly shunned by his classmates, just like his mother had been. Addison had a sense of humor—so he thought. More often than not, when he thought he was being funny, it sounded sarcastic to his classmates. Most viewed Addison as an odd duck and a bore and constantly bullied him.

With his exceptional good looks, Addison could have dated regularly. However, he had difficulty expressing himself to his female classmates. Inevitably, he would begin to stammer.

Unlike Lacy, Addison ended his twelfth year at the top of his class. He balked when he learned he would be asked to deliver the traditional valedictorian speech at the commencement exercises.

"I can't stand on the stage before all those people, Mom."

"What's the big deal? You deliver a few lies about a bright future and get off."

"She's right," Ben added. "It's not that big a deal."

"I don't know. Maybe I'll think about it."

"No, son, you'll do it and make us proud. Now get to your computer and write something."

"I'll try it, Mom, okay?"

"Don't do us any blooding favors, Addy," Lacy snapped.

Addison spun around, tossed up his arms, and walked off. "Now, who's being sarcastic?"

"Watch your mouth, boy," Lacy called after him.

Ben rolled his eyes.

On graduation night, Addison approached the podium, never making eye contact with his teachers or classmates. He set a single sheet of paper on the podium and read from it.

"I want to thank the school and my teachers, for without them, we would not possess the knowledge we have gained. The question for all of us remains: what will we do with that knowledge? Let us not be guilty of sticking our heads in the sand and going along for the ride. Stay curious, continue to learn, and let your voices be heard. Thank you. I wish us all well in our future endeavors, whatever they may be."

That was it; that was his entire speech. The applause was timid at best. Addison didn't care; he was happy to have gotten through it without stammering once.

When the ceremony ended, everyone exited to the lobby. John McGuire, who had often bullied Addison, hooked his arm through Addison's and pulled him into a semi-dark corner.

"Your speech sucked, Stone."

"John, for once in your life, let it be, will ya'?"

"You're an asshole, Stone. You'll always be an asshole."

This time proved to be one too many times McGuire had bullied him. Addison's face turned red. He balled his right fist and cold-cocked McGuire. With a stunned look, McGuire stumbled back several steps.

"You're the asshole, John, and always will be. Now, take a minute or two and grow up."

"Jesus!" McGuire howled, holding his jaw, "Why did you do that?"

Addison rubbed his hand and grinned. "I should have done that long before now. Have a nice life, John."

And with that, Addison, pleased with himself, walked off smiling.

At breakfast the following morning, Lacy asked Addison

about his future plans.

"Jeez, Mom, graduation was yesterday; I have no plans yet."

"With your grades, you could easily get a college scholarship."

"Maybe."

"Well, son, time stops for no one. I suggest you give it serious thought."

Weeks passed, then months, and Addison still had not decided what he wanted to do with his life besides his addiction to his computer. It was his connection to the outside world without having to participate in the outside world. He spent most of his time in his room scanning YouTube, especially anything related to music.

When Addison turned nineteen, he still had not decided on his future. Frustrated with her son's inability to adapt to or engage with reality, she sat him at the kitchen table for a talk.

"Addy, I won't allow you to spend the rest of your life sitting in your bedroom in front of that computer. You either take some college courses or get a job. Your choice."

"I told you, Mom, I have no interest in college."

"That eliminates choice number one. So, find a job. The clock is ticking."

"And what kind of job would I find?"

"How about computer science?"

Addison smirked but made no comment.

"In case you haven't noticed, there's no free ride in this world. I'm running out of patience with you."

Addison abruptly stood.

"Where are you going?"

"To my room."

"Why am I not surprised?" Lacy said with a sneer. "Get going and look for a job, any job. I'll be waiting for your decision with bated breath."

"That's better than holding your breath, Mom."

"Watch your tongue, boy."

"And you should watch yours."

Lacy popped to her feet. "Who the hell do you think you're talking to?"

"You, Wonder Woman."

Lacy lost it; she marched around the table and slapped Addison across the face.

Until that moment, Lacy had never once set a hand on Addison. She looked confused and glanced at her open hand; it was shaking.

Addison looked stunned and took a step back. "For God's sake, Mom, what's wrong with you?"

Lacy looked confused. "I… I don't know what came over me, Addy. Please forgive me."

"Mom, you need help. That's it. I'm out of here." Addison stormed off.

In an angry flash, Lacy lashed out at him again. "Damn you, Addison Stone, come back here right now!"

Addison tossed a hand over his head, entered his room, and slammed the door behind him.

Lacy, wide-eyed and looking like she had no idea why she had slapped Addison, returned to her seat at the kitchen table, lowered her head in her hands, and began to cry. "Dear God, what did I do?"

As soon as Lacy had left for her shift at Chick's, Addison went to Ben's and told him what had happened. "She's not well, Ben; I swear she's losing it."

Ben washed a hand over his face. "I'm sorry, Addy."

"What do I do, Ben? Tell me."

"You know her background, Addy."

"Only what I see, Ben. She's never talked to me about it."

"Addy, you're gonna have to be the grown-up in the room when she acts out the way she did."

"That's like asking the blind to lead the blind, Ben. I'm a mirror of her in so many ways, and you know it."

"Because you're able to recognize and admit that, you're going to have to be patient with her."

"Easier than said than done, Ben. I question our relationship as well as my own identity. Am I me, or am I a clone of my mother?"

For the next several days, Addison and Lacy tiptoed around one another, never mentioning what had happened.

One day, while Addison was on YouTube, he came across his favorite song, *Your Love,* sung by renowned Italian Tenor Andrea Bocelli. It was the first time he had heard the song with lyrics. Bocelli's extraordinary voice and range captivated Addison; he listened to the recording repeatedly, Googled the lyrics, and began singing along with Bocelli.

While pruning bushes on the side of his house one afternoon, Ben heard Andrea Bocelli singing *Your Love.* He had heard it coming from Addison's bedroom before. Then, a second voice joined at the beginning of the second verse. Whoever it was singing had a beautiful voice, going toe to toe with the Italian tenor in perfect harmony.

Curious, Ben approached Addison's window and peered in. To his utter surprise, the second voice was Addison's.

"Well, I'll be damned," Ben whispered. He had no idea that Addison had such an outstanding voice. He listened until the song ended. "Wow, he whispered, Addy's voice is unique."

That's when an idea popped into his head that he thought might get Addison interested in something and out of the house.

The following day, Ben approached Addison. "Hey, Addy, I heard you singing with Andrea Bocelli yesterday."

"You heard me?"

"Yes, I did. Wow, I had no idea you sang so well."

"I like to sing, Ben. I'll bet I don't sing as well as you and your church choir."

"Huh, how would you know? Neither you nor Lacy has come to Sunday services."

Addison grinned. "We hear you singing in the shower, Ben."

Ben laughed. "These houses are too close. Say, why don't you and Mom come and listen to the choir this Sunday? I think you'd both enjoy it."

"Thanks, Ben, but I'm gonna pass. Maybe another time. Besides, Mom's an atheist and won't step inside a church."

Ben frowned, "Yeah, yeah, I know. Well, at least think about it."

Ben wasn't about to give up. He told Lacy about Addison singing along with Bocelli. "He's more than good, Lacy."

"My Addy? He never sings when I'm around."

"He sings during the day when you're at work. Trust me; the boy has a unique gift, a voice like none I have heard. Why don't you bring him to hear the choir on Sunday?"

"Ben, I haven't been in a church since the end of the Civil War. And, if there is a God, she'll have me removed from the building."

"Oh, stop. Do this for Addy. It's time he exited his bedroom and met other human beings."

"You are a persistent pain in the ass, Ben Dickey."

"Yeah, but I'm your pain in the ass, Lacy Stone."

"Okay, okay, already. I'll go if Addy goes, but you know how bullheaded he can be."

"As I recall, he gets that from his mother."

Lacy smirked. "And I love you too, Ben."

Lacy approached Addison about attending the services on Sunday.

He shrugged. "So, Ben told you?"

"He told me he was impressed with your voice."

Addison shrugged again.

"Look, Ben's always been there for us. He helped me through my early years and helped raise you.

"That's because I had no father around. I still don't know who he was because you won't tell me. Maybe one day you'll share that with me."

Lacy's expression turned dark. "I've told you before, I don't talk about that."

"You don't talk about the past at all, Mom. Why? Afraid to finally come to grips with it? You slip in and out of your dark moods, and I don't believe you are aware of it half the time."

"I'm gonna' ignore that remark."

"You always do, but you know it's the truth."

Lacy threw up her hands. "We're getting off the subject, Addy. I have no interest in attending church, but I will do this for Ben if you will."

Addison blew a breath and shrugged.

"Stop shrugging and answer me."

"Okay, okay. We'll go for Ben just this once."

"You know, son, you're not too old to be spanked."

"You and who else, Mom?"

"Just me, wise guy."

The conversation sounded more like sister and brother than mother and son.

Sunday morning, Addison insisted they sit in the last pew next to the door.

The service opened with the choir singing a *praise song*. Pastor Bruce Landford made several announcements, followed by his sermon. Then, the congregation joined the chorus, singing two more songs and ending with *Love Gifted Me*. The Pastor wished everyone well, and the service ended.

Addison was on his feet and first out the door.

When Ben returned home, he was anxious to know if Lacy and Addy enjoyed the choir. He knocked on their door—Lacy answered—Addison was standing behind her.

"Well, what's the verdict."

"Not bad, Mr. Dickey, not bad," Lacy said.

"Addy?"

"Yeah, Ben, the choir is pretty darn good."

"Good enough for you to consider joining us?"

Addison laughed. "Are you joking?"

"You have a gifted voice, son. Share it."

"I don't know, Ben. I'll think about it."

"I have a better idea. On Saturday mornings, we hold choir practice. It would be the perfect time to see if it interests you."

Addison raised an eyebrow and looked at Lacy.

"Don't look at me, Addy; the invitation is yours. Besides, I can't sing."

"If I agree to come once, Ben, will you leave me alone?"

Ben laughed. "I seriously doubt it."

"That's what I thought. All right, I'll go to your rehearsal but just once. That's it."

Lacy smirked. "How easy was that, Addy?"

"Painful, Mom, very, very painful."

When Ben and Addy left for choir practice on Saturday morning, Lacy hugged them. "Break a leg, boys."

Addison's face crinkled. "Break a what?"

"That's what they say in show business."

"Why?"

"Oh, never mind. Go and try to enjoy yourself."

The Church choir consisted of seven women and five men, along with choir director Millie Andrews, who accompanied them on piano. When Ben introduced Addison to the group, Addison forced a smile.

"Addison, sing along with us," Millie said.

"Oh, I don't know, Ms. Andrews. I don't know the lyrics."

"The first song will be *Come to the Water*. Just follow the lyrics in the book, and then you can join us when we rehearse it again."

Addison hesitated. "Okay, but if I goof up—"

Millie chuckled. "That's why we call it a rehearsal."

With the songbook in hand, Addison followed the lyrics. Millie suggested a few changes, and the choir sang the song again. This time, Addison joined in, and lo and behold, he really got into it. When they were finished, the choir and Millie complemented Addison on his voice.

"You have quite a gift, young man," Millie said. "Do us the honor and join us for tomorrow's services as our guest singer."

"Oh, I don't know, Ms. Andrews. Maybe I need more

practice."

"Go on, Addy," Ben said, "Give it a try."

"Let's finish the rehearsal and see how it goes," Millie said. "Take the songbook home and get comfortable with the lyrics of each song we'll be singing tomorrow."

"Ah, ah, okay, Ms. Andrews."

Ben was beaming. *Finally! Something other than his computer has caught Addy's interest. Thank God for small favors.*

When Ben and Addison returned home from rehearsal, Lacy met them at the door. "How did it go, boys?"

"Fine, Mom, fine."

"Are you joining the choir?"

"Just for tomorrow, but you have to come." And with that, Addison returned to his bedroom and his computer.

Ben placed a hand on Lacy's arm and grinned. "That settles that; you're going to church tomorrow."

"Wipe that smug look off your face, old man."

The following morning, when the choir took their positions, Addison and Ben were in the second row with the other men.

Lacy was sitting in the third pew. When the choir began, she could not believe it was her son singing. His voice was strong and clear and stood out above the others. Best of all, Addison looked like he might actually be enjoying himself.

"Well, I would have never guessed." Lacy beamed and whispered. "The boy can really sing."

The lady beside her said, "Sorry, did you say something?"

Lacy smiled and pointed to Addison. "That my son up there."

Following the service, Ben introduced Lacy to Millie Andrews.

"Your son has an amazing gift, Ms. Stone. His voice has a warm, emotional quality to it. You could see the positive response on the faces of the congregation."

"Thank you; I hope he'll continue with the choir."

"He will," Ben said, "I'll see to it."

No one could have predicted what would happen next. By the third week, word had spread about the young man with the golden voice. Sunday crowds grew until services drew a full house to hear young Addison Jordan Stone sing.

Millie Andrews knew Addison would be popular, but she was so overwhelmed by Addison's reception that she took it upon herself to explore where his unique talent might take him beyond the choir. She did so without consulting either Addison or Lacy.

Chapter 5

Langston *'Lang'* Sherman sat at his desk on the fifth floor of The Fuller Building on Fifth Avenue in New York City. Lang lived and breathed show business from the time he was a young teenager. After graduating college, he landed a job as an assistant to one of the agents at a New York talent agency. In time, he would work his way to becoming one of their top agents.

Following his wife's untimely death, Lang opened *The Sherman Agency*, a successful boutique music talent agency representing singers and singing groups. With a lean support staff of thirteen, The Sherman Agency's client roster grew to in-demand, top-earning musical performers.

Lang's secretary buzzed him. "Lang, Richard Jacobson is on line two."

"Thanks, Nancy." Lang picked up. "Dick, how is the publishing business these days?"

"Ever since self-publishing allowed anyone to write a book and publish it for a buck, ninety-five, it's the *in* thing. Everyone is writing a book, some very good, and some downright awful. How's the talent business?"

"Full of overblown egos as always."

"Lang, I know how busy you are, so I'll get to the point. I received a call from my cousin Millie Andrews in Cullman, Alabama."

"Never heard of the place."

"It's fifty miles north of Birmingham, where I grew up; our mothers were sisters. Anyway, Millie's the choir director at the Cullman Baptist Church. She asked if I knew of any talent agents interested in a young man who sings in the church choir. Millie says he has the most extraordinary voice she's heard in years. His name is Addison Stone, and he's nineteen years old. Since you, Langston Sherman, handle the best of the best, I thought I'd call you first."

"Thanks for the compliment, Dick, but I'm not looking to add to my roster."

"Lang, Millie said people pack the church on Sundays just to hear this kid sing; that's how good he is. Can I at least give Millie your email?"

Lang thought for a moment. "Okay, Dick, as a favor to you because we've been friends for over a hundred years now. But only email, no phone call."

"Thanks, Lang, you're a gem."

"Yeah, that's me, Lang, the Gem."

"Dinner on me the next time out."

"That's deal, Dick."

Just before the office closed for the day, Lang received an email from Millie Andrews with an attachment. She had not consulted with Addison or Lacy before sending it in case Lang wasn't interested.

Dear Mr. Sherman. I have attached a video of the choir I shot on my cell phone during one of our rehearsals. It features nineteen-year-old Addison Stone. I hope you will be as excited as we are with this young man's exceptional God-given talent.

I look forward to hearing from you if you are interested in pursuing this matter further. Thank you, Mr. Sherman.

Sincerely, Millie Andrews.

"Well, at least the lady kept it short. Let's see what all the crowing is about."

Lang clicked on the attachment and sat back. Up came a shot of the choir. Addison, lean and tall, stood in the middle of the ensemble with his full head of wavy brown hair. Lang couldn't help but notice the young man was movie-star handsome.

With the choir backing him, Addison began singing, *You'll Never Walk Alone*, one of the most inspirational songs ever. His phrasing was flawless, his intonation pitch-perfect, delivering the song with such passion, zeal, and intensity that it gave Lang a chill.

As Addison neared the end, his voice rose to a heart-stopping crescendo, holding the last note so long that Lang thought the young man would run out of breath. The video ended, and the screen went black.

Lang sat quietly for a moment. "Wow," he said softly.

He watched the video a second time. "Wow, again!"

He stood, crossed to a window, peered down at the congested Fifth Avenue traffic five stories below, and said aloud, "That kid has a golden voice like none I've heard. I'd be one damn fool to let this one get away. He's a rough-cut gem, waiting to be polished and delivered, and I'm going to give it a shot."

Returning to his desk, he stared at Millie's email for several moments before placing his fingers on the keyboard. "*Dear Ms. Andrews, this young man has an extraordinary talent. I would like to pursue this further. I will need a better demo than one shot on a cell phone. Maybe you could find a local wedding videographer to shoot an audition in a single full shot against a generic background. Be sure he sings, **You'll Never Walk Alone**. I'll cover the cost, and we'll go from there. Besides his talent, he's one handsome young guy. He'll have the ladies eating out of his hand.*" He added a happy face emoji. *Thank you. Lang Sherman.*

Fifteen minutes later, his email pinged with Millie's reply. *Thank you, Mr. Sherman, that's exciting. I'll send you the audition tape as soon as I have it. If you need to speak with me, my cell number is below. Thank you again.*

Sincerely, Millie Andrews.

Millie called Lacy later that evening and asked if she could come by the house and meet with her and Addison after work the next day.

"Of course, Millie; what's up?"

"I'd rather explain when I see you, Lacy."

"Hmm, okay, how about seven?"

"Perfect, see you then."

The following evening, Millie met with Addison and Lacy and told them she had sent a rehearsal tape to a New York talent agency to see if they might be interested in Addison. "A cousin of mine in New York is in the publishing business and is friends with Langston Sherman, who owns the Sherman Agency, which only represents singers. My cousin connected us via email. I sent Mr. Sherman a note and a video of one of our rehearsals."

Lacy shot a quizzical look at Addison. "You knew about this?"

Looking as confused as Lacy, Addison shook his head. "No."

"I'm sorry, Lacy. I suppose I should have consulted with you both. But—."

"Yes, you should have, Millie."

"If it had not gone well, I would have never brought it up to either of you, so nothing ventured, nothing gained. The good news is Mr. Sherman viewed the rehearsal video and is very interested. He wants to follow up but with a better demo tape."

"Besides singing in your choir, Addy has no professional experience, Millie."

"Neither did most when they began their careers. Addison has a unique talent. The overflowing crowds on Sunday morning confirm that. A top agent like Langford Sherman and his staff can shape, guide, and accelerate Addison's potential singing career. That's if he wants one. What do you think, Addison?"

Addison drew a breath. "*I-I,* I don't know what to say. I've never given thought to singing professionally." Addison looked to Lacy.

Lacy placed her hand on Addison's. "If this interests you, Addy, it's your decision. I can't make it for you."

Addison shifted uneasily in his chair, "If I was interested, Millie, how does it work? What would I have to do?"

"Mr. Sherman has requested an audition tape. There's a wedding photographer in Cullum who could shoot it, and Mr. Sherman will cover the cost."

"An audition tape?"

That's it; that's all you'd have to do. Mr. Sherman would take it from there."

"Whew, you've overwhelmed me, Millie. Mom?"

"Like I said, it would be your decision. I never heard you sing before last Sunday."

"But you have an opinion, Mom."

"Well, you do have a wonderful voice. But to be honest, I have reservations, Addy."

"What kind of reservations?"

"Son, besides singing with the choir on Sundays, you barely ever leave this house. If this were to become real, shy as you are, you could find yourself singing before hundreds, maybe thousands, of people. That's a hell of a lot different than singing to the Sunday morning congregation. Are you ready for that? If this were to happen, it could change your life in ways you're unprepared for."

Lacy was right, and it gave Addison pause. "Maybe I could do the audition and wait for Mr. Sherman's comments before deciding anything. Like Millie said, nothing ventured, nothing gained."

"Is that a yes, Addison?"

"I guess it is, Millie." Addison looked at Lacy; she turned away.

"I'll set it up with the photographer, send it off to Mr. Sherman, and we'll go from there."

Lacy stood. "Excuse me, I need to visit the bathroom. Thanks for coming, Millie."

Addison folded his hands and whispered. "She's only

looking out for me, Millie. She'll come around. Thank you for doing this."

"Your voice needs to be shared, Addison. Let's see if Mr. Sherman and his team can make that happen."

Four days later, Lang received an email from Millie with an attachment.

"I hope you like the audition," Millie wrote. *"Addison and his mother appreciate your interest, as do I. Looking forward to hearing from you. Thanks again. Regards, Millie."*

Lang clicked on the attachment. Addison, dressed in dark blue slacks and a blue striped shirt, stood before a gray backdrop. He sang *You'll Never Walk Alone,* back by an instrumental version he found on YouTube.

Addison's voice had a unique quality that Lang was hard-pressed to pin down. Addison's phrasing and intensity were overwhelmingly emotional, and despite not having any professional experience, Addison delivered the song like a seasoned performer.

"My God, not only does the kid have a golden voice, but there's real chemistry there," Lang whispered. "I'm gonna' roll the dice and go big and hope we come up with a seven or eleven."

He forwarded Millie's email with the audition attached to Stan and Sally Potts, the producers of *Sing America Sing*. This top-rated weekly music competition is broadcast worldwide every Friday night.

Stan, Sally, Lang wrote, *watch the attachment. Call me when you can.*

An hour and a half later, Stan Potts called.

"What took you so long, Stan?"

"You know how to get our attention, Lang. I have you on speaker—Sally's with me."

"Hi, Sally."

"Hi, Lang. Stan and I watched the video four times. Amazing, just amazing. Where did you find this talented young man?"

"Singing in a church choir in the Cullum, Alabama."

"You struck gold with this one, Lang," Sally said. "His voice is—I don't know how to describe it. He'll have audiences on their feet screaming for more. Lang, we have to be the ones who present him to our worldwide audience."

Lang's face lit up, and his lips curled into a grin. "I never doubted it for a minute."

"Lady luck is running with you, Lang," Stan added. "You couldn't have called at a more opportune time. Just so happens we had a slot unexpectedly come open. The young lady who was scheduled was in an auto accident. She was banged up a bit and had to postpone to a later date. We were about to fill the opening with another young singer until we watched Stone's demo."

"Wow! When would this be, Stan?"

"Ah, yeah, that; a week from this Friday's broadcast."

Lang's brow went up. "Whoa, Stan! The kid's only public appearances have been in that church choir. I need time to prepare him."

"Well, it's up to you. But as good as this Stone kid is, I'd grab that date and run with it if I were you."

Lang thought for a moment. He knew it was risky, but Stan was right. Catch the brass ring when it comes around, or punt. "Okay, lock it in; we'll make it happen."

"Good decision. But, if there are any problems, we need to know quickly."

"Ten-four, Stan. I'll get back to you."

Lang's next call was to Millie Andrews. "Millie, are you sitting down?"

"As a matter of fact, I am."

Lang filled her in on his conversation with the producers of *Sing America Sing*. There was no response from Millie.

"Millie, are you there?"

"I'm speechless, Lang."

"Addison is booked for a week from Friday."

"A week from Friday!"

"I know it's short notice, but I had to jump on it or wait for another opening sometime in the future. So, I went for a bird in the hand and committed. But the producers want confirmation ASAP. If there is a problem, I need to know immediately."

"Let me talk to Addison and his mother tonight."

"This is a once-in-a-lifetime gift; they better go for it. We'll need young Stone here in New York this Sunday. By the way, what are his parents' names?"

"His mother, Lacy, raised Addison alone. My God, this is so exciting."

"I'll send you the standard representation agreement. Let Addison know he needs to have a second song ready in case he is to win.

"How can we ever thank you, Lang?"

"Thank Addison, it's his talent that's making this possible. Hang on, Millie, we're off to the races."

Lang hung up and buzzed his secretary. "Nancy, ask everyone to join me."

One by one, his staff members filed in.

"Make yourselves comfortable; I want to share something with you."

Lang turned his computer around, pushed it to the front of his desk, and played Addison's audition.

The staff's reaction was precisely what Lang expected; they were blown away.

"His name is Addison Stone," Lang said, "and he's nineteen."

Andrew Crawford, Lang's longtime second in command, spoke. "I think I can safely speak for all of us, Lang. Stone has one hell of an amazing voice. He's star material."

The staff nodded in agreement.

"Prepare a news release that the Agency has signed a new talent named Addison Jordon Stone, who will make his public debut on *Sing America Sing* a week from Friday."

"Whoa," Andy said, "are you kidding? How did you pull that off?"

"An unexpected opening occurred when a contestant had to

delay their appearance. Stan and Sally raved about the demo and wanted Addison to replace them. I jumped on it. Let's get to work and make this kid a star."

In the morning, Lang received a call from Millie. "All is okay, Lang. Addison and his mother said yes. I just sent you an email with the signed agent agreement attached."

Lang sighed with relief; step one was signed, sealed, and delivered. "Addison and his mother must be beside themselves by this news, Millie."

"Addison is more than overwhelmed. He had no idea anything would happen so quickly. I think it's scared him."

"Huh, I'd be disappointed if he wasn't. And his mother?"

"She has expressed some reservations. I'm not sure what they are. That is between her and Addison. Ah, they both have requests."

Land drew a breath and blew it out. "Alright, lay it on me."

"Addison doesn't want the house band to back him up."

"Huh? Is he going to sing acapella?"

"He wants recorded instrumental tracks for both songs, preferably Andrea Bocelli's 'for the two songs he's chosen—*Your Love* and *Time to Say Goodbye*,' the two songs he's chosen."

"He wants what? Does he have any idea what those tracks might cost? That is, assuming we could even get them. What else?"

"Addison's never been away from home; Lacy doesn't want him traveling alone. She wants Ben Dickey, a close family friend, to accompany him."

"Before we even get to the starting gate, this kid and his mother are making demands?"

"Not demands, requests."

"Millie, because I believe Addison has the goods to make it, I'll see what can be done to secure the tracks. Please make it clear to Addison that if the tracks are unavailable from any source, he'll have to settle for the house band. If he balks, that's the end of my involvement."

"I understand, Lang."

"The agency will advance upfront expenses to bring him and his friend to New York. If we strike out, it's on our ticket; that's how much confidence we have in Addison's talent."

"Thank you again, Lang."

"We're off to the races, Millie, and I expect us to win."

Lang called Stan Potts and filled him in. "I can handle the family friend accompanying the kid, but what the hell do we do about the music tracks?"

"That's a tall order, Lang. Even if we obtain permission, they won't come cheap. I'll reach out to the right people. But what about the cost?"

"I've already agreed to cover upfront expenses; let's go big. The agency will cover the cost."

"You're putting your money behind a winner, Stan."

"Let's hope, Stanley, let's hope."

Three anxious days passed before Lang heard back from Stan Potts.

"By decree of the music gods and my exceptional negotiating skills, we have the music tracks for one-time use only. If the kid doesn't win and you only use the one track, there's no charge for the second."

"Whose tracks are they."

"Andrea Bocelli's."

"How'd you pull that one off?"

"I sent Stone's audition tape to my connections with Bocelli's people. They all reacted similarly; the young man possesses a unique gift that needs to be shared with the world."

"That's amazing. Thank you and the music gods for big favors, Stanley."

"Want to hear what the tracks are gonna' cost?"

Lang drew in a breath. "Break it to me slowly."

Chapter 6

Incredibly, the go light had turned a bright flashing green in record time.

Lang called Millie. "Millie, we secured the music tracks from Bocelli's album."

"Oh, thank goodness."

"Things are moving faster than a speeding bullet. We need Addison and his family friend on a plane this Sunday, no excuses. My office will arrange the flight and call you with the details. When they arrive at LaGuardia, our guy will meet them in the baggage area and take them to the hotel. Tell them to plan on having dinner with me Sunday night."

"This small-town girl is overwhelmed with joy, Lang. We appreciate your putting yourself on the line like you have."

"Only because I think he has the talent to make it, Millie. Be well; we'll talk soon."

Lang hung up, sat back, and ran a hand through his hair. "I feel like a fart in a whirlwind on this one."

Addison sat quietly, staring at his computer screen, trying to absorb everything happening as fast as it was. It was then that

Addison decided to keep a journal. He bought himself a 6X9 notebook and wrote his first entry.

> *I can't believe this is happening. Sunday, this small-town boy is going to New York to appear on a major television broadcast. I'm scared as hell. Thankfully, my rock, Ben, is going with me. What still bothers me is Mom. I'm not sure she is entirely on board with this, but that's Mom; she always sees the negative first. If all goes well, she'll come around; I know she will.*

At 9:30 Sunday morning, Addison and Ben boarded the flight from Birmingham to New York's LaGuardia Airport. Addison sat nervously, gripping the armrests as the plane sped down the runway.

Ben tapped him on the arm. "Are you okay, Addy? You look nervous."

"Just wondering what's going to keep this thing in the air, Ben."

Ben laughed. "A flock of birds attached to the underbelly."

Addison raised an eyebrow. "Big birds, I hope."

In the baggage area at LaGuardia, Ben was the first to spot a man by the exit holding a white card with Addison's name.

Ben chuckled low. "Either that's our ride, or he wants your autograph." Ben raised his arm and got the guy's attention.

The man called out to them. "Mr. Stone?"

"Yes," Addison responded.

"I'm Julio Sanchez. I work for Mr. Sherman."

Julio and Addison shook hands.

"This is our neighbor and family friend, Ben Dickey."

"Nice to meet you both. I'll be your driver during your visit with us. Been to New York before, Mr. Stone?"

"This is my first time."

"Ah, well, let me be the first to welcome you to the Big Apple."

As they drove into the city, Addison's eyes were as big as

golf balls as he viewed the city. "My God, Ben, who knew they built buildings higher than five stories?"

"It's an amazing city, Addy. I've been here before, back when I was pulling trains."

Julio maneuvered through the dense downtown traffic until they arrived at the Hilton Garden Inn on 52nd Street, less than a mile from Lang's office.

"You're pre-registered." Julio handed Addison his card. "Call me if you need anything."

"Thank you, Julio."

When they checked in, there was a message from Lang to meet him at seven that evening at Fabio Cucina Italian restaurant, a short walk from the hotel.

Addison and Ben's rooms were side by side on the third floor.

"Addy, after we unpack, how about we catch a bite in the restaurant downstairs."

"Okay, Ben."

Once settled in his room, Addison took out his journal and made an entry:

> *We made it to New York, although my first plane ride was a little scary. The city is enormous; I feel out of place like I don't belong here, like I'm pretending to be someone I'm not. I know that sounds silly, but what's happening is just beginning to sink in. What if I've made a mistake? How do I turn this speeding train around now?*

There was a knock at the door. Addison closed his journal and stuffed it beneath his underwear and socks in the dresser's top drawer. "The doors open, Ben." He went to the window and stared out.

Ben strolled in. "Did you remember to call your mom to tell her we arrived?"

No reply from Addison.

"Quite a sight out there, huh?"

Still no response from Addison.

"Hey, Addy, anybody home in there?"

A moment passed before Addison answered in a soft voice. "Where are we, Ben?"

"You're looking out the window, son. It's still New York City."

Addison hesitated, sucked in a breath, and exhaled slowly. "Do I belong here?"

"What?" Ben crossed the room and stood behind Addison. "Addy, look at me."

Slowly, Addison turned. His expression signaled he was troubled.

"Addy, what's wrong?"

Addison breathed in and out slowly. "Did I choose this, Ben, or did it choose me? Am I living a predetermined path because of my voice?"

"What? That's crazy talk."

"Is it?"

"Hey, this was your decision, remember?"

"Was it, Ben?"

"I don't know what you're talking about, son. Look, Addy, I realize this is all happening fast. But think of life as a merry-go-round; it only goes in one direction. You grab that brass ring when it comes around, or you don't; it's your choice. The open road is there; only you can decide where you want it to take you."

"You make it sound simple, Ben."

"But it is. Turn around, look at me."

Addison turned slowly.

"You've been locked away in your room with that damn computer for too long. It's time to breathe fresh air out in the real world. Each of us is given a finite amount of time; what we do with it is up to us. Yesterday's narrative is not necessarily today's; things change, and we must change with it. All that lives on after we're gone is what we left behind. In your case, you have a gift to leave one day—Addison Stone's legacy."

"You mean my voice's legacy."

"That's gibberish, Addy."

Addison walked to the bed and sat. "What if I'm not ready, Ben? What if I blow it and fail?"

"It's only failure if you don't try." Ben walked over and sat beside Addison. "Where is all this doom and gloom coming from? I thought you wanted this?"

"What about Mom? I feel like she's distanced herself from it."

"She hasn't."

"You couldn't prove it by me, Ben. She told Millie she had reservations but didn't articulate them. That's just like her, isn't it?"

"She's only looking out for you." Ben placed a hand on Addison's arm. "Look, we both know the baggage Lacy carries from her childhood, and we both know how it's affected you, but —"

"Mom never shared any of her past with me. She's like two people. There's Mom, and then there's Lacy, who withdraws, becomes distant, and often acts irrationally. It's maddening. I don't know how to reach her when she's in those spaces. Sometimes, I feel like I'm just an inconvenient part of her life that she had not planned on."

"No, it was not planned, but it happened. I know one thing for certain: you are the most significant thing that came into Lacy's life. She's told me that on more than one occasion."

"Really, Ben?"

"Yeah, really." Ben slipped an arm around Addison's shoulders. "I know it hasn't been easy dealing with her at times, but—"

"That putting it mildly, Ben."

"Let me finish. You are being given an opportunity to put all that behind you and become who *you* are. Go with it. Don't waste your life and talent lamenting about the past and singing to your computer in your bedroom. Enough said. Come on, I'm hungry; let's get lunch."

Ben stood and walked to the door.

"Ben," Addison called.

"Yeah?" Ben said without turning back.

"Who is my father?"

Ben was taken aback. That was the first time Addison had ever asked him that. "Why do you bring that up now?"

"Because mom won't tell me." Addison stood and returned to the window.

Ben paused for a moment, then lied. "I don't know who your father was. Your mom never shared it with me, either."

Addison shook his head and shrugged.

"Lacy has her demons, Addy; let them be hers, not yours. Now, come on, let's get lunch."

"You go, Ben; I'm not hungry."

"Suit yourself. Get some rest. We have dinner with Mr. Sherman at seven."

As soon as Ben left, Addison retrieved his Journal:

> *Damn, you, Addison, damn you. Make up your mind. You either want this or you don't. If you don't, act like a grownup and stop wasting everyone's time, especially Ben's; he's on your side. Don't burden him with your self-doubts or what other phobias are plaguing you. You can do this; in your heart, you know you want this, so stop whining, and damn well, go for it. Easier said than done.*

Chapter 7

That evening, they received directions from the hotel desk clerk and were off to meet Lang for dinner. When they arrived, the maître d' showed them to Lang's table. There was another man with him.

Lang stood. "You must be Addison and Ben?"

Ben smiled. "That would be us."

Lang shook Addison and Ben's hands. "A pleasure to meet you both. This is Andy Crawford, our top agent who will be at your side every step of the way."

"How was your flight?" Andy asked.

"It was my first, sir," Addison said unsmiling.

"That must have been exciting."

Addison nodded. "Yeah, kind of."

"Well, young man, all of this has crystalized for you with dizzying speed," Lang said. "What's going through your mind?"

"I don't know where to begin, sir. I'm excited, but I'm also anxious. I've never performed in public other than with the choir. It's intimidating when I think that millions will be watching."

"I'll share a little secret with you. The four judges will be sitting on the stage floor right before you, with over a couple of thousand audience members behind them. The natural instinct is to play to them. Don't. If you do, you'll lock eyes with one or more, which could throw you off. Play just slightly over their heads to the back of the studio, moving your gaze from left to right and back. Everyone will think you're looking at them. As for the TV audience, you can't see them, so don't dwell on them. Just sing your heart out." Lang held up the menu. "The food is excellent here. Let's eat and get to know one another. We'll talk business after we eat."

Dinner was filled with small talk. Addison was quiet. Ben was more expressive, discussing life in a small Southern town with fewer than a thousand residents.

Following dinner, Lang got down to business. "Addison, let me begin by saying we believe you have an extraordinary voice that audiences will fall in love with. That's why we pulled out all the stops on your behalf. There is a quality to your vocal cords that is difficult to define. You have a gift, Addison. But the passion and emotion you placed on the lyrics also came through in your demo. That is important for the songs you have chosen to sing."

"Thank you. I'm not even aware of it; that's how it comes out."

"Then you have two gifts, your voice and your passion for each song."

Addison smiled.

Andy took over and explained how a talent agency worked and their plan to present Addison to the public following his appearance on *Sing America Sing,* win or lose. Addison answered questions politely but offered little in the way of conversation.

"I assume you watch *Sing America Sing?*"

"Every week, sir."

"Good, then you're familiar with the format. The contestant that receives the highest score wins a ten-thousand-dollar prize. Unlike other talent shows, that's it. There are no other levels to compete in, and the winner is under no further obligation to the show. After each broadcast, there is a reception for the contestants and guests. Win or lose, you'll get to meet some important industry people who are in a position to help boost your career. Tomorrow is a day of rest. Enjoy New York. We'll have you rehearse both music tracks on Tuesday before a small audience."

Addison shot a nervous look at Ben. "An audience?"

"Just our staff," Andy said. "Since they'll all be working for you in one capacity or another, it's an opportunity to meet and hear you sing. On Thursday, each contestant is given a walk-through at the studio. Yours is scheduled for 10:30 in the morning. Any questions?"

Information was coming fast—Addison was trying to keep up. He forced a smile. "No, sir."

"It's time you began calling us Lang and Andy, young man."

"Yes, of course—Lang, Andy."

"I'm about to give you the same speech I give all young clients just starting out," Lang said. "A musical career can be exciting and rewarding, but it can also be heartbreaking."

"How so, sir—I mean, Lang?"

"It's show business, son, with a capital *S*. It's as much about chemistry and connecting with audiences as it is about talent. To succeed, you need both."

"You think I'm good enough, *M-m*, Mr. Sherman?"

"If he didn't, you wouldn't be sitting here," Andy added. "Lang doesn't toss out compliments unless they're deserved."

Lang continued. "Talented songwriters and arrangers, beloved singers like Frank Sinatra, Bing Crosby, Vic Damone, Peggy Lee, Barbra Streisand, and many others left an indelible mark on what became known as *The American Songbook*, the kind of songs you sing. But times change, the public's tastes change, and pop singers come and go. You have a unique voice, Addison, that will evoke people's emotions. That's important, that a special gift. We're confident you're destined to rank up there with the greats. That's how much faith we have in you.

Sing the music you love; sing it well, and people will follow you."

With a soulful look, Addison looked to Ben, then to Lang. "Do you think *I-I'm-I'm,* I'm good enough to be in their company?"

That Addison even asked that question riled Ben. "Listen to Lang, Addy. He should know."

"Let's take this one step at a time," Lang Continued. "Don't think of *Sing American Sing* as a win-or-lose proposition. Think of it as a significant exposure introducing Addison Stone to millions of viewers. If you win, great; if not, you will have been seen and heard by a worldwide audience. That alone is worth a million bucks in exposure for any new talent. Are you with me?"

"Yes, Lang." Looking nervous, Addison stood and looked around. "Excuse me; I need to find the men's room."

Andy motioned to the rear. "Back there past those tables."

Addison left. A long silence followed until Lang said, "He's, ah—how shall I put this—he seems a bit shy and not very communicative, Ben."

"Yeah, he seems a bit awkward," Andy added.

"I'm sure you'll agree that this is all happening fast," Ben said. "Addison is, after all, nineteen with no professional experience. That's enough to rattle anyone."

Lang nodded in agreement. "Yes, it is.'

"And, ah…" Andy paused. "We noticed he has a slight stammer?"

"Oh, that, it's nothing. It sometimes happens when he's stressed or under pressure. Right now, he's feeling the pressure."

"On the positive side," Lang said, "none of that came through on the audition tape. Addison sang like a polished, seasoned performer. But what happens offstage when he has to meet people and do endless interviews?"

"With your guidance, he'll find his way soon enough."

"We hope so, Ben. Okay, we're off to the races."

As soon as they returned to the hotel, Addison made an entry in his journal:

> *Dinner with Lang and Andy was a wake-up call. They confirmed how little I understand the impending changes that are about to encircle my life. I have much to learn. But how do I shed these feelings of inadequacy that continue to shadow me? As difficult as it is to believe, I will sing before a worldwide audience of millions in a few days. I must find a way to do as Lang suggested and block out everything except what I'm there to do: sing my heart out. I will find a way... I will.*

After sleeping in Monday morning, Addison and Ben caught a quick breakfast and then ventured out on the busy streets of New York City.

"Wow, look at this place, Ben. I had no idea. But, then again, Cullum is still a big deal to me."

"There's no place quite like New York City, Kiddo."

The city overwhelmed Addison but in a good way. He was excited to finally leave his small world behind and join the outside world that had eluded him until then.

Tuesday, at 10:00 AM, Julio drove Addison and Ben to the *Dolby 24* screening room on the Avenue of the Americas. Addison did not say two words during the drive. As they entered the building, Ben touched Addison's arm.

"Imagine you are playing centerfield for the Yankees. The batter hits a high fly ball right to you. If you catch it, the game is over—your team wins. Now, take a deep breath, go in there, and catch that ball."

"I'll do my best, Ben."

"I know you will. Go big or go home."

Addison forced a smile and shrugged. "If you say so, *Sir Ben.*"

Inside the screening room, Lang introduced Addison and Ben

to his staff. Addison smiled and nodded to each of them.

Lang motioned to the film screen. "Addison, we'll have you stand before the screen."

Addison looked like a deer caught in the headlights of an oncoming eighteen-wheeler. "*O-o* okay, Lang."

"Nod when you're ready, and we'll start the music. Sing just as you did on your audition tape."

Hesitantly, Addison moved to the movie screen and stared at it momentarily. He closed his eyes, took a deep breath, held it, and wiped his mind clean before slowly exhaling until his lungs were empty. He took a deep breath, turned, and nodded. The music track for *Your Love* began. After finishing *Your Love*, he stunned everyone by singing the first stanza of *Time to Say Goodbye* in Italian. Everyone was on their feet with zealous applause. Several had tears in their eyes.

He had caught that high-flying ball—at least with Lang's staff.

"Do that on the show, and I promise you will win."

"Ah, I don't know about that, Lang."

"Trust me, son, you will."

As Julio drove them back to their hotel, Ben asked, "When did you learn Italian?"

"I Googled the lyrics in Italian and listened carefully to Bocelli's version on YouTube. It took me a week to get it right."

"You never cease to amaze me, young man."

Addison smiled. "Humble as I am, I try, Ben, I try."

Although Addison was thrilled by the reception he received from Lang's staff, inside, he felt like a scared rabbit running for his life from a fox on the hunt. In his journal, he wrote.

> *Why do I keep having these self-doubts? If I'm aware of them, why can't I bury them once and for all? Lang would not have put his agency on the line if they didn't believe I could do this. What is so difficult to understand about that, Addison? If I bring this up again, Ben will swift-*

kick me in the ass. Remember what he told you; this is your opportunity to become you. Take it, run with it, stop living in the past—put all your angst behind you and catch that high-flying ball.

Early Wednesday morning, Addison received a call from Lang.

"Good morning. I hope I didn't wake you."

"No, Ben and I were about to get breakfast."

"You had everyone in the palm of your hands yesterday. I haven't seen the staff that excited about a new client in a while."

"Thank you."

"Tomorrow, you get to see the studio. You're in for a treat."

"I've seen it lots of times on TV."

"Trust me, Addison; It's a whole different experience seeing it in person."

"Ben and I are looking forward to it, Lang."

"Good. Now sit back, relax, and enjoy the ride because your train is about to leave the station."

Thursday morning, Julio drove them to the Steiner studios in Brooklyn.

"Addy, in your wildest dreams, did you ever think this could happen?"

"You know the answer to that, Ben. It never once crossed my mind until Millie stepped in and contacted Lang. I sang in the choir for fun, end of story."

"Well, it's happened, kiddo. Whoop it up a little."

Addison tossed his hands up. "Whoop, whoop, whoop. How's that?"

"That'll do, for now, smart ass."

At the studio gate, Julio provided the guards with their names. The guard waved them to the vast production center that was once the busy Brooklyn Navy Yard. Julio drove past several sound stages until they reached Stage Five.

"Here we are, gentlemen. Straight ahead through that door.

I'll catch a cup of coffee in the cafeteria. Have Andy call me when you're ready to leave."

"Thanks, Julio," Ben said.

As they approached the door, Addison stopped. "Wait, Ben." He turned away and began pacing.

"Now, what's wrong, Addy?"

"Give me a minute." Addison took deep breaths with each step.

Ben fumed and raised his voice. "Damnit it, Addy, enough already. I can't be shoring you up every damn time you fall into a funk! Stop acting like your mother."

It was the first time Ben had ever raised his voice at Addison.

"Ben, you don't understand."

"Yes, I do. It's you who doesn't understand. When you step through that door, your life is about change, and in a good way, because you have a unique talent to make something of yourself. I believe in you, Millie, and Lang and his people believe in you, and he's put his money where his mouth is. Son, everyone hopes to live their lives with purpose. In your case, you have a unique gift. Think of yourself as a flower bud."

Addison's brow furrowed. "A flower bud, Ben? I don't follow you?"

"Think of those who are supporting you as the sun and rain, the nourishment you need to blossom."

"Wow, that's deep, Ben. I had no idea you read Shakespeare."

"Okay, smart ass, enough. Are we going through that door or joining Julio for coffee?"

Addison wavered for a few beats before walking to Ben's side. "I'm sorry; let's go in."

"Are you sure?"

"Yes."

"Okay then, let's go." Ben turned the handle and swung the door open.

"Ben?"

"What now?"

"Please don't be mad at me."

Ben placed a reassuring hand on Addison's arm. "I'm not; I was trying to get your attention. It seems to have worked."

As they stepped into the studio, what confronted them brought them to a complete stop. Addison's mouth flapped open, but nothing came out.

"My God," Ben breathed, "It looks like something out of Stars Wars."

Off to their right was the main stage. In the center was an elevated round platform with three stairs that descended to the main stage. Four plush chairs were positioned in front of a long table on the studio floor facing the stage. A round red button the size of a half-baseball protruded in front of each chair on top of the table. Next to it was a small TV monitor. Several feet behind the table were row after row of audience seats extending to the rear of the massive studio.

Andy, standing on the stage, waved to Ben and Addison. "Good morning."

"Good morning, sir," Addison answered.

"*Andy*, remember?"

"Sorry… Andy."

Andy motioned to the stairs to the far right of the stage. "Come on up."

Overwhelmed with the set's enormous size and complexity, Addison and Ben climbed the stairs to the stage.

"Before I forget, Addison, you'll be the last of the four to perform."

"Why is that, Andy?"

"They do it the old-fashioned way. Each contestant's name is on a slip of paper, dropped in a bowl, and withdrawn. Yours came up last."

A middle-aged man appeared from the wings and joined them. "Is this the young man you were crowing about, Andy?"

"Yes. Addison, this is George Smith, the Stage Manager. George, this is Addison's family friend, Ben."

Addison and Smith shook hands with both men. "Welcome

to the show, Addison.”

“Thank you, Mr. Smith.”

“Addison, George is going walk you through what happens when it’s your turn.”

“*Oh-oh*, great.”

Smith motioned to the three steps leading to the elevated round platform area. “Come with me, Addison.”

Addison followed Smith up the three steps.

“This is a rotating stage.”

“Yes, Mr. Smith. I watch the show regularly.”

“Good. Let’s go around back.”

Addison followed Smith until they reached the rear of the platform.

“When it’s your time, I’ll come to get you from your dressing room and position you on this mark on the floor. When host Billy Wonder introduces you, the stage will begin to rotate. When it’s about halfway to the steps, your music will begin. With me so far?”

“Yes, sir.”

“Okay, follow me.” They walked back to the three steps leading to the stage. “You’ll go down these steps to that X marked on the floor. The mike stand will be right in front of it. You can leave the mike on the stand or hold it in your hand. Billy will join you when you're finished, ask a few questions, and then poll the judges. You’ll be asked to sing a second song if the judges award you the highest score. You know about the red buttons?”

“Yeah. The contestant receives five bonus points if a judge hits their button.”

“Right. Any questions?”

“No, I don’t think so, sir.”

“You need to arrive here tomorrow no later than 4:00 PM. See you then. Good luck.”

Smith walked off. Addison held back momentarily, gazing in awe at the enormous soundstage. His heart was racing, and his mind was reeling.

Later that evening, Addison wrote in his journal:

> *Went through the show's routine today. Very exciting. But, despite Ben's speech, I can't help thinking I'll wake home in my bed in the morning to find this was all a dream. Just kidding— nothing funny about that. Pump yourself up, Addison, not down. DUH!*

Next, Addison called Lacy.

"Well, it's about time," Lacy said.

"Sorry, Mom, they've kept us busy. I wish you were here."

"Me too, Addy."

"I hope I do well."

"You will. Just pretend it's Sunday and you're singing with the choir."

Addison chuckled. "Oh, yeah, sure, easy for you to say."

"I'll be watching the show, sweetheart. I love you."

"Love you too, Mom."

Addison turned in early, but sleep was slow in coming. At 3:30, he woke with a start and sat up. He had been dreaming that the audience had booed his performance. "Jeez, Addy, get a grip." Slipping out of bed, he went to the bathroom, splashed water on his face, and stared at his image in the mirror. "Here we go, Mr. Stone. Don't screw it up now. And stop talking to yourself in the bloody mirror, or Ben will have you committed."

3:00 PM Friday; Julio drove them back to the studio. Addison said little during the drive.

Ben tapped at Addison's temple. "How's it going in there?"

"How do you think?"

"I don't know what you did on the audition tape and again in front of Lang's staff,

but I think I saw you slipping into another time and place; It was just you and the music."

"I don't know how I do that, Ben; I just do."

"Do it again tonight, and you'll be just fine."

When they arrived at the studio, Julio shook Addison's hand. "Best of Luck tonight, Addison. I'll be in the audience rooting for you."

"Thank you, Julio."

The studio was a hub of activity as the crew was busily preparing for that night's broadcast. Six television cameras were now part of the setup.

A production assistant came to take Addison to a dressing room.

Ben hugged him. "I'll be sitting with Lang and Andy. This is your night, son. Catch that high-flying ball."

Addison smiled and gave a thumbs-up.

At 5:30, a production assistant escorted Addison to hair and makeup, where he came face-to-face with three other contestants for the first time: one woman and two men who looked not much older than him. Beyond polite introductions, there was little conversation, which was fine with Addison.

Chapter 8

One of the young men was the first to perform. Addison had already forgotten his name. The guy was good and scored well, with the judges giving him two out of four red buttons. The audience cheered.

The young lady was next, and she, too, scored well, receiving two red buttons.

When the third contestant began, the Stage Manager came to get Addison. "Ready, young man?"

"*Y-yes*, sir."

"There will be a commercial break following this contestant; then you're on."

All four judges gave the third contestant a good score, but only one gave him a red button.

The commercial break began, and Smith led Addison to his position on the rotating stage.

"It'll be dark back here until the break is over, so be careful and don't move around."

"*G-g*, got it," Addison quietly said.

When the break ended, Billy Wonder began Addison's introduction. As Wonder said, "Ladies and Gentleman, Addison

Stone," the stage slowly began to rotate. Halfway around, the music for *Your Love* began. A spotlight struck Addison like a lightning bolt. A chill went through him. Smith had forgotten to inform Addison that would happen—he blinked and flinched. Suddenly, the painful years of his youth flashed through his mind. *Stop,* he told himself, *concentrate, or you'll blow this.*

When the rotating stage reached the steps, Addison descended to the stage, took a deep breath, and removed the mic from its stand with his right hand. He closed his eyes and took a deep breath. When he opened his eyes, there were no judges, audience, or cameras, just him and his music; he was in a zone all by himself, following Lang's instructions to keep his gaze just above the heads of the audience.

At the end of *Your Love*, the applause was deafening. The audience was on their feet with hoots, hollers, and whistles. Seven young ladies rushed to the edge of the stage with their hands outstretched, calling Addison's name.

Addison looked baffled. He had no idea why they had rushed the stage or why they were reaching out to him. The ladies were quickly returned to their seats by two security men.

When the applause finally subsided, Billy Wonder joined Addison. "It appears, young man, you've captured the hearts of our audience."

Addison looked like a petrified Doe.

"Tell us where you're from."

"Ah, Addison, Alabama."

"You're named after your hometown?"

"Yes, sir, I am."

"Man, that's cool. How come I never thought of that? I could have been Baltimore Wonder."

The audience roared with laughter.

"Okay, let's hear what our judges have to say. Cory Benson, you get to go first."

Cory Benson was a successful singer, songwriter, and one of the show's original judges. He stared at Addison for what felt like an eternity. Addison waited, shifting uneasily from one foot to the other.

"No comments from me, Billy." Benson brought his hand down on the red button, which lit up.

The audience roared.

"Wow!" Billy Wonder said. "Home run! Patricia Reed, your comments, please."

Patricia Reed, a well-known songwriter, musician, and music producer, smiled. "Congratulations, young man. You have an amazing gift." She pushed her red button.

The audience cheered.

"Wow, another home run," Billy Wonder boomed.

"Okay, Jack Orwell, go for it, man."

Singer Jack Orwell, a famous rock singer, had the number two song in the country. "I'll make this short and sweet, Billy." He raised his right hand over his shoulder, lowered it slowly, and pushed his red button.

Now, there was no restraining the audience: they were on their feet cheering.

"Last but not least, let's hear from the venerable, guitar-strumming Hank Gorman."

Hank Gorman was a top country and Western singer. He shook his head from side to side. "What an incredible gift you have, young man." Gorman pushed his red button.

Addison looked bewildered and stared blankly at the audience. He heard what each judge had said and saw their glowing red lights, but, at that moment, it didn't register. Had he heard right? Had he really won?

"Wow, and wow again!" Billy Wonder roared. "That's all she wrote, baby." He took Addison's right hand and raised it over Addison's head. "Addison Stone, you are the newest and brightest star of *Sing America Sing.* Never in the five years of this broadcast has any contestant received four red buttons!"

The audience roared again, but Addison didn't hear them; he was in a trance.

Billy patted Addison on the back. "Young man, this audience and those watching around the world get the pleasure of you singing a second number. What will it be?"

Addison hesitated. "*Time to Say Goodbye.*"

"Ladies and gentlemen, tonight's powerhouse winner, Addison Stone, singing appropriately, *Time to Say Goodbye.*"

Addison's mind was racing. *Yes, I won, I really did. Now, bring it home, Addy, bring it home.* He withdrew into himself again and sang *Time to Say Goodbye.*

The audience remained standing, some singing with Addison, others cheering him on. Then, as quickly as it had begun, it was over; he had caught that high-fly ball with both hands.

In his dressing room, Addison sat alone, reliving all that had transpired in the last five days. He dropped his head into his hands and wept.

Lang, Ben, Andy, and Julio entered.

"Hey, those better be tears of joy," Lang said with a broad smile, "because you, young man, just won the lottery like we knew you would."

Addison stood, walked to Ben, and hugged him. "Thank you, Ben, thank you for everything."

Ben's face splayed into a wide smile. "Just about now, the little old town of Addison, Alabama, is celebrating big time, Addy."

Lang shook Addison's hand vigorously. "You were amazing. Now we wait for the offers to roll in, and they will."

"Wipe those tears away," Andy said, "toss some cold water on your face, and let's go to the reception and meet some of your new fans."

"Gentleman, can we give him a minute to call his mother?" Ben handed Addison his cell phone. The room cleared, and Addison called Lacy.

"I did it, Mom, I did it!"

Lacy was crying. "I'm so proud of you, Addy. My phone's been ringing off the hook. Now, you go enjoy yourself, and remember to hold your head high."

"I will, Mom."

"When do you get to come home?"

"I don't know yet; that's up to Lang and what happens next."

"Call me when you know. Love you, son."

"Love you, Mom."

When they arrived on the stage, the reception was underway.

Lang whispered to Addison. "There are many music industry big shots here. Don't be intimidated. Tonight, you're bigger than them all."

Addison smiled, but inside, he was scared to death.

As Addison entered the reception area, the entire gathering applauded. Stan and Sally Potts were the first to approach.

"Hi, Addison, I'm Stan Potts, and this is my wife, Sally. We're the producers of the show."

"Oh, yes, nice to meet you. Thank you for this opportunity, Mr. and Mrs. Potts."

"Believe me when I tell you your life is about to change dramatically, and that's an understatement," Sally said. "Congratulations on your amazing first-class performance."

"My wife knows when a talented newcomer is about to fly high, young man," Stan added. "Stay focused, and you'll fly higher and higher."

The four judges came to Addison and shook his hand. As Addison moved through the crowd, he smiled and thanked well-wishers but did not converse with them. His head was swirling. None of this felt real; he would need time to process it all.

Someone tapped Addison's shoulder as he and Ben approached the buffet table. He turned and came face-to-face with a beautiful young woman with large, penetrating blue eyes that sparkled like diamonds, reddish-blond hair that touched her shoulders, and a great figure to boot.

"Hi, I'm Hanna." She took Addison's right hand in hers, cupped her left over the back of his, and gently squeezed. Her grip was firm and warm. "That was one hellacious performance, Mr. Stone."

Addison's heart skipped a beat. He couldn't take his eyes off this stunning young woman. "*P-P*, please call me Addison. Are you in the music business?"

"No, not, not me. A friend on the production staff slips me a ticket whenever I can make the show."

"Nice friend to have, um—"

"Hanna—H-a-n-n-a—without an *h* at the end. It was my mother's idea."

"Hanna without the *h*," Addison repeated.

"After tonight, everyone will know the name Addison Stone."

Addison blushed. "Oh, I don't know about that."

"Trust me; they will. What's next for you?"

"That's up to the Sherman Agency who represents me."

"Well, Addison Stone from Addison, Alabama—"

"That was my mother's idea."

"I'm happy to have this opportunity to have met you." Hanna glanced at her watch. "I promised to meet up with friends after the show. Good luck to you, Addison." She hesitated before turning to leave and stared at Addison as if to say something, but she didn't. She just stared.

"Were you going to say something?"

"Huh, no, I mean yes. When you sang *Your Love,* several people near me had tears in their eyes. The same is true with *Time to Say Goodbye*. You sing with great emotion. That's a gift."

"Thank you, Hanna."

"Well, I have to go. Best of luck to you.

Hanna turned and began to walk away."

Addison blurted, "Boyfriend?"

Hanna turned back. "What?'

"I was just wondering if you were meeting a boyfriend."

"Ah, I don't have one."

"Me neither… I mean a girlfriend."

"Then," Hanna said with a chuckle, "We both need to get a life. You take care now, Addison."

"Hanna?"

Hanna looked back over her shoulder. "Yes?"

"*I-I*… I was wondering if… I, ah, I would like to see you again sometime?"

Hanna thought for a moment. "I would like that. How long will you be in New York?"

"I don't know yet."

Hanna took a small pad from her purse, wrote her cell number, and handed it to Addison.

"If you're gonna' be in town for several days, call me."

"*O-o*, okay," Addison smiled. "I will, I promise."

Hanna tossed him a thumbs up and began walking away but stopped, turned back, and smiled. "Enjoy yourself. Tonight, you are on top of the world. Be well, Addison Stone. Call me if you can."

Addison, the shy introvert, was smitten by this lovely young creature. "Hanna," he whispered low as she walked into the crowd. His eyes remained on her until all he could see was the top of her reddish-blond hair. Like a wisp of wind, she was gone.

Ben had been watching the exchange with amusement. He inched closer to Addison and whispered, "See something you like?"

"What?"

"There will be many pretty young women circling you before long."

"Don't know what you're talking about, Ben. Let's eat."

Lang and Andy watched from nearby as guests continued to congratulate Addison.

"He has no idea what's about to happen to him," Andy said. "His unique voice and good looks are about to propel him to the Moon."

Lang nodded in agreement. "Yes, but remember that his entire singing experience has been in that church choir. We'll have to protect him and carefully walk him through the process. Tomorrow will tell where we go from here. Come on, let's boost his ego."

They approached Addison and Ben. "You, young man, are

about to begin the most exciting time of your life," Lang said. "You get the next two days off, enough time to let what happened sink in. We'll meet at the office on Monday. Julio will pick you up around one. Until then, take it easy and savor the pleasures of New York City."

Addison couldn't wait to return to his hotel room and write in his journal.

> *Tonight was magical. Not only did I win the show—a mind-blower in itself—but I met a beautiful angel named Hanna, who moved me in ways I have never experienced. She took my breath away. I hope to spend time with her before Lang and Andy send me off to parts unknown. God, was she beautiful, or what? My challenge now is taking Ben's advice and moving beyond the past into the future. Will I be able to do that? Why is it so difficult for me?*

Saturday morning, Addison awoke with a start. The unbelievable events of the previous night came flooding back. He won the show and a $10,000 prize to boot. Unfortunately, the prize money would go to securing the musical tracks.

His phone rang, and it startled him; it was Ben.

"Hey, you gonna sleep all day? I'm hungry; let's get breakfast already."

"Sorry, Ben, I overslept. Give me fifteen minutes."

"Hey, kiddo, congratulations. Last night, you caught the ball —game over. Have your feet touched the floor yet?"

Addison chuckled low. "No, not yet, Uncle Ben."

"Trust me, son, they will be, they will be. Now, let's get breakfast."

They spent Saturday and Sunday exploring more of New York. Ben had traveled extensively with the railroad, so he was used to big cities and knew how to get around. Addison gawked at the high-rise buildings and the dense traffic like it was CGI created for a movie.

Chapter 9

At 1:05 on Monday, Julio drove Addison and Ben to the Sherman Agency. When they entered the office, Lang, Andy, and the entire staff greeted them with applause, which embarrassed Addison. He smiled and nodded.

They entered Lang's office and sat at the conference table.

"Congratulations again, Addison," Lang said. "Today, the whole world knows your name."

"A little scary when I think about it, Lang," Addison answered with a sullen expression.

"Not to worry, you'll get used to it. Now, we have much to review. Andy will get us started."

Andy slipped a copy of *USA Today* across the table. "Open to page twelve."

Addison opened to page twelve, which was the entertainment section. The top feature story was about Addison, accompanied by a shot of him performing on *Sing America Sing*. As he began to read, his eyes grew big. "Ben, read this."

Ben took the paper and began to read. '*Addison Stone stole the show Friday night by winning the hit TV series Sing America Sing. Young Addison, named after his hometown of Addison,*

Alabama, is without exaggeration America's next singing sensation.'

"Wow," Ben said. "Pretty damn impressive."

Andy continued. "We have requests for interviews from Rolling Stone, Music Connection, and Billboard, just to name a few. Entertainment Tonight wants an on-camera interview, and one of the network late-night shows wants you on as a guest."

Lang took over. "Our phones began ringing Saturday morning with offers for you to appear in concert in Los Angeles, San Francisco, and Denver: more will come in."

Addison's brow went up. "I can't wrap my head around that, Lang."

"That's not all. This morning, Micro Records offered you a recording contract. When I told them we had a cross-country tour in the planning stages, they offered to record an album wherever your first venue might be."

Ben playfully slapped Addison's arm. "Wow, Batman, you're flying high today!"

"Wow, is right, Ben," Lang added. "Never in all my years have any of our clients ever clicked with audiences this fast following a single public performance. It confirms yet again the reach and influence of television."

Still overwhelmed by it all, Addison sat quietly, showing little emotion.

"We'd be crazy not to take advantage of these early responses. We need to get you on tour as soon as possible, beginning on the West Coast, continuing across the country, and ending in New York City."

Unsure he had heard right, Addison glanced at Ben and then at Lang. "A tour—this soon?"

"We strike when the iron is hot, and after last night, you're as hot as it gets. Not because of anything we did but because of how you and your unique voice resonated with *Sing America Sing's* massive worldwide audience. If you doubt that, check social media. It has exploded with stories about you."

"Really?"

"Like Lang said," Andy added, "that's the power of television. Now, for more good news. It's highly unusual for a venue to tamper with their schedule once locked in. The management of the Hollywood Bowl in LA called Andy a couple of hours ago. They would like your first live tour appearance to be with them if possible."

Addison's eyes widened in surprise. "Hollywood Bowl?

"They have a dark Saturday in three weeks and want to fill it with you. I called Micro Records. They agreed to record your performance for an album titled *Addison Stone at the Hollywood Bowl.* I mean, that's unheard of for a first-time out."

Addison's head was spinning again.

Andy smiled. "It doesn't stop there, Addison. Following the Bowl, Davies Symphony Hall in San Francisco and the Fillmore Auditorium in Denver are ready to commit. By the time you play Denver, we'll have the rest of the tour firmed up. Think of it, Addison; fresh out of the gate, you're already in high demand."

"I don't know what to say, Andy."

"How about… *Is this really happening to me, Andy?*"

"Now, to the business end," Lang said. "These tours deliver substantial paydays. That's why so many entertainers hit the road. You're going to need to get organized with a corporate entity."

"A what?"

"A company that oversees your business," Lang said. "Something simple like A. J. Stone Enterprises, LLC."

"Ah, sure, whatever you think."

Lang smiled and slid some papers across the desk. "Sign them, and you're all set."

Addison grinned when he saw the name A. J. Stone Enterprises. "You were that sure of me?"

Lang smiled. "Just a guess, my friend."

"Guys, I know nothing about running a company."

"There's not much to it. It amounts to writing checks and accounting for income and expenses so you don't end up in a federal prison for tax evasion. Your accounting firm will handle all that."

"Where would I find time with me on tour?"

"Maybe Ben could help out. You could make him your Chief Operating Officer if he was game."

Now, it was Ben's turn to roll his eyes and frown. "Me? I was a railroad engineer; I drove trains."

"There's really nothing to it, Ben," Lang said.

"Whew, I don't know, guys." He turned to Addison. "What do you think?"

"It's up to you, Ben."

"I guess I could try it if it helps you, Addy." Ben chortled. "Hell, I know how to sign checks."

"Are you sure, Ben?"

"I'll give it a try, Addy."

"Great. That solves that." Lang. "You'll need a corporate address."

Ben raised a hand. "How about mine to get us started?"

Andy nodded. "Problem number two solved."

Ben playfully smacked Addison's arm. "How can I ever thank you for getting me into this mess? That's what I get in return for spoiling you all those years."

"Did you spoil me, Ben? I don't remember that."

"Sign the papers, smart ass, and pronounce me COO of A. J. Stone Enterprises."

Andy passed a pen to Addison, and he signed the corporate papers.

"We'll overnight those to Henry Jackson, an attorney we've worked with in Birmingham," Lang said. "Once his office files, it'll take nine or ten days for the State to process them. Ben, when you receive confirmation, open a bank account for A. J. Enterprises and hire a local accounting firm. Let us know when that's done, and we'll begin wiring Addison's earnings to the bank as we process them. Until then, the Agency will continue to front all expenses. Addison, Ben tells us you're the only person on the planet without a cell phone."

"I've never needed one, Andy."

"You do now. We'll loan you one of ours before you leave, then, when the company is legal, Ben, get one for both of you issued to Stone Enterprises."

"When do we get to go home?" Addison asked.

"In a couple of days when everything is wrapped up here. Before you leave, we'll need a list of the songs you plan to sing on tour."

"How many?"

"Enough for an hour and a half show at a minimum."

Addison's face scrunched, and he leaned forward. "An hour and a half? That's a lot."

"Audiences expect no less, Addison. Your show will be in two parts. Following your first set, the backup singers will fill in with a short set while you rest off-stage. When they finish, you'll return, do your second set, and end the show. As soon as we receive your list and we're in sync with your selections, the list will be sent to Lawrence Ley, the Bowl's music director. Since this is your first time out, we've arranged a full rehearsal with Ley, the orchestra, and the Noble Street Singers, a highly in-demand L.A.-based backup chorus."

"Be sure to toss in a few numbers to demonstrate your versatility. Songs to get the audience on their feet, clapping and dancing."

"I'll work on the list when we return to the hotel."

"Oh, before you leave, Hillary Garcia, our PR Director, will take a few headshots of your handsome face. Be sure to smile. Okay, kid, we're off to the races."

Addison turned to Ben with a forlorn expression and swallowed hard.

Ben touched Addison's arm and said low, "Time to catch that next high-flying ball, son."

When Addison and Ben returned to the hotel, Addison opened his computer and began making a list of songs. After much thought, he chose *Your Love* as his opening number and *Time to Say Goodbye* to end the show. Now came the challenge of filling in the rest. He began typing the names of his favorite songs, the ones he loved, the ones he most wanted to sing, and there were many to choose from.

For the show's first half, he added *A New Day Has Come, I Dream a Dream, Love Changes Everything, The Music of the Night, Moon River, Don't Cry for Me Argentina, At Last,* and *You Raise Me Up.*

"Lang wants me to mix it up and demonstrate versatility. Huh, I didn't know I had any. Okay, if this doesn't get their hands clapping, nothing will."

He added a tribute to ABBA, his favorite singing group. Before the break, he would sing *I Have a Dream, The Winner Takes It All*, and *I Surrender.*

For the second act, he would begin with, *Be My Love, Lara's Song, Have You Ever Been in Love, Send in The Clowns, The Phantom of the Opera, You'll Never Walk Alone, Thank You for The Music,* and finally, *Time to Say Goodbye.* He Googled the running time of each song; the total was just short of an hour and forty-five minutes.

He emailed the list to Andy and waited.

An hour and a half later, Addison received an email from Andy. "Lang and I and a few others went over the list. Congratulations, it was unanimous. Go with this list. And the tribute to ABBA is brilliant. That'll have the audience on their feet for sure."

Addison emailed back. 'Thanks, Andy. As Lang would say, we're off to the races.'

As overwhelming as all of this was, for the first time, Addison believed he could begin to cut the strings of his past and start a new life filled with excitement, fame, and, hopefully, financial reward.

He called Lacy to tell her he and Ben planned to be home in two or three days, but the call went to her voicemail. Now, his top priority was to get in touch with Hanna and spend time with her before he left. When he dug around for the slip of paper containing her number, it was nowhere to be found. He searched everywhere—nothing—her phone number was lost.

"Damn it all to hell; that's the end of that! I'll never find her now! And she never said what her last name was. A dead end of all dead ends!

Friday morning, Addison and Ben flew to Birmingham with three performance dates set, a deal with Micro Records for his first album, and his own company.

He was quiet during the flight. It was Ben who did most of the talking.

"It's like you pulled back the curtain on the Wizard of Oz, Addy, and he handed you a pot of gold."

Addison smiled and nodded in agreement.

"That's it, that's your reaction?"

Addison made a silly face. "Twinkle, twinkle, little star, how I wonder—"

"Okay, okay, wise-ass, I got it."

When they arrived at the house, they were surprised by a dozen placards on the lawn congratulating Addison on winning *Sing America Sing*.

"Whoa," Ben said, "take a look at these, will ya? Nice welcome home."

Lacy met them at the door. "Well, the conquering heroes return." She hugged them both. "Ben, thank you for doing this."

"I should be thanking you, Lacy. It was the thrill of a lifetime being with this kid of yours as he introduced himself to the world. Pretty damn impressive."

"Oh, Ben," Addison said with a sly grin, "You're just saying that because you're the new COO of my new company."

"What company?" Lacy asked.

"Addy will tell you all about it, Lacy. I'm going to bed for the next two days. Addy, I suggest you do the same. Dream well, kiddo."

Lacy hugged Ben again, and he left.

"Who placed the signs on the lawn, Mom?"

"I have no idea, but I think our little town is quite proud of you."

Over dinner, Addison provided Lacy a blow-by-blow on everything that happened and was about to happen. He told Lacy about his new company and how Ben would oversee it.

"I'm still pinching myself, Mom."

"As well as you should. How long will you be gone on this tour?"

"That depends on how many venues the agency books. It could be six, seven weeks, or more."

Lacy's face slackened.

"We should make plans for you to visit me on the road at one of the venues."

"We'll see."

"Oh, look at this." Addison reached into his pocket and pulled out a cell phone.

"Where did you get that?"

"The agency loaned it to me until Ben gets two issued through the new company."

"I'll add your number to my contact list for you and add that number to mine.

"Mom, I have a better idea. Instead of visiting me in some city, you'll come to Los Angeles for my show at the Hollywood Bowl."

Lacy ignored the question, picked up their empty plates, and placed them in the sink. "Chick gave me the day off tomorrow to spend with you. You're going to need new clothes. You and I will go to Cullum and buy you some spiffy new clothes."

"Great. On the way home from the airport, I called Millie and offered to sing with the choir on Sunday, my way of thanking her and the gang for all they did."

"Good, Addy. That was the right thing to do."

Addison yawned. "I'm beat. I'm gonna hit the sack."

Lacy hugged and kissed him. "When you wake, we'll go shopping.

Following Addison's nap, Lacy drove them to a menswear outlet in Cullum. There, they picked out a dark gray suit, grey slacks, a dark blue blazer, and two long-sleeved shirts to go with them.

At 7:30 the following morning, Addison awoke, put on his robe, and went to the kitchen. Lacy wasn't there, which surprised him; it was a work day, and Lacy had always been an early riser. He fixed himself a cup of coffee and sat at the table. By 8:15, Lacy still had not gotten up. Concerned, he went to her bedroom door, lightly knocked, and waited, but there was no answer. Opening the door, he peeked in and saw Lacy was still sleeping even though the bright morning sunlight streamed in from the window.

As he approached her bed, two items on her nightstand caught his attention—a small amount of residue of dark liquid in a spoon next to an empty syringe. Repulsed, he backed away. He saw Lacy breathing normally, so he left, quickly paced to Ben's door, and knocked.

"Good morning, Addy." Addison's dour expression signaled something was wrong. "What's up?"

Addison walked further into the living room.

"Addy?"

"Moms always up early. This morning, she wasn't, so I checked on her. I entered the room and approached her bed. Ben, there was a spoon with the remnants of a brownish liquid next to an empty syringe on her nightstand."

Ben turned away, tossed his hands up, and wailed, "Damn it, damn it!"

"What was it?"

"It sounds like heroin."

"Heroin! You knew about this, Ben?"

"Hell no. I knew she used cocaine sometimes, but—"

Addison raised a clenched fist and punched the air. "She was using cocaine?"

"When I found out, I confronted her. She said she needed it sometimes and to mind my own damn business."

"She needed cocaine for what?"

"Addy, you know as well as me Lacy still deals with deep emotional scars from the abuse she received from her blood-sucking, alcoholic, drug-using grandparents."

"And for that, she needs Heroin?"

Ben folded his arms across his chest and paced across the room. "Addy, get used to it; Lacy is not emotionally ready to take this ride with you. She fears losing you to your budding career."

"She told you that?"

"Yes, a couple of times."

"Oh, for God's sake, that's utterly ridiculous."

"Addy, listen to me, she's—"

"No, Ben, you listen. I won't stand by and watch her kill herself as her parents did. We have to confront her now."

"No, Addy," Ben said adamantly, "*you* won't do *anything*. I'll take care of this *after* you leave for California."

"I want her with me in California, Ben."

"Addy, that's not going to happen."

"Then screw it all; Mom comes first."

"Now, you're talking crazy talk." Ben moved to Addison's side and rested his hands on Addison's shoulders. "Listen to me. The best way you can help Lacy is to stay focused on you and your future. I said I'd take care of this, and I will."

"After what I saw on her nightstand, how am I supposed to face her now, Ben?"

"You just do."

Addison tossed his hands up. "With all that's gone down between us over the years, that's easier said than done."

"You'll find a way, Addy. Now go before she gets up and wonders where you are."

When Addison returned to the house, Lacy was drinking coffee at the kitchen table. Her eyes were glassy, and she looked pale and tired.

"Good morning, Mom. Aren't you working today?"

"I just called Chick and told him I'd be late. Where have you been?"

"Checking up on Ben."

"Oh, your phone rang while you were gone. It was your agent, Andrew Crawford. He asked that you call him. Your phone is by your computer."

"Thanks, I better see what he wants."

Addison went to his bedroom, closed the door, and sat on the bed with his head in his hands. "Mom, Mom, what are you doing to yourself?" Finally, he returned Andy's call.

"Sorry I called so early, Addison, but we've scheduled an interview with a reporter from the Northwest Alabamian Newspaper for later today."

"Today? Jeez, I just got home, Andy."

"It'll take no more than an hour. We've also scheduled an interview tomorrow with WVTM-TV, the NBC station in Birmingham."

"Whoa, slow down, Andy. I don't want to get swallowed up with a bunch of damn interviews."

There was a momentary silence before Andy said, "Get used to it; it goes with the territory. We also have other requests for interviews and TV appearances in L.A. to coincide with your appearance at the Hollywood Bowl. The office is working on those. Now, how about 4:00 this afternoon for the Northwest interview?"

"Don't I have a say in this?"

"Not unless you know more about this business than we do."

"All right, Andy, point made. I'll do the newspaper interview."

"And the TV interview?"

"I'll think about it."

"You'll think about it? Hmm, okay, I'll let Lang know. I'll check in with you later."

At 3:55 that afternoon, the reporter from the newspaper showed up. Addison gave him twenty-five minutes and agreed to one photo to accompany the article.

At 5:30, his phone rang. "Addison, it's Lang. You did the newspaper interview?"

"Yes."

"Andy tells me you don't want to do the TV interview."

"It's not that I don't want to; I just want to take it slow."

"Addison, turtles go slow; dolphins go fast."

"Lang, I, ah—"

"Don't interrupt. I understand this is all coming at you fast. But you chose it, and now your job is to go with it. The staff is working hard on your behalf: An Addison Jordon Stone website, a Facebook fan page, a Twitter account, TikTok, and Instagram accounts are all in the works. That's what we do for our clients. You, in turn, get to support what is being done on your behalf."

"Sounds like I'm being chewed out, Lang?"

"In the nicest way, I know how. Look, Addison, winning *Sing America Sing* was a big deal. There will be constant media attention, the paparazzi, butt-kissers, hangers-on, and public adulation, especially after you appear at the Hollywood Bowl. We understand how difficult it is for a young man with no previous experience to grapple with all this. But know this: you're not alone. I'll be there for you every step of the way, as will Andy and the entire staff. We *will* protect you."

"*I-I,* I know that, Lang."

"Good. Then we're in sync?"

Addison took a breath and hesitated. "Yes."

"You'll do the TV interview?"

"Yes."

"Andy will set it up for tomorrow. Stay loose, smile, and don't look at the camera during a TV interview. Keep your eyes on the interviewer."

"Got it, Lang."

"Okay, we're off to the races, kid. Hang in there, and whatever you do, don't panic."

Addison hung up, sat back, ran his hands through his hair, and sulked. "You're off to the races, kid. Lucky me."

Reluctantly, Addison sat for the TV interview. He never thought that in his lifetime, he would be featured on TV for any reason, let alone winning *Sing America Sing.* He followed Andy's advice: *relax, answer questions honestly, and don't look at the camera.*

Addison felt good about the interviews and thought it had gone well. To his surprise, he seemed to enjoy it.

Lacy's drug addiction continued to gnaw at Addison like a wound that refused to heal. He wished he had not entered her room and found the spoon and syringe. Now, he felt compelled to do something about it.

He marched over to Ben's and knocked on the door.

"Addy, come in."

"Ben, I would never forgive myself if I didn't try to do anything to help her."

"Addy, I already have."

"You already have what?"

"I spoke with a lady at the Gulf Coast Treatment Center in Grand Bay in Southwestern Mobile County. She agreed Lacy was an immediate candidate for treatment. They want her to meet first with the drug rehabilitation counselor at their satellite office in Cullum. The challenge will be convincing her to go when she finds out that, based on what I told the lady, it will require inpatient treatment; she may not go for that."

"What if she refuses?"

"One step at a time, Addy. And don't you let on that you know any of this until she agrees to go."

Addison walked to the door, stopped, and turned back—there were tears in his eyes. Ben went to him, put his arms around him, and held him.

"It's going to be okay, Addy, I promise you. I'll take care of Lacy. Go, do what I told you. Go catch that next high-flying ball. That'll make us happy and proud."

"Okay, Ben."

When word got out that Addison was home and would sing with the choir on Sunday, the church parking lot was overflowing by 9:00. There was insufficient seating to accommodate everyone who had come, and fire regulations forbade people to stand. Addison suggested a second choir performance to accommodate those still waiting outside.

"These kind folks came to hear me and the choir sing. We should not disappoint them."

The pastor agreed and made an announcement to the crowd waiting outside. A loud cheer went up.

After the second choir performance, the crowd waited outside to glimpse their soon-to-be-famous hometown boy. With Lacy and Ben by his side, cheers, hoots, and hollers greeted them. The media was there in full force.

Addison seemed to relish every second. Lacy and Ben beamed.

Andy called to tell Addison the office had booked him on a Tuesday morning flight to Los Angeles. Addison's short vacation had come to an end. He made no other further mention of Lacy joining him since Ben was working on getting her into rehab.

After a tearful goodbye with Lacy Tuesday morning, Ben drove Addison to the Birmingham airport to catch his 11:00 a.m. flight.

"As soon as you hear anything from the rehab people, call me."

"Of course, Addy. Now, Mr. Big Shot, knock them dead at the Hollywood Bowl just like you did on TV."

Addison forced a smile. "I'll give it my best, Ben."

"I know you will."

Chapter 10

After a six-and-a-half-hour flight with a stop in Dallas, Addison arrived in LA. Andy and another man met him in the baggage area.

"Good flight?"

"Ah, a little bumpy out of Dallas, but otherwise okay."

"You remember Ty Webber. You met at the Dolby Theater in New York."

"Yes, of course. Good to see you again, Mr. Webber."

"Good to see you too, Addison. And please call me *Ty*."

"Since this is your first outing, Ty will travel with you; he'll handle all details from city to city."

Addison looked relieved. "Whew, Andy, that's a relief."

"You didn't think we'd let you go out there alone, did you?"

"Since this is all new to me, it never crossed my mind."

"By the time you get to New York, you and Ty should be fast friends."

Ty laughed. "Let's hope you're not bored with me by then, Addison."

"Where are we staying? I promised to let my mother know."

"No far from the Bowl at the Hollywood Roosevelt Hotel,"

Ty said. "You'll meet Lawrence Ley and Noble Street tomorrow morning. The LA-based seven-member Noble Street Singers is your backup group. We've hired them to accompany you on tour instead of dealing with a new group in each city."

Addison looked relieved. "Yeah, I like that."

"After lunch tomorrow, you're all set up for interviews with Rolling Stone, The Hollywood Reporter, Entertainment Weekly, and a TV interview with Entertainment Tonight. By the way, Lang negotiated a 30% cut of the gross with the Bowl, and tickets are going fast. Given the response you received on *Sing American Sing*, we expect your performance will be sold out."

"Sold out? Wow!" Addison's head was spinning yet again.

Thursday morning, they drove the short distance to the Hollywood Bowl.

"We're going to do a full rehearsal, Andy?"

"Yes."

"Let's hope I don't screw it up."

"You'll be fine. The orchestra and the singers will do their thing, and you'll do yours."

Addison grinned. "Tell me again, Andy, what is it I do?"

"As I recall, it has something to do with your voice."

The orchestra and the Noble Street Singers were already on the stage when they arrived.

Addison walked to the end of the stage and stared out at the arena. The sheer size of the place gave him a chill.

Ty walked up to him and saw the look on Addison's face. "Just over 17,000 seats. A little intimidating, isn't it?

Addison scanned the amphitheater from one side to the other. "Yeah, just a little."

A man appeared from the wings and waved. "Good morning, gentlemen."

"Larry, there you are," Andy called to him.

"Good to see you guys again. It's been a while."

Andy placed a hand on Addison's shoulder. "Say hello to *The Voice*—Addison Stone. Addison, this is music director extraordinaire Lawrence Ley."

Ley shook Addison's hand. "Young man, you have the purest voice I've heard in a long time."

"Thank you, sir."

"I look forward to working with you, young man."

"Okay," Andy said. "Quick introductions before we begin." Andy waved to a lady standing with Noble Street. "Ivey?"

Ivey walked to them and hugged Ley. "Good to see you again, old man."

Ty motioned to Addison. "Ivey, meet Addison Stone. Addison, Miss Ivey Wagner creator and lead singer of the Noble Street Singers."

Addison thought she looked young to be the creator of the group. She was very attractive, with short blond hair and light green eyes.

"I watched your appearance on *Sing America Sing,* Addison. I know you've heard this a hundred times already, but you have an amazing talent. The gang and I are excited to be joining you on the tour."

Addison smiled and nodded.

Ivey pointed to the other singers. "That raggedy bunch over there from left to right is John, Carl, Cathy, Elizabeth, Julie, and Margaret."

The group waved and, in unison, called out, "Hello, Addison."

Ivey held up several sheets of paper. "Now, to business. We've broken down our participation in each of the songs. It pretty much follows what is standard for the songs you've chosen. If you want anything changed, let me know."

"Thank you, Ivey."

Ley pointed to the conductor. "Standing on the raised platform over there like he owns the place is the Bowl's musical director, the amazing Henry Zimmer."

Zimmer waved. "Good luck, Addison."

Addison waved back. "Thank you."

The orchestra's drummer did a rim shot, and all the thirty

musicians waved.

Ley continued. "I gathered the standard arrangements for each song you've chosen. We'll tweak them if you hear anything that feels off. Here's how the show is broken down. You'll sing all songs through the three ABBA numbers, then take a break off stage while Noble Street sings ABBA's *Mamma Mia, Chiquita,* and *Dancing Queen.* That should have the audience on their feet. You'll come back and sing the rest of your numbers except *Thank You for the Music, We Will Meet Again,* and *Time to Say Goodbye.* You'll pretend the show's over and leave the stage."

"How do I do that?"

"Thank the audience for coming, take your bows, shake hands with the conductor, and leave. The applause will persist until you return for an encore. You'll come back and sing those last three songs, and the show's over. Any questions?"

"None from me, sir."

"Okay then, Ladies and gentlemen, boys and girls, let's rehearse."

When he sang his last song, the orchestra, and Noble Street gave Addison a loud round of applause. "Bravo," voices called out.

Addison was pleasantly surprised at how the orchestra and Noble Street brought his songs to life.

"Well done, Addison. Your eclectic selection of songs will have the audience begging for more."

"I hope you're right, Mr. Ley."

After thanking everyone, Addison walked to the edge of the stage and stared at the vast seating area again.

"They're just seats, Addison."

"Yeah, Ty, but they'll be full of people."

"Think of them as contributing to the growth of your bank account."

Addison found that funny and laughed. Little did he know that, like a garden of roses, how much his bank account was about to grow.

As they left, Addison whispered to Ty, "Ivey looks kind of

young to have created this singing group."

Ty whispered back. "Would you believe she's twenty-six and easy on the eyes? Talk about young talent."

That afternoon, in a meeting room at the Roosevelt, Addison sat for interviews with Rolling Stone Magazine, The Hollywood Reporter, Entertainment Weekly, and finally, an on-camera interview with Entertainment Tonight.

When the interviews were over, Ty complimented him. "You did quite well."

"Did I come off too stiff?"

"Not at all. Remember to treat each interview as your first; you'll come off sounding and looking great each time."

Except for a breakfast meeting with Andy and Ty to review details again; Thursday and Friday were free days for Addison.

"Use your free time to see a little of Hollywood, Addison," Andy said. "This town has a special magical vibe."

Addison took to the streets of Hollywood, touring Madame Tussauds Museum and the famous Grauman's Chinese Theater with the foot and handprints of the stars embedded in the walkway out front. He had lunch at the Hard Rock Café, walked along the Walk of Fame, and viewed the Hollywood sign atop Mount Lee.

It would not be long before he found walking the streets nearly impossible without being recognized.

When he returned to his dark room at the hotel, something or someone was swaying by the window, and it frightened him; he quickly turned on the light. There, by the window, were six balloons tied together.

"What the heck?"

There was an envelope attached to the end of the balloon strings. To Addison's surprise, it was a birthday card from Lacy and Ben. In all the excitement, Addison had forgotten it was January 28th, his 20th birthday.

When Addison told Andy and Ty it was his birthday, they

treated him to dinner at Musso & Frank Grill, a legendary hangout for the Hollywood elite.

Andy raised his wine glass. "Happy Birthday, Addison. One more year, and you'll be a responsible adult."

Addison smiled. "At least according to the law."

When Addison, Andy, and Ty arrived at the Hollywood Bowl on Saturday, the Stage Manager escorted them directly to Addison's beautifully decorated dressing room. One wall displayed framed photos of the famous performers who had appeared at the Bowl over the years.

"Someone will be by at 5:30 to see what you'd like for dinner," the Stage Manager said. "Expect the makeup lady around 6:45. I'll come for you around 7:30 and get you settled in the wings. Okay, best of luck to you."

Andy glanced at his watch. "Unless you need us for something, Ty and I will leave you to get some rest before the show. It's best if you eat a light dinner. After the show, it's customary to greet well-wishers here in your dressing room."

"Oh? Will you be here?"

"No. People feel less intimated if they can meet with you alone. Break a leg, kid."

"I'm gonna' have to Google that one, Andy."

His cell phone rang as Addison prepared to lie down for a brief nap. It was Lang.

"Hey, Addison, ready for your big debut?"

"As ready as I will ever be, Lang."

"Sorry I couldn't be there, but I have multiple alligators to deal with here in New York. I'm confident you'll wow them tonight."

Addison sighed. "From your lips to—"

Lang finished Addison's comment. "… to the music god's ear."

"Thank you, Lang; I appreciate everything you've done for me."

"Addison, on *Sing America Sing*, I swear I saw you

disappear into yourself. I don't know how you did it, but from then on, it looked like you had blocked out the world, and it was just you and the music. Am I right?'

"Yeah, Ben told me that, too. I can't explain it, but yes, I somehow do."

"Well, do it again tonight. Break a leg, kid."

After the call, Addison slept for about an hour. At five, he took a shower. At 5:30, recalling what Andy said about eating light, he ordered a Caesar salad and an iced tea. At 6:40, the makeup lady arrived. When she left, he put on his new grey suit and open-collar powder blue shirt, sat in one of the lounge chairs, and entered a note in his journal.

> *I'd be lying to myself if I didn't admit being scared as hell. This isn't the church choir on Sunday morning. This is the real thing in front of 17,000-plus people. What if I freeze? What if I forget some lyrics? My head is not clear; it's fogged. Damn it, I need to pull it together.*

He put the journal aside, sat facing the wall of photos, and marveled with great respect at the famous performers' photos who had preceded him. *This is it*, He thought. *Tonight will determine if I can live up to their standards. Unless, of course, I have a massive panic attack and fall into a puddle of urine after I wet my pants. With the blessing of the music gods', and this voice I was born with, all will be well. Repeat ten times while standing on one leg.*

Chapter 11

7:30 PM. The Stage Manager escorted Addison backstage to a lounge area with a sofa, two matching chairs, and a coffee table. Andy and Ty were there.

"You guys look comfortable."

Ty grinned. "We've done our work, Addison; the rest is up to you. Are you ready?"

"Nervous."

"That's normal, even for seasoned performers," Andy said. "That'll melt away once you're into it."

Addison began to pace.

"Come, sit. You still have twenty minutes."

"I'd rather pace, Ty."

"Suit yourself, but they say pacing is how shoes get worn out."

Addison raised an eyebrow. "Funny, very funny."

At exactly 8:00, the unseen announcer began.

"Good evening, ladies and gentlemen, and welcome to the Hollywood Bowl. On August 14, 1943, Frank Sinatra was the first singer to appear on this stage, followed over the years by an endless lineup of legendary performers. Tonight, the Hollywood Bowl has the honor of presenting a new young performer making his first public appearance after winning *Sing America Sing* with the highest score ever. Without further ado, please give a warm and rousing Hollywood Bowl welcome to Addison Jordon Stone."

The applause was electrifying. As Addison entered from the wings, the curtain rolled back, revealing the orchestra and the Noble Street Singers. He shook hands with the conductor, gave a thumbs-up to Noble Street, and glanced out at the crowd of 17,376. His back stiffened, and a cold chill ran through him. Sheepishly, he smiled and bowed his head slightly.

The rhapsodic applause continued. Addison turned to the conductor and nodded. The Orchestra began playing the forty-three-second intro to *Your Love*. Addison removed the microphone from the stand, walked a few feet to his left, and stood stiffly.

Thirty seconds before the musical intro ended, Addison closed his eyes, took a deep breath, and slowly pivoted to the audience; his eyes were still closed. He had withdrawn deep into himself as he had done before; now, it was just him and his music. He opened his eyes and began singing *Your Love*. He poured his heart into it as he had done before. When he finished, the audience was on their feet; the applause and cheering were overwhelming. Addison smiled and bowed.

The zealous response from the audience was just what Addison needed to calm himself and bolster his confidence. He was totally into it now.

When Addison finished singing *You Raise Me Up*, he removed his jacket and hung it on the microphone stand.

"Let's mix it up a bit. One of my all-time favorite singing groups is ABBA. Agnetha Fältskog, Björn Ulvaeus, Benny Andersson, and Anni-Frid Lyngstad are Sweden's Gift to the World. ABBA is among the most commercially successful bands in the history of popular music. Let's hope I pronounced their names correctly."

The audience laughed and went wild when Addison sang, *I Have a Dream*, *The Winner Takes It All,* and *I Surrender*. When he finished, and the applause died down, he motioned to Noble Street and said the line Ty had him memorize. "Ladies and gentlemen, please give a warm reception to the amazing Ivey Wagner and the Noble Street Singers."

As Noble Street began singing *Mamma Mia*, Addison tossed his jacket over his shoulder, put the mic back on its stand, and exited stage left to the wings.

Andy was smiling from ear to ear. "Addison, you have them; that audience is yours, baby."

Addison took a deep breath and exhaled slowly. "Let's hope I don't have a heart attack before the show's over."

Ty shook his head. "Bad joke, Addison, bad joke."

"Okay, Ty, how about this? Three singers entered a bar, and —"

The Stage Manager interrupted Addison and handed him a bottle of water. "Kid, I've been working here for nine years, and I've never seen the audience go this nut. Congratulations."

Addison responded with a sheepish grin. "Thank you."

"Drink up." Ty said, "Get ready to wow them with your second half."

"Whew, I didn't expect the enthusiastic response I've received so far."

"Addison," Andy said, "You forget that millions upon millions watched you win *Sing America Sing*. Overnight, you became the darling of social media. This audience was primed, and so are those to come."

The Noble Street Singers began singing *Chiquita*. The audience was on their feet, clapping in rhythm with the music. The aisles filled with people dancing; this audience was pumped. The group ended their set with *Dancing Queen*.

Addison returned to the stage to a rousing greeting. He waved to the audience. "Ladies and gentlemen, the Noble Street Singers. Are they great, or what?"

The audience responded with another round of applause.

When Addison finished the rest of his repertoire, he said the line he had practiced. "Thank you; you've been a wonderfully generous audience."

He shook hands with the conductor, waved to Ivey and Noble Street, and exited to the wings. The audience was on their feet, clapping their hands in unison and yelling *Encore* as Addison watched from just off stage.

Andy called out to Addison. "Go wow them with your encore, tiger."

Addison returned to the stage and began singing *Thank You for The Music*, followed by *We Will Meet Again,* and finally, *Time to Say Goodbye*, singing the opening stanza in Italian. The audience went wild, gifting Addison with a standing ovation lasting several minutes.

The magical, fantastic night had come to an end. It was the beginning of Addison Jordon Stone's meteoric rise to worldwide fame.

Following the show, Addison greeted well-wishers in his dressing room. One older, retired, beloved pop star, who had performed at the Bowl many years back and whose framed photo was on the wall, came by.

"Son, that was as prodigious a performance as I've ever heard. You're going places fast." He pointed to the wall of photos. "Your photo will be there with the rest of us long after you and me are gone. Congratulations."

"Coming from you, sir, means a great deal to me. Thank you."

"Can I give you a bit of free advice?"

"Yes, of course, sir."

"You're young, talented, and just starting out. Don't let this business swallow you up as it has others. Fame and money can be dangerous aphrodisiacs. Never forget that you're just a human being who happens to be blessed with a special gift. Remain humble, respect and protect that gift, and this business will treat you well."

"Thank you."

"Good luck, Addison." The man shook Addison's hand and left.

Ty entered. "I saw who just left. Gracious of him to stop by."

"Yes. It was a thrill for me, Ty."

"Oh, Andy checked with Micro Records' chief engineer. All went well with the recording of the show."

Addison blew a breath. "Whew, Ty, my nerves were so on edge, I forgot about the recording."

"Oh, one more fan asks to see you."

"Okay, Ty, send them in."

Ty left. A minute later, the door opened halfway, and a young woman peeked into the room.

Addison's eyes bloomed, and he swallowed hard. "Hanna?"

"You remembered my name."

Addison was beside himself with excitement. "*I-I*-I'm so pleased to see you."

"I was hoping we'd get together in New York before you left, but you never called."

"I had every intention of calling you." Addison slapped the back of his head. "Would you believe dumb me lost the slip of paper with your number? But here you are. I'm pleased to see you again."

"I loved your show, and obviously, so did that audience."

"I admit I was a nervous wreck; I hope it didn't show."

"It didn't, you were fine."

"Hanna, what are you doing in L.A.?"

"Have dinner with me, my treat, and I promise to reveal all."

Addison beamed, "Yeah, dinner, okay."

"Tell your man I will deliver you to your hotel unscathed."

Addison explained to Ty that he had met Hanna at the reception in New York after the show. They would catch a bit to eat, and then she would drive him to the Roosevelt.

"First autograph seekers are lined up outside."

"Oh crap, Ty, I forgot about that. Why do people want my signature anyway?"

Ty grinned. "Ours is not to reason why Addison, ours is but to do and die."

"Whatever that means, Ty."

Addison explained the autograph situation to Hanna. He asked where she had parked; his driver would meet her there.

Outside, there was a long line of autograph seekers waiting. Addison quickly signed as many as he could as he made his way to the waiting limo. Hanna would be waiting for him in Lot B.

"Hanna, for the love of me, I have no idea why people stand in long lines to get my signature."

"That's what fans do. It makes them feel closer to their idols."

Hanna drove to a nearby all-night dinner. Over burgers and fries, they chatted away, getting to know one another.

"You still haven't told me what you're doing here in L.A."

"I'm studying filmmaking at the American Film Institute."

"You're going to direct movies?"

"No, no, my interests are corporate films and documentaries. I still have a year to go. Now, about you. That was one heck of a knockout performance. Your wonderfully creative song list has something for everyone. And you pour so much emotion into each song. You had people in tears."

"They're the songs I love to sing. By the way, I never did get your last name."

"It's Potts."

Addison's eyes narrowed. "Potts?"

Hanna laughed. "How else do you think I get into the shows for free? I'm the one and only child of Stan and Sally, producers of *Sing American Sing*?"

"Wow, if I had known, I could have called the production office for your phone number."

"Now that we have that cleared up, what's next for you, Addison?"

"A cross-country tour. This was the first stop."

"Whoa, so quick. Congratulations are in order."

"It took me by surprise, too. Next is The Davies Symphony

Hall next week in San Francisco, then on to Denver. The agency will have the rest of the tour lined up by then. The final stop is New York City."

"How exciting that it has come together for you as quickly as it has."

"Yes and no, Hanna; it's all I can do to keep up."

Hanna reached across the table, took his hand in hers, and squeezed. "I know, Lang Sherman. You're in good hands. He and his staff are the best."

They spent the next hour chatting away like teenagers on their first date. Clearly, Addison was infatuated with Hanna. He felt comfortable with her as he never had with the fairer sex. Unless it was his ego working overtime, Addison felt Hanna might be interested in him or why she would come tonight. "It would be great if we could see one another again to compensate for New York."

"I would like that, Addison. But I don't know when with me in school and you on the road."

"We could start by keeping in touch by phone."

"Yes, of course, we can FaceTime. Hand me your phone."

Addison dug in his pocket and handed Hanna his phone. She entered her number in his contacts list. Then she put his number in hers.

"There. Now, there's no excuse for losing them."

Addison chuckled. "Assuming I don't lose my phone."

"Don't you dare, young man. It's getting late. I have a class first thing in the morning, and you must be exhausted. I better get us both home."

"Gosh, I wish we had more time."

"Your wish is my command, but unfortunately, circumstances will keep us apart."

"Lots of phone time."

"Count on it, Addison."

When they arrived at the Roosevelt, Hanna walked Addison to the door. Addison took her hand in his. "Thank you for coming, Hanna; it was the highlight of my night."

Hanna laughed. "I don't think so, but it was kind of you to say so." Hanna smiled, hugged him, and kissed his cheek. "Good luck on tour. And don't forget you promised to call."

"A promise is not a promise unless you keep it, and I will."

"I'll hold you to it, *Megastar*."

Addison laughed and clapped his hands. "Megastar in training—*maybe*."

Hanna hugged and kissed him again, and then she was off.

For Addison, their time together had been magical and all too short. He felt a connection to this gentle, beautiful woman, one he could not readily explain. Was it nothing more than an infatuation with this pretty young lady, or was it something more, something deeper that he didn't yet understand?

He watched Hanna drive away until, like a whisp of wind, she was lost in traffic.

Returning to his room, he took out his journal.

> *I barely know Hanna, yet our time together this evening continues to awaken suppressed feelings I didn't think I was capable of sharing with anyone, let alone understanding. I pray that I'm right, but something was happening between us; I know it and felt it.*

Chapter 12

Andy flew back to New York; Addison and Ty were on their own for the rest of the tour, with daily support from the New York office. Addison and Ty flew to San Francisco to prepare for Addison's performance at the Davies Symphony Hall. Even though Davies Hall had 2,743 seats as opposed to the Bowl's 17,376, it was a prestigious venue where top performers jumped at an opportunity to appear.

Thanks to Lang's negotiations, Addison was guaranteed a minimum of thirty top local musicians at each venue, primarily members of local symphony orchestras. Along with Noble Street Singers, he would be accompanied by the best.

Addison's performance went exceptionally well. After singing his encore, the Davis Hall audience thanked him with a standing ovation and a chorus of *Bravo, Bravo*! Addison Jordon Stone, the insecure and shy kid from Addison, Alabama, was on a role, and it was just beginning.

Following the show, Addison and Ty sat in Addison's dressing room, about to greet guests. The press interviews Addison had sat for in LA were coming out. Ty handed him the entertainment section of the Los Angeles Times.

"Read the first paragraph out loud, Addison."

"Okay, Ty. *Last night, I had the pleasure of listening to a truly talented rising young star. On the first stop of his cross-country tour, Addison Stone, a recent winner of 'Sing America Sing,' wowed the audience at the famed Hollywood Bowl. Young Mr. Stone has an extraordinary voice that defies definition. His range appears to have no boundaries as he transitioned easily between classic and contemporary songs. Amazingly, young Stone has no formal training other than singing in a church choir in Cullum. Alabama. Bravo, Mr. Stone, for a genuinely moving performance. You are about to take off like a rocket ship.*"

"Well?"

"Nice review, Ty."

"Just nice?"

"Okay, more than nice. So many of the questions in the interviews I've done so far are all the same and strike me as endless gossip."

"I'll give you a pass on that one, Addison, because this is all new to you. But reviews and interviews are worth a million bucks of free PR. Would you prefer the press ignore you?"

Addison frowned. "No, I suppose not."

"Right. Okay, people are waiting to shake your hand. Wipe off that frown and put on a happy face."

When the last well-wisher had come and gone, Ty returned with a mischievous grin. "One more, and you're finished for the night."

"Whew! Okay, okay, send them in."

Ty left, and Addison waited. Finally, the door opened slowly, and a head of reddish-blond hair appeared.

Addison's face lit up, and he popped to his feet. "Hanna!"

"I drove five hours and thirty-eight minutes to arrive in time for your performance, so please tell me you're happy to see me."

"*Of-of*, of course. I'm just surprised. Please, *c-c*, come in."

"Hanna went to Addison and hugged him. "Well, like a bad penning, here I am again."

"You mean like a silver dollar. I'm so pleased. Sit and be comfortable. Can I get anything?"

"No, I'm good." She sat on the sofa; Addison sat next to her. He was at a complete loss for words.

Hanna blew a breath. "Whew, I'm pooped from the drive. That was another great show tonight. I thought you were more at ease than in LA."

"You think so?"

"Yes. Say, have you had dinner yet?"

"Just a little something before the show."

"I'm starved, Addison; feed me."

Addison asked Ty to recommend a nearby restaurant. He suggested Uccello Lounge and gave Hanna directions. "It's not far from here. It's a collaboration of experienced restaurant professionals and the West Coast's premier music academy. And the food is excellent. I'll call ahead and reserve you a table."

Addison and Hanna followed the same routine; Addison would leave, sign autographs, and instruct his driver to take him to where Hanna had parked her car.

When Addison and Hanna arrived at the Uccello Lounge, heads turned.

"I think some of these folks recognize you from the show."

As they settled in at their table, an elderly couple approached. They had attended Addison's concert and had high praise for his performance. Addison smiled and thanked them.

"You see, two shows in two cities, and you're already famous. Your career is locked and loaded for success."

"It's not me, Hanna; it's the voice."

"Huh?"

"I'm the vessel that houses the voice, and I'm along for the ride."

"That's silly."

"I can't explain it, Hanna; it's how I feel."

"Addison, how can you separate yourself from your voice? That doesn't make sense."

Addison looked away briefly before turning back, leaned into the table, and said low, "Why did you come all this way?"

"To see your show."

"You've already seen me perform twice."

"Would you rather I hadn't come?"

"Oh, no, just the opposite. Will I see you in Denver next?" Hanna laughed. "No, I think not."

"Not even for the weekend if I sent you a ticket?"

"Oh, Addison, you don't have to do that."

"But I would love to see you again. Let me have Ty arrange for a flight the week I'm there. Come on, say yes."

"Yes, on one condition."

"Name it."

"No argument, I buy my own ticket."

"If that's the only way I get to see you again, so be it."

"I have a room booked at your hotel for the night. Let's plan breakfast together, and then I drive back to LA.

Following breakfast in the morning, Hanna and Addison said goodbye at the hotel's front door. Hanna hugged him and kissed Addison on the cheek.

"Be well, Addison; we'll see each other in Denver."

Then, like a whisp of wind, Hanna was gone again."

Back in his room, Addison opened his journal and began writing.

> *Wow, what just happened? Hanna has me dancing on air. She makes me feel—hell, I don't know, I can't put it into words. I know that Hanna has my head spinning in all directions in a wonderfully exhilarating way that I have never experienced before. How lucky I am to have found this beautiful young lady. Now, let's hope I don't screw it up.*

Chapter 13

Addison placed a call to Ben.

"Hey, how is it going, superstar?"

"Good so far, Ben. I'm off to Denver in a couple of hours. What's going on with Mom?"

"I was planning on calling you. Lacy surprised me and agreed to meet with the counselor in Cullum without an argument. This time, I believe her when she says she wants to get clean, or she wouldn't have agreed to the interview."

"That's great news, Ben. Let's hope this is a new beginning for her. Call me after she meets with the counselor."

"I will. In the meantime, Addy, call her. And *do not* let on that you know anything."

"I'll call her now. Take care, Ben."

"You too, Addy. Keep wowing those audiences."

Knowing what he knew, Addison dreaded calling Lacy. When she answered her phone, he lied and told her he was about to leave for the airport and only had a few minutes to talk. He assured her all was well and that he would call again from Denver. He made no mention of Hanna.

About an hour after they checked into the hotel in Denver, Ty came to his room with the schedule for the rest of the tour.

"Hot off the press from the New York office. Following Denver, it's the old Vic Theater in Chicago, the James L. Knight Center in Miami, the Atlanta Convention Center in Atlanta, Heinz Hall for the Performing Arts in Pittsburg, John F. Kennedy Center for the Performing Arts in Washington D.C., Symphony Hall in Boston, and Radio City Music Hall in New York City."

Addison's brow furrowed. "That's eight more weeks on the road, Ty."

"And your point would be?"

Addison shrugged. "It's a lot, that's all."

Ty ignored Addison and moved on. "The office has been flooded with interview requests and television appearances. Lang placed them all on hold until you finish the tour except for local stuff at each venue."

"Well, that's one for me."

"There's one more item."

Addison gave him the evil eye. "Break it to me gently."

Ty handed Addison a slip of paper with a series of numbers on it. "What's this?"

"Your take from the LA Bowl and San Fransico concerts after we paid Noble Street, agency advances, and commissions."

Addison stared at the number with disbelief. It was more money than he had ever imagined possible. "Is this number real?"

"As real as real gets, Addison; don't spend it all in one place."

The morning after arriving in Denver, Addison and Ty visited the Fillmore Auditorium and met with the Conductor and the Stage Manager to review the show. That would be the routine they would follow from city to city.

As promised, Hanna flew in for the weekend. She arrived at Addison's hotel Friday evening, the night before Addison's performance. Addison met her in the lobby. They hugged like they had known one another forever."

"Welcome to Denver, Ms. Potts."

"Thank you, Mr. Stone, I'm happy to be here."

"I made reservations in the hotel's restaurant. Hungry?

"Famished."

Once settled, they ordered dinner and chatted away like old friends.

"You have a front-row seat reserved for the show."

"Ah, nice to have connections. I fly back early Monday morning."

"Then, let's make the most of our time together."

Hanna's turned away. Her hand went to her mouth, and she ran a finger along her lower lip.

"What is it, Hanna?"

"Addison, I, ah—"

"Just spit it out."

"When we met in New York, I, ah—" Hanna leaned in and looked deep into Addison's eyes. "When we met, I felt this connection to you. I can't explain it, but it was there. I thought maybe it was just… if it was a momentary attraction to the handsome and talented guy who had just stolen the show. God, I must sound like a silly schoolgirl."

"No, not all."

"With you about to fly off with the show business gods, I dismissed it; I put it out of my mind." Her eyes began to tear. "Then you showed up in Los Angeles, and I had to see you again; I had to know if what I had felt in New York was real." She wiped at her right eye and looked away. "Am I embarrassing you?"

"Just the opposite, Hanna." Addison's heart was racing. Reaching across the table, he took Hanna's hand in his. "What if I told you I felt the same way."

Hanna wiped away another tear. "You did?"

"Like you, I couldn't explain what I felt, but there it was; it felt real."

Hanna leaned back and laughed low. "God, Addison, I went over this a hundred times during the flight here. I kept asking myself, what if Addison doesn't feel the same? I'd be sitting there looking and feeling foolish."

Addison squeezed her hand. "So, here we are, Hanna. What happens now?"

"Whatever we want."

"I'm at a loss for words, Hanna. Help me out here."

Hanna tossed her head back and laughed.

"What's funny?"

"Don't they teach you boys anything down there in Alabama? Kiss me, seal the deal already, and we'll go from there."

Addison smiled and stood, sauntered around the table, took Hanna's hand, lifted her to her feet, and wrapped her in his arms. He had never kissed a girl before and wasn't sure how to go about it. With his eyes open, he lightly brushed his lips over hers. With her arms around Addison's waist, she pulled him closer, and they kissed.

There was a rousing round of applause from the other guests. Addison and Hanna looked embarrassed.

"Oh, hell, Addison, ignore them; kiss me again."

He did, and they received another round of applause. Together, they took a playful bow.

"And that, sir, settles that," Hanna said with a satisfied grin. "Now, to business. Since I failed to book a room, I guess I'm staying with you. The desk clerk was kind enough to hold my bag."

Addison Jordon Stone was about to cross yet another one of life's significant thresholds. A night of heavenly bliss followed for two young souls who had found one another.

Hanna sat in the second row for Addison's Saturday night performance. Although the audience didn't catch it, he played to her.

Following breakfast Sunday morning, Addison and Hanna

spent the entire day holding hands and meandering the Denver Botanic Gardens, followed by a scrumptious dinner at the A5 Steakhouse. That was capped with a second night of heavenly bliss wrapped in each other's arms.

Early Monday morning, Addison and Hanna waited at the hotel's front door for Hanna's Uber to take her to the airport.

"I'm off to Chicago later today," Addison told Hanna. "The final stop is in New York.

"Great. I should be home for spring break by then."

Hanna's driver arrived.

"I don't want to leave, Addison. I want to stay by your side and join you on tour."

"Wouldn't that be perfect?" Addison took her in his arms. "We'll phone one another often."

With her head buried in Addison's chest, Hanna cried softly. He lifted her head and kissed her. When they parted, Addison whispered, "I love you, Hanna."

Hanna wiped away a tear and smiled. "I love you more, Addison."

Hanna entered the car and was gone like a wisp of wind again.

Chapter 14

Addison scheduled a Zoom call with Hanna at midnight after his Chicago performance.

"Well, if it isn't, Mister Megastar. How are you doing, Cowboy?"

"Convincing myself that I'm not a flash in the pan."

"Bite your tongue, boy. You need a refresher injection of confidence."

"You boost my confidence, Hanna. You've turned my life around in a way I never believed possible." He paused for a couple of beats and scratched at his chin. "Um, Hanna, is it too soon in our relationship to say I love you enough to ask you to marry me?" He couldn't believe what had just come out of his mouth because he had not planned it.

Hanna was quiet—Addison waited. He heard her breathing. "Hanna?"

"You don't waste time, do you, Mr. Stone?"

"Time is a precious commodity, Hanna; don't waste it. So, what do you think?"

Hanna hesitated, giggled, and responded, "I accept on the condition that our engagement is not official until I have an engagement ring on my finger."

"Fine. We'll pick you out a fabulous ring when we meet in New York."

"God, Addison, I can't believe we did this over the phone."

"I know, it's crazy."

"Mr. Stone, have made my day."

"And mine, Hanna."

"This was Kismet. If we hadn't met in New York, we were destined too somehow somewhere."

"I love you, Addison. Call me again next week."

"Count on it, Hanna. And, oh, by the way, I love you more."

As soon as the call ended, Addison entered his journal.

> *Is it possible to love someone so completely that I proposed to Hanna after only four face-to-face encounters? It was love at first sight; it was Kismet, just like she said. I should share this with Mom and Ben. No, I'll wait until I get to New York and seal the deal with a ring and proper proposal. I've never been happier in my life. My feet have yet to touch the ground.*

By the time the tour reached New York City, Addison had become a confidant—some would say brash—young entertainer. No longer was he the shy, withdrawn Addison Stone from Addison, Alabama, but Addison Stone, who had entered a dark, lonely tunnel of self-doubt at an early age only to exit a performer who was on his way to the pinnacle of success. Despite warnings that money, fame, and public adulation could damage or ruin a career, it had become Addison's aphrodisiac. The tour was making him a star that people fawn over. He began playing that ace of spades to the hilt on and off stage.

In New York, the demand for tickets for his engagement at Radio City Music Hall was overwhelming. The Music Hall management contacted Lang, requesting a second performance the following night.

Lang called Addison. "It's up to you, Addison."

Addison grinned. "I recall someone telling me that when you're hot, you take advantage of every opportunity because it may not come around again."

"I seem to recall I was the one who gave you that sound advice."

"Then, by all that's holy, let's do it, Lang; then I'll take a vacation."

"You have my full support on both. You've earned it."

Addison laughed. "Can I get that in writing?"

That evening, Addison received a call from Hanna.

"Addison, I have one final exam before spring break. I don't get home for another bloody week and a half."

"Send me your flight information. I'll pick you up at the airport."

"I miss you so much, Addison."

Addison chuckled. "I miss you more."

"No, no, I miss you more."

"I'll wrestle you for that title."

Hanna laughed. "And it'll be your loss."

"We'll see about that. See you in New York, Ms. Potts, soon-to-be Mrs. Stone."

"Hmm, sounds delicious to me."

If Addison's previous tour stops had been sold-out smash hits, New York topped them all with two consecutive nights attended by the most exuberant audiences he had encountered. Young and old danced in the aisles, and young women rushed to the edge of the stage. At times, it looked like an out-of-control frat house bash.

Following his second night performance, he left the theater to sign autographs. He was met by a larger crowd than usual. As he moved along the line signing autographs, several young men began pushing those in front of them, trying to get closer to Addison. A fight broke out; there was pushing and shoving. A young woman was caught in the middle and pushed to the ground. The crowd began to scramble. Security quickly surrounded Addison and Ty and escorted them safely to their waiting limo.

Addison was shaken by the incident. "What the hell was that?"

"A couple of jerks who spoiled it for everyone," Ty replied angrily.

"Jeez, Ty, for an autograph scribbled on a piece of paper, for God's sake. What the heck is wrong with some people?"

Addison was relieved when he returned to the relative safety of his hotel room. He drove his fisted right hand into the palm of his left hand. "Damn it, someone could have been hurt," he yelled. "And for what, a worthless signature? I've had enough of the damn fools!"

He undressed, haphazardly tossed his clothes on a nearby chair, visited the bathroom, and crawled into bed. A couple of minutes later, there was a knock at his door.

"What now, Ty?"

There was a second knock.

"Hold your horses; I'm coming."

He slipped into his robe and swung the door open, expecting to see Ty. Instead, standing about six feet away were two beautiful twenty-something ladies.

"Hi," the lady on the left said with a big smile. "We wanted to tell you in person how much we loved your show."

Addison took a couple of steps into the hallway. "Thank you, that's very kind of you. Was there anything else? An autograph, maybe?"

The second girl smiled and spoke. "Well, you could invite us in."

Before Addison could respond, she stepped past him, entered his room, and had her blouse unbuttoned and off by the time she reached the bed.

Addison was confused and had no idea what was happening. "Hey, what the—?"

"Time for fun and games," the second girl said. She stepped

to Addison and hooked her arm around his. "Are you up for this?"

"Ah, ladies, I don't know what's going on here, but—"

"Do you want us to leave?"

"Look, I don't know what you two are up to, but—"

The girl smiled, lifted her blouse, and exposed her naked breasts. "This is what's happening, bright eyes."

Addison's eyes went briefly to the woman's breast, glanced up and down the hallway, then met the lady's eyes. "Really ladies, it's late and—"

"I'll ask you again. Do you want us to leave?"

Addison scanned the hallway again. Only some guy on his phone was waiting by the elevator thirty or so feet away and paying no attention to them. Addison's eyes came back to the women.

"That's what I thought, handsome. Come with me."

The young lady hooked her arm through Addison. He did not protest as she led him into his room and closed the door.

The following night, in honor of their successful tour, Lang treated Addison and the Noble Street Singers to a celebratory dinner in a private dining room at New York's La Mercerie French café. Stan and Sally Potts were also there. Addison assumed Hanna had not told them of their relationship because neither Stan nor Sally brought it up.

Addison awoke to the sound of the phone ringing. "Who's calling this early?" He picked up the phone. "Yeah!"

"It's Lang."

"Oh, Lang, hi. What time is it?"

"Nine thirty."

"Whoa, I overslept. What's up?"

"What took place in your room the night before last?"

Addison hesitated. "What are you talking about?"

"Don't play dumb with me, Addison. This morning, I was alerted to a video on TikTok showing you and two young women outside your room. One of them walked past you into the room. The other one led you into your room a few seconds later."

"Ah, Lang, I—"

"Was there anyone else in the hallway?"

Addison thought for a moment. "Um, only some guy waiting for the elevator."

"By any chance, was he on his phone?"

"The elevator isn't that close. Yeah, I think he was."

"For God's sake, Addison, you were set up. The girls were pros, and the guy by the elevator was taking video of the whole thing with his phone. It's running on the Internet with the title, *Addison Stone whooping it up in New York with two fine-looking ladies after his show.*

Addison hesitated. "Lang, I did *not* invite them; they just showed up, and—"

"And, like any red-blooded male, you took them up on their generous offer."

With his head bent forward and his eyes on the floor, Addison said low, "Yes."

"Okay, it's done. Now we have to deal with the PR disaster that follows."

"How?

"Andy has been on the phone with various execs explaining that it was a setup, that the ladies entered your room without your permission, and you promptly escorted them out. Every step is being taken to remove the video. Unfortunately, by now, it has been viewed by millions."

"Who would want to do this to me, Lang?"

"Any number of evil lowlifes for any number of evil reasons. I'm surprised you didn't get a ransom call before it was posted. That's how some sub-humans get their jollies off on the Internet these days. Be in my office at 11:30. Julio will come and get you."

Lang hung up.

Addison turned on his computer and logged into one of his

social media accounts, typed his name in the search box, and the video of him and the two ladies appeared.

Addison moaned. "What the hell have I done? You damn fool! Oh, dear God, Hanna! I have to get to her before she sees the video."

He checked his watch—it was 9:15, 6:15 in LA—too early. He decided to shower, dress, grab breakfast, and then call her.

It was 6:20 in the morning in LA. Hanna sat in front of her computer. A girlfriend had called, woke her up, and alerted her to the video. There were tears in her eyes as she watched. When it ended, she slammed her laptop shut.

At 7:30, as Hanna was getting dressed, her phone rang. It was Addison. She let the call go to voicemail.

"Hanna, it's Addison. Call me, please."

Hanna hissed, "Yeah, sure, as soon as the Moon turns a bright pink." With tears streaming down her face, she deleted Addison's message.

At 11:10, Julio was out front waiting to take Addison to the agency.

"Good morning."

"Good morning, Julio. You heard?"

"The whole office knows, Mr. Stone."

When he arrived at the office, Addison received a cool reception from Lang's secretary, Nancy.

"They're waiting for you in Lang's office."

Andy was there with Lang. Lang pointed to the chair in front of his desk. "Take a seat."

Addison sat, his shoulders slumped with his eyes to the floor. He said just above a whisper, "I royally screwed up."

"Yes and no, Addison," Andy said. "The temptation to participate with two lovely ladies is understandable, especially in this business where some ladies make themselves readily available to celebrities." He shook his head from side to side. "I will never understand the mindset of the jerks who get their kicks doing this stuff, but there it is."

Addison took in a breath and exhaled slowly. "I need to go home to Alabama and hide out for a while."

"That won't solve anything," Lang said. "No one will believe either of those women once we reveal their chosen profession. This was a prank, pure and simple. We're issuing a news release stating that you promptly escorted the ladies out of your room. If a reporter approaches you on the subject, and they will, don't answer them; refer them to our release. Are we in sync on this?"

Added sighed and nodded. "Yes."

"They didn't take pictures inside your room, did they?"

"Hell no, Lang."

"The media will have fun for a few days, but it will become yesterday's news when our side of the story is out there. Then, it becomes about those two women and whoever was behind it."

"You're sure of that?"

"Yes, Addison, I'm sure. Now to business. With the tour over, Micro Records had planned to release the Hollywood Bowl album next week."

"God, Lang, I forgot about the album."

"With the video thing taking center stage, they've pushed it back by two weeks. That's not a problem."

"Whew," was all Addison could say."

"You do recall we told you road tours can be lucrative?"

"Yes."

"We haven't received the final Radio City numbers yet," Andy added, "so theirs is an estimate, but the figures from the other venues are final. You will have earned—better yet, here." Andy handed a sheet of paper to Addison. "Each city is listed with totals next to them. Check out the bottom total."

Addison's eyes went to the bottom of the page.

"That's your take from the tour after whatever advances were deducted. You, Addison Stone, are becoming a wealthy young man.

Wide-eyed, Addison stared at the numbers. "This doesn't register as real, Andy."

"Trust me; it is. Now, we have to keep the train steaming ahead. The time has come to get you an assistant who travels with you, looks after your every need, and hopefully keeps you out of trouble like this recent incident. You have become a full-fledged entertainment phenomenon. Like it or not, your life is about to get more complicated. So, trust us when we tell you that you need a majordomo; you can well afford one now."

"And where would I find this—what did you call them?"

Lang spoke up. "Majordomo is a highly trained chief steward, butler, secretary, and whatever else is needed. Every successful entertainer has one. We have someone in mind. His name is Jonathan James, and he's an Englishman trained in his chosen field. He's been working for some years now for the president of a hedge fund here in New York. The guy died three weeks ago, so James is looking for a new gig. He's got a top-notch reputation and is in high demand. Still, he agreed to meet with you before considering other offers. We've set up a meeting for the day after tomorrow."

"I'm not sure about this, Lang."

"Addison, you're where you are because of your talent and because we held your hand and guided you. We booked, negotiated your fee, provided the best support, and protected you. Your sold-out tour has established you. To prove it, we have a lucrative offer from EURO6 Entertainment in London for a European tour. If you accept, we're sure as hell not going to let you go alone; that's where someone like James comes in."

"Another tour? When would it begin?"

"In six weeks, beginning in London, then to Scotland, Germany, Switzerland, Stockholm, Sweden, Finland, France, and Italy.

Addison realized if he agreed to another tour, it would be months before he saw Lacy, Ben, or Hanna again—if she answered his calls. Another tour so soon gave him pause. He trusted Ben to look after Lacy, but what about Hanna? She must have seen the video, or why else would she not return his call? He shifted uneasily in his seat and thought for a moment. *The hell with it,* he thought; *I'm steamrolling like a champ. I'd be nuts to put the brakes on now.* "Okay, Lang, I'll do the tour."

"Good decision," Lang said. "How about you give some thought to new songs."

"Why? I haven't performed in Europe. The song lineup will be fresh to them. No, I don't want to change anything yet."

"Okay, keep the show as is for this tour, but when you return, it'll be time to change your repertoire. You can't sing the same songs for the rest of your career."

"Oh? Why not?"

"Hopefully, you're joking. Now, moving on, do you know who Jimmy Hudson is?"

"Can't say I do."

"Jimmy is one of the top lyricists in the business with a wall of awards for the hit songs he's written for major stars," Andy said. "He's the best of the best."

"What's that got to do with me, Lang?"

"Hudson approached us about writing an original song for you."

Addison's face scrunched. "Huh?"

"He has a few ideas for a song he wants to discuss with you."

"Ah, no, I'm not interested."

"Why?" Lang asked. "The man is a hitmaker. You should be excited that he wants to work with you."

"Lang, I sing standards, songs that people love, songs that have endured, songs that will endure for generations to come. So far, it's working just fine, and that's how I intend to keep it. So, no, I have no interest in an original song that would eventually be covered by other artists."

"Addison, you're making a big mistake."

Addison's face slackened. He stared at Lang for a few beats, then said rather brusquely, "Well then, it'll be my mistake, won't it, Lang. And what happens if I did sing an original, and it flopped?"

"You'd wear it around your neck to prove everything you touch doesn't turn to gold."

"Okay, so now I've pissed you off."

Lang pushed back in his chair, glanced at Andy, shook his head, and turned to Addison. "It's your decision, Addison."

"Right. Anything else?"

Andy laid a sheet of paper on the desk in front of Addison. "We have a firm offer of two hundred and fifty thousand for one night's performance at the twenty-five-thousand-seat Honolulu Stadium in Hawaii. They want it to be in the round to add another thousand seats on the infield circling the stage.

Addison's eyes grew wide. "Whoa, Andy! Two fifty."

"Whoa, is right," Andy answered. "The event producers want an answer ASAP to have time to promote. You mentioned a vacation. Hawaii would be a great place to kick back before you leave for the European tour.

Addison washed a hand over his face. "Look, guys, I'm sorry if I came off sounding like a spoiled brat about working with Hudson on a song."

"No need to explain," Lang said.

"You know I came into this business not knowing my ass from my elbow. I can never thank you enough for what you've done for me. But becoming a star was never on my radar. Yes, it's brought me early rewards beyond my wildest imagination." Addison placed a flat hand on his chest. "But all the fame and the money don't make the man what he is not in here. I'm not looking for more and more but maintaining what I build along the way."

"You should have no trouble with that, Addison," Lang said. "Frankly, I wish we had this conversation sooner. It's all the more reason you need a full-time assistant who understands the man behind the public façade and protects you. If you and Jonathan James hit it off in your meet and greet, take him to Hawaii with you. That'll give you time to get to know one another during your vacation. Then it's off to Europe and beyond."

"How much is James going to cost me?"

"We'll negotiate his salary and benefits for you. With his

reputation, he won't come cheap, but from what we've learned, he's worth it."

"All right, Lang, I'll meet with him."

"Good. I think that's it for now." Lang paused and grinned. "Just avoid hookers in the future."

"Ouch!" Addison said. "That hurt."

"Good. Many ladies who are not hookers would love to spend time with you. Stick to them."

As soon as he left Lang's office, Addison placed another call to Hanna. Again, his call went to her message box. "Hanna, honestly, I can explain. It was a setup. I took no part in it. Please, Hanna, call me."

Addison hated lying to Hanna, but as Lang instructed, the news release from his office would be their side of the story, and he was to stick to it.

His next call was to Ben, who did not mention the internet video. Either he was unaware or didn't want to embarrass Addison.

"Addison, you were on my radar to call. Lacy received a call from the Town Manager. They want to hold an Addison Stone Day to celebrate his success."

"A what?"

"A day to celebrate your success."

"Would I have to be there?"

"Well, yeah. Addy."

"Oh, jeez, I'm off to do a show in Hawaii, and then I'm off to tour Europe.

"Geez, Addison, that's wonderful."

"I may be gone for a couple of months, Ben. I don't know when I'll be able to come home."

"Oh, well, I'll tell Lucy. Maybe when you get back."

"Yeah, maybe."

"Don't worry about Lacy, Addison. She's coming along fine. I'll take good care of her."

"I know you will, Ben. Tell Mom I'll call when she's back

home."

"We're proud of you, kiddo."

"Take care, Uncle Ben. We'll talk soon."

Over the next two days, Addison placed several more calls to Hanna, but none were returned. He became depressed, but he refused to give up and made note of it in his journal.

> *Damnit it, she's not going to answer me, or she would have by now. I think she's made up her mind that because of my slip, it's over between us. But in my heart, I cannot accept that and will continue to reach out to her.*

That night, with Hanna at the forefront of his mind, Addison cried himself to sleep.

Sure enough, Lange's prediction would prove correct. Despite denials by the two ladies, with the assistance of a private detective, they were able to establish they were, in fact, prostitutes, and the incident shifted from Addison to whoever had set him up. Although there was an intense effort to track down the prankster, they were never discovered, and soon, the story became yesterday's news.

Addison met with forty-three-year-old Jonathan James as planned. James was a handsome fellow, six feet tall, well-dressed in a black suit, white shirt, black tie, black socks, and shoes, and perfectly groomed with slightly graying black hair and light gray eyes.

Following introductions, Lang left the room to allow the two men to speak alone.

"I'm sorry to hear of your employer's passing, Mr. James."

"Thank you, Mr. Stone. He was a kind and generous man. I was by his side for eleven years and will miss him."

"Lang tells me you're from England, Mr. James."

"Please, call me Jonathan. I was born and raised in Bristol, two and a half hours east of London on the Bristol Channel.”

“Ah, sounds lovely. Lang filled you in about my upcoming European tour?”

“Actually, Andy did. Your career appears to be humming along nicely. Congratulations.”

“Thank you, Jonathan. Out of curiosity, why would you want to work in an industry that can be brutal and requires constant travel? Heck, I’m still learning to walk in this crazy business.”

Jonathan grinned. “From what I know, you learned to walk pretty quickly. You seem to have enjoyed a prodigious rise in a very short time. To answer your question. I’ve had many offers from entertainers in recent years but turned them down out of loyalty to my late employer.”

“Married, children?”

“Widower, no children, and presently unattached.”

“Oh, sorry about that.”

Jonathan laughed. “So am I.”

The two men spent the next half hour getting to know one another. Jonathan was outgoing and easy to talk to, and Addison felt quite comfortable with him.

“I’m off for a vacation in Honolulu, Hawaii, then a one-nighter there before I begin the European tour. Would that interest you?”

“I’ve worked my entire career for highly successful industry businessmen. It is time for a change. The entertainment business has always interested me, so I would accept your offer and consider it an honor to work with you.”

“Great, Jonathan. Lang will speak to you about your employment package. Then we’re off to Hawaii and wherever else this world drags us kicking and screaming.”

The two men shook hands. Addison had found his Major-domo; perhaps *Babysitter* would be a more appropriate title.

One week later, Addison and Jonathan boarded a plane for Honolulu. The agency booked them at the Espacio Hotel and Resort, in separate Ocean View Emerald Suites directly overlooking Waikiki Beach.

Despite his professional life going in a straight line, Addison remained anguished over his loss of Hanna. No matter how often he reached out to her, Hanna never responded. It was over; in a moment of weakness, he had blown it with the woman he loved, the woman he looked forward to spending his life with, all because of one night's lust with two hookers.

And then there was Lacy. He remained hopeful that she would get sober now that she was in rehab, but knowing her as he did, he feared his mother might never rid herself of her. But her demons were hers; he would no longer allow them to be his.

Addison and JJ took advantage of everything Honolulu had to offer, including its beautiful beaches. While sunbathing on the beach one day, Addison stared at the ocean and said, "I love it here, JJ; it's beautiful."

JJ smiled. "What's not to love, sir? Lucky are those who get to enjoy this lovely place year-round."

Later that day, Addison received a copy of Ben's email to Lang. Ben had received State confirmation that A. J. Stone Enterprises had been activated. He opened a bank account and provided Lang with bank transfer instructions and the name and address of the new accounting firm in Cullum. Addison wrote Ben and instructed him to add Lacy as an administrative employee of A. J. Stone Enterprises with a sufficient salary so she would never have to waitress again.

It was no surprise that Addison's appearance at the Honolulu Stadium before a crowd of over twenty-seven thousand was another sold-out smash hit. It was the first time Addison had appeared in the round. The orchestra was positioned on the stadium floor directly in front of him. For this performance, he wore a traditional Hawaiian shirt, khaki slacks, red socks, and white sneakers. He followed Andy's instructions and played to all sides of the stadium, which, nervous as he was, he seemed to enjoy.

Addison received an email from Andy informing him that *Addison Stone at the Hollywood Bowl* was the number-one best-selling album.

"Congratulations, Addison!" Andy wrote. "What are you going to do with all your money?"

Addison wrote back. "I plan on spending every last nickel on wine, women, and song, and not necessarily in that order." He added two happy face emojis.

Chapter 15

Addison and JJ flew to London to kick off the tour at the sold-out London Palladium. It was news in all the newspapers and TV.

"It appears, sir, that you are the talk of the town."

"None of which I dwell on, JJ. If I do, it sends me crazy."

"I thought of something that would make each of your stops special."

"What is it, JJ."

"Consider adding a beloved native song in each country. I will research and print the lyrics for you in English."

"That's a great idea, JJ. Let's do it."

"Here in England, that song would be *Jerusalem*, based on the William Black poem. It goes like this. *'And did those feet in ancient times walk upon England's mountain green? And it was the Holy Lamb of God on England's pleasant pastures seen?'*"

"You know the lyrics?"

JJ laughed low. "I would not be a true Englishman if I did not, Mr. Stone."

Since they had two days until Addison's performance, JJ hired a driver to take them to some of the more famous sites.

First, they met management at the Palladium to be sure all was set for the show. Then, their driver drove them past Buckingham Palace, Westminster Abbey, and Westminster Palace while JJ provided background notes on each. They toured the Tower of London and the British Museum. Addison was speechless when he viewed the notebook there displaying Paul McCartney's handwritten lyrics to the 1968 hit *Hey Jude.*

Following the massive success of his American tour, Addison was feeling his oats. That was freely displayed when he sat for an interview with the BBC, answering each question confidently and with more than a bit of swagger.

Addison's performance at the sold-out Palladium wowed the audience. He was playful and cocky at times and told stories of growing up in small-town Addison, Alabama. He received several ecstatic standing ovations, especially after singing *Jerusalem.*

Following the show, he greeted well-wishers in his dressing room. He offered one young lady he found quite attractive to join him for dinner. The lady immediately sensed where that was heading and made an excuse about having a previous engagement.

Strike one, two, and three.

The next stop was the Edinburgh Playhouse in Edinburgh, Scotland, home to several educational institutions. Addison's performance drew many young students who had watched his appearance on *Sing America Sing* and continued to follow his remarkable rise to stardom.

As usual, he greeted well-wishers in his dressing after the show. One pretty fetching young lady—a second-year student at the University of Edinburgh—was the last visitor.

"Forgive me for gushing, Mr. Stone, but I'm a huge fan. I'm honored to meet you." She extended her program guide. "Would you autograph my program?"

"Of course. Your name?"

"Cynthia Cron."

Addison signed her program, smiled, and handed it back.

They chatted easily for a few minutes before he invited Cynthia to join him for dinner. She excitedly accepted.

He had hit a home run!

Outside, autograph seekers were waiting. Cynthia was at Addison's side as he walked through the crowd, signing whatever someone placed before him, including several T-shirts, a photo of himself, and some baseball caps. When they reached the end of the line, Addison and Cynthia entered the limo together.

Watching from nearby, JJ frowned. He disapproved, knowing the press would have a field day. He could not do anything about it, so he returned to the hotel while Addison and Cynthia were off to the French Mediterranean restaurant La Garrigue.

When word got out that Addison Stone was at La Garrigue with a young woman companion, the paparazzi swarmed the place and shot photos of them when they left the restaurant. The paparazzi followed Addison's limo and shot pictures of him and Cynthia entering his hotel. The following morning, several photographers caught Cynthia leaving alone wearing dark sunglasses. Photos splashed across the front page of The Guardian, the Sun, and the Daily Mail and quickly spread to the tabloids back in the States.

Since Hanna had kicked him out of her life, Addison tossed caution to the wind, no longer caring if he was seen with women on his arm in public. To the joy of the press, he became constant fodder for their articles. But in truth, he preferred the woman on his arm be Hanna, whom he still loved deeply.

They were off to Berlin, Germany; Geneva, Switzerland; Stockholm, Sweden; Helsinki, Finland; and Paris, France. Addison played to sold-out audiences at each venue. In Berlin, he spent the night with a lady Yoga instructor. In Geneva, a forty-something chef. In Stockholm, he struck out. In Paris, he hooked up with a real estate saleslady. Celebrity had its benefits, and he thought nothing of using his leverage to his advantage. He didn't care who disapproved, least of all JJ. Oddly enough, he never heard a word from Andy or Lang about his public amorous toying and flirtations.

Considering Addison's turbulent and confusing upbringing resulting from Lacy's erratic mood swings and inability to deal with reality, Addison was traveling on the fast track, quickly becoming one of the most popular entertainers of his time. His fans fawned over him; the constant adulation proved a potent aphrodisiac, slowly turning him into what he had fought against becoming. This was *Show Business*, baby; this was the big time, and he was determined to run with it.

The final stop on the tour was Rome, where he would perform in the Piazza Theater in the MAXXI Museo Nazionale Delle Arti del XXI Secolo, one of Rome's top contemporary art museums. The performance was scheduled for January 28th, Addison's twenty-first birthday.

Lacy and Ben sent him a Blue Mountain birthday card with a dancing pig with bright red lipstick singing Happy Birthday. The Sherman Agency sent a large bouquet of white Lillies. His social media sites crashed with birthday wishes.

Following the show, to celebrate Addison's birthday and the end of a successful tour, Johnathan and Noble Street took Addison to *Ristorante Aroma* on the rooftop of the Palazzo Manfredi Hotel overlooking the Roman Colosseum.

JJ and Ivey sat with Addison, the Noble Street gang, at the next table.

Addison gazed out at the Coliseum with awe. "Despite the inhumanity that took place in there, that's one spectacular sight."

JJ raised his glass of wine. "A toast. Happy Birthday, Mr. Stone. May you enjoy many, many more."

"Here, here," Ivey added.

When they finished dinner, Ivey stood. "Sorry, boss, but we have an early flight to LA in the morning." Ivey hugged Addison. "Happy Birthday, my friend."

"Thank you for making the tour a success, Ivey. I couldn't have done it without you guys."

In unison, the Noble Street group stood and raised their

glasses." Happy Birthday to the King."

"See you on our next outing," Ivey hugged and kissed him on the cheek.

Several minutes later, looking quite annoyed, a young man approached their table. He glared at Addison and brusquely said, "Pensi di essere una merda, non è vero."

Addison could see the man was upset about something. "Sorry, sir, but I don't speak Italian?"

The man glared at Addison and spoke in halting English. "I said-*a*, you think-*a* you're hot shit-*a*, don't you?"

Jonathan raised a hand and shot the guy a terse look. "Excuse me, sir, but—"

"Excuse-*a* me, sir, I wasn't speaking to-*a* you."

"Did you attend my performance?" Addison asked.

"Si," the man snarled.

"Well, sorry you didn't enjoy it. Now, why don't you go back to your table."

The guy glared at Addison. He stepped to his right and pointed to a young lady sitting four tables away. "Anyone look-*a* familiar to you?"

Addison froze. He did indeed recognize the young woman. She had come to his dressing room alone after the show to express how much she had enjoyed his performance. Addison signed her program, and they took a selfie. Finding the young lady quite attractive, he initiated a conversation that led to his inviting her to dinner and hinting they might return to his hotel afterward. The young woman became visibly upset, called him a few names in Italian, and left in a royal huff.

The young man's face was contorted into a snarl. Angrily, he thrust his right hand in front of Addison's face and snapped his fingers. "Cat got-*a* your tongue-*a*, Mr. Stone, big-*a* shot?"

"What is he talking about, sir?"

Before Addison could answer JJ, the angry man cut him off. "That-*a* lady sitting there is-*a* my fiancé, the one you-*a* propositioned in your-*a* dressing room." He looked hard at Addison. "Ti frega! You arrogant American bastard." He tossed

Addison the finger and left.

JJ looked confused. "Mr. Stone?"

Addison hesitated and took in a breath. "She came to my dressing, JJ. I invited her to have dinner with me. I may have said something about going back to my hotel later."

"You may have? Sir, if what just happened ever found its way to the press—"

"It happened, JJ; the guy got it off his chest, end of story."

"But, sir—"

Addison stood. "Book us a flight to Honolulu and two suites at the resort."

"We're already booked on a flight to New York, sir."

"Cancel it."

"Why are we returning to Honolulu?"

"You'll understand when we get there."

The next afternoon, Addison and Jonathan flew back to Honolulu. During the flight, JJ brought up the incident of the night before. Addison made it clear there would be no further discussion on that subject, nor would he explain to JJ why they were returning to Honolulu.

"JJ, if New York calls with additional bookings, tell them no more for at least a month."

"We're spending a month in Honolulu, sir?"

"Ask me no question; I will tell you no lies."

"I beg your pardon?"

"Hang on, JJ, it's about to get interesting."

After checking in at the resort, Addison emailed Ben asking how much cash was in the corporate account.

A half-hour later, Ben wrote back." So far, we've received 4.5 million, Addy. Can you believe that?"

"Unbelievable!" Addison wrote back. "Safeguard that money with your life. More to come."

Next, he called local real estate agents Terri and Ray Hewitt and arranged to meet with them the next day.

"We're going to look for a permanent residence, JJ."

"What? Here in Honolulu? That's quite a distance from your home in Addison, Alabama, sir."

"Home is where I choose, and I choose to live here. I won't be happy, but I'd understand if you decided you don't want to live here."

Without hesitation, JJ replied, "I work for you and live wherever you do, sir."

"That means a great deal to me. I don't know how I'd get along with you." Addison smiles." You've cast a magic spell over me."

"Ah, so you noticed."

"It was hard to miss, *Sir JJ*. Okay, let's look at properties."

Flush with cash, it only took forty-eight hours for Addison to find what he was looking for.

JJ approved. "Excellent choice, Mr. Stone."

Addison signed a contract to purchase a fully furnished, two-acre beachfront estate on Miomo Loop just north of Kamehameha Highway.

The property was magnificent, with a pool and rolling manicured flower gardens. To the left of the main house was an attached three-car garage. Beyond that was a stand-alone two-bedroom guest house. The main house's interior was just over four thousand square feet. The second floor featured four En-suite guest bedrooms. Across the hall, at the back left, was a self-contained maid's quarters. Forward of the maids' quarters was a large room that functioned as a meeting and entertainment area with a floor-to-ceiling fireplace and windows that overlooked the swimming pool and the blue Pacific beyond.

The first floor featured a high-ceiling entryway with a half-corkscrew staircase to the second floor. To the right of the entry was a dining room, gourmet kitchen, and large pantry. To the left of the foyer was a large living room with a floor-to-ceiling stone fireplace. Foreword of that was the lavish master bedroom and a private study and library that also looked over the ocean.

Addison Stone, who grew up in a twelve hundred square foot rental house, was walking on a cloud.

Once a price was set with the sellers, Addison called Ben. "Hey, Chief Operating Officer, I need you to do something. I bought a house in Honolulu, and—"

"Slow down, Addy; say that again. You bought what?"

"A house; I'm going to live here in Honolulu."

"So that's why you asked about the bank account balance."

"Yeah. I need you to transfer 2.1 million to my personal account. I'll email the house address and the bank transfer info."

There was silence on the line.

"Did you hear me, Ben?"

"That's a lot of money for a house, Addy."

"It's more of an estate, Ben. The guy who lived there passed away and left the place to his son and daughter. They must need the money desperately. I never thought they would accept my lowball offer, but they did. It was a steal, Ben. You and Lacy will come to visit. Better yet, you could move here. Lord knows I have enough room, and nothing keeps either of you in Addison."

There was silence on the line.

"Still there, Ben?"

"Yeah, I'm trying to wrap this around my brain."

Addison could hear it in Ben's voice; his friend and mentor disapproved.

"Okay, Addy, if this is what you want, I'll get it done."

"Thanks, Ben. Be sure to tell Lacy what I said about moving here."

"Yeah."

He then called Andy to let the agency know he had purchased a home in Honolulu that would be his home base.

"Why Hawaii, Addison?"

"Why not, Andy? It's beautiful here."

"How much?'

"Two point one. It was a bargain."

"Have you discussed this with your accountant?"

"No, and I don't intend to. Besides, Andy, Ben tells me I'm a millionaire three times over."

"But, Addison—"

"Whatever you were going to say, Andy, don't. I don't need to explain my actions to anyone, least of all my booking agency." Addison bit his lip. "Oh, crap, Andy, I didn't mean it to come out like that."

Andy hesitated. "No problem, Addison, I'll let Lang know. Um, how's it going with Jonathan?"

"Couldn't be better. He keeps me on the straight and narrow."

"Great. Look, I've got another call waiting. Good luck with the new house. Send pictures."

In New York, Andy leaned back in his chair and thought for a long moment. Finally, he pressed the intercom. "Lang, are you there?"

"Yes, what is it, Andy?

"I need to speak with you about Addison."

"Go ahead."

"He just bought a waterfront estate in Honolulu. He said that's his home base now."

"Honolulu? Jesus, how much did he spend?"

"Two point one."

"Whoa, what!"

"Addison's success has gone to his head, and he's becoming arrogant, Lang. He's awash in money for the first time in his life. He's on an ego trip and a spending spree."

"Well, we've seen this before, haven't we?"

"Sadly, yes."

"Andy, we can't tell Addison how to spend his money or where to live. We can only advise him. Whether he listens to us or not is up to him."

"He's our top money earner, Lang. Let's hope he gets his act together before he goes broke."

After moving into the new house, JJ arranged to retain the landscaping company. Through a local employment agency, he hired a housekeeper named Aria Akina, a Hawaiian-born lady who lived nearby.

"Does the lady cook, JJ?"

"The agency says she's an excellent cook."

"Great. When does she start?"

"The day after tomorrow, sir."

"Fine. Until then, find a restaurant that delivers."

That evening, Addison called Ben.

"Well, if it isn't the *Lone Stranger* who lives in a beachfront estate in Hawaii. I'm still trying to understand why you bought a place halfway around the world."

"Ben, it's a state, remember? Did you tell Mom?"

"Yeah."

"And?"

"To be honest, Addy, she was pretty blasé about it and didn't say much. Why haven't you called her?"

"Ben, if you knew the pressure I was under on the European tour—finish in one city, catch a plane to the next, then repeat. Let me make up for it by sending you and Mom tickets to come visit."

"Addy, take it easy on the spending."

Addison laughed. "What good is money if you can't spend it? Talk to Mom again, and let's get you two to Hawaii."

"Alright, I'll talk to her."

When he got off the phone, Addison went to the patio, sat, and stared at the water. His thoughts went to Hanna. He had read in Variety that she had graduated from The American Film Institute with honors. She opened Hanna Productions in New York City with the help of her well-known industry parents. Hanna Productions' first project was to produce a series of shorts showing the behind-the-scenes activity of *Sing America Sing*. That led to a contract with a cable network for a one-hour documentary on the rise and use of Fentanyl in America, which won Hanna an EMMY.

Addison still loved Hanna and desperately wanted her back,

but that was no longer in the cards. "Damn you, Addison, you blew the best thing that came into your life in exchange for one night's lechery."

"Did you say something, sir?"

Addison looked up to see JJ standing by the door. "Just talking to myself, JJ."

"Beautiful day."

"Couldn't be better."

JJ sat next to Addison. "Ah, Mr. Stone, forgive me, but there is an issue I would like to discuss with you."

"Go for it, JJ. I'm all ears."

"That incident in Rome with the young lady."

"Past tense, JJ."

"Using your celebrity in that way is quite dangerous to your career. That unfortunate encounter in Rome could have easily become physical."

"What can I say, JJ? Women want to be with me, and that, sir, is a fact."

"Not with that particular lady, it seems. At the very least, inquire if a lady is attached before you—"

"Yes, yes, JJ. Anything else?"

In Edinburgh, you threatened a photographer."

"He was in my face, and I told him to stop, JJ."

"Sir, you told him you were going to knock him on his ass if he didn't stop."

"He stopped, didn't he?" Addison got up and strolled to the door.

"Mr. Stone, you have become a beloved entertainer in an extraordinarily short time. You have a reputation to protect.

Addison raised a hand and waved JJ off. "Got it, JJ—lesson learned."

"Ah, sir, there is one other issue."

"Get it off your chest?"

"Your sense of humor. I'm used to it, but others are not. Sometimes, it comes out sounding like sarcasm."

"Boy, you're all wound up and in lecture mode today."

Addison turned and entered the house: the phone in his study was ringing. He walked quickly to his desk and answered."

"Hey, Addison, it's Lang."

"Mr. Sherman, it's always a pleasure to hear from you."

"Andy told me about your new digs."

"You need to come visit, Lang."

"I look forward to it, Addison. I'm calling to ask how you feel about playing Vegas?"

"Not anytime soon, Lang. Didn't JJ make it clear I'm taking a month off?"

"He did. That's not a problem. Caesars has extended an invitation to play there whenever we want."

"For how long and what kind of money?"

"Tuesdays through Sundays for one month for two million."

"You sure know how to get my attention, Lang. Explore a date that works for them after I finish recuperating."

"When will that be exactly?"

"A year and a day from now."

"How about six or so weeks from now."

"Alright, Lang, go for it."

"Good. Remember what we talked about before you left for Europe. You need to change your repertoire."

"Ten-four, Boss, I'm on it."

Chapter 16

Sixty-two-year-old housekeeper Aria Akina arrived. She was short and thin with graying hair and a stone-face expression that would kill a cat. JJ introduced her to Addison.

Unsmiling, Aria said, "You're that singer, right?"

Addison grinned and replied, "Yeah, I'm *that* singer."

"Nice to meet you." She turned to JJ, "Okay, show me around."

Addison and JJ quickly learned Aria was a lady of few words. She would arrive each day at 10:00 AM, clean the house, make lunch and dinner, and leave around 7:00 PM. That was it. At the end of the first week, Addison dubbed her *The General*.

Addison began assembling his new song list. He would continue opening the show with *Your Love*, the tribute to *Abba*, and close with *Thank You for The Music*, We'll Meet Again, and *Time to Say Goodbye*. All the other songs would go, replaced by *Easy on Me – All I Ask of You – You're Still You – That's What Friends Are For, Memory, Without You, I'm Alive, Fly Me to The Moon, If I Can Dream, Can't Help Falling in Love, Softly as I Leave you, Killing me Softly,* and *My Way*.

"Not bad if I say so myself." He sent the new list to Andy, who responded with a thumbs-up.

The laidback life in paradise would end when Addison received an email from Andy. "Are you cool with a Las Vegas start date in five weeks?"

Addison emailed back. "Book it."

Andy responded. "Great, details to follow. The Caesars Music Director and Noble Street will get up to speed with your revised song list."

Addison thought Vegas presented an excellent opportunity for Lacy and Ben to visit. He called Ben. "How's it going, Chief Operating Officer?"

"Well, if it isn't the kid I helped raise."

"And a good job you did, Ben. How's Mom since she was released from rehab?"

"Getting her life back on track is rough, but she's working at it."

"Please let her know I'm pulling for her, Ben."

"And the reason you don't call and tell herself is?"

Addison glossed over Ben's jab. "Listen, Ben, in five weeks, I'll be playing in Vegas for a month. It would be a perfect opportunity for you two to visit and see the show."

"Good idea. I'll run past your mother."

"This would be a business trip, a board of directors meeting, so pay for it out of the company account. I'll email you the dates."

"Okay, Mr. Businessman, your mom will be excited about seeing you on stage for the first time."

"You're going to perform where?" Aria asked Addison when Addison told her he and JJ would be leaving.

"Las Vegas."

"That's that gambling place in the desert."

"Yes, Aria, it is."

Aria turned and walked off. "I disapprove of gambling; the

House always wins. Have a nice trip; see you when you get back."

Addison shook his head and mumbled, "Sometimes I wonder if she's in control of all her marbles."

Addison and JJ arrived in Las Vegas four days before he was to begin performing at Caesars Palace to go over the new orchestral arrangements and Ivey's plan for Noble Street. During the trip, Addison wore a ballcap and sunglasses. They made their way to baggage, then to the waiting limo sent by Caesars Palace without Addison being recognized once.

As they drove into the city, Addison's eyes lit up like a kid in a candy store.

"Wow, JJ, look at this place! Disney World for adults! Who pays the electric bill?"

JJ stared out the window with a look of wonderment and whispered, "I've never seen anything like it."

As the limo entered Caesars, they were wowed by the grand splendor of the Caesars complex and the colossal billboard announcing Addison's upcoming appearance.

"Well, if they don't come to the show, at least they'll know my name," Addison joked.

The driver took them to Nobu Tower, one of six towers on the property. Ned Eastman, one of Caesar's vice presidents, greeted them.

"We are truly excited about your appearance, Mr. Stone," Eastman said. "You are the talk of Vegas, and all of your performances are sold out."

Addison glanced at JJ and grinned.

Eastman escorted them to two spacious suites high in Nobu Tower.

"Let us know if there is anything you require, anything at all, Mr. Stone."

"That's kind of you, Ned; thank you," JJ said.

In the morning, over breakfast in Addison's suite, Addison,

Ivey, and Caesars' musical director, Franklin Parsons, reviewed the arrangements for the new songs.

At 10:00 AM, they were on the stage in the Colosseum Theater for rehearsal. Parsons would accompany them on the piano.

Addison's eyes grew big when he strolled to the edge of the stage. "Good God, this place is enormous."

"Forty-one hundred seats, to be exact," Parsons pointed out. "It's one of the most popular venues in Vegas."

The rehearsal went like clockwork. When the rehearsal ended, Addison clapped his hands. "Great job, everyone. What do you need me for?"

"Because, Addison," Ivey joked, "You get the big bucks."

"And, Ms. Wagner, don't you forget it."

That evening, Addison and JJ dined at the Old Homestead Steakhouse on the Caesars Palace property. Addison's enormous popularity made him vulnerable to being constantly approached in public. He had grown weary of it and instructed JJ that when they visited a restaurant, he was to request a reserved table in the back of the room against the wall with his back to the other guests.

As they were shown to their table at Old Homestead, heads turned.

"God, JJ, will they never leave me alone?"

"It goes with the territory, sir."

"Yeah, well, it's beginning to piss me off. I can't go anywhere like a normal human being anymore. I feel like a caged animal."

No sooner had their food arrived than JJ spotted a young woman walking toward their table with a pad and pen in hand.

"Ah, Mr. Stone, a young woman is coming this way."

"Damn it," Addison cursed under his breath.

The young lady stopped behind Addison. "Excuse me, Mr. Stone."

Addison pretended he had not heard her.

"I'm a big fan, Mr. Stone, and I love your new album. Could I get your autograph?"

Addison placed his fork down, twisted in his chair, and snapped. "Young lady, is your eyesight in good working order?"

The girl frowned. "I beg your pardon?"

"Can't you see we're here for a peaceful and quiet dinner?"

The young lady's jaw dropped, and she took a step back. "Um, I'm terribly sorry. Please forgive me." Embarrassed, she turned to leave.

Addison sighed. "Oh, wait a minute. Sorry, that was rude of me."

"It's okay, Mr. Stone; I understand. My mistake."

"No, miss, there's no excuse for what I said. Here, give me your pad and pen. What's your name?"

"Shelly—Shelly Fisher."

Addison wrote on the pad: *To my new friend, Shelly Fisher, best wishes, Addison Stone.* He handed the pad back to her.

Shelly read the note and smiled. "Thank you very much, Mr. Stone. I'm sorry for interrupting your dinner. I should know better."

"Me too, Shelly. Are you in town for a while?"

"Yes, my girlfriend and I are on vacation. We're staying at Caesars."

"Write your name and your girlfriend's name on that pad and give it to me."

Shelley looked confused but wrote down the names and handed them to Addison, who passed them to JJ.

"There'll be complimentary tickets for opening night at the entrance for you and your friend, Shelly."

Shelly's right hand went to her mouth. "Oh, my, thank you so much."

"The show is sold out, so I don't know how good the seating will be, but they'll work it out. Enjoy the show, and please accept my apology."

Shelly was almost in tears. "Bless you, Mr. Stone, bless you." She spun around and left with a broad smile on her face.

"Bravo, sir, that was the right thing to do."

"Yeah, well, JJ, there's no excuse for rudeness. Feel free to slap me silly if I ever do that again."

"At which time you will fire me and charge me with assault."

Addison grinned. "Probably."

Addison agreed to a live interview on the ABC affiliate's Sunday morning show, *Morning Blend*. That afternoon, he was interviewed on KQLL radio. Then, he called Ben to confirm he and Lacy were still planning to visit him in Vegas.

"Yes, yes, Lacy's coming. I'm making flight reservations for next Thursday. She's back to work at Chick's, by the way."

"What?"

"She said she won't have you paying her bills."

"Why not?"

"Because your mother is stubborn and insists on paying her own way. She said she wouldn't know what to do with herself if she didn't work. Addy, it is Lacy's decision, not yours. If she wants to work, let her."

Addison blew a hard breath. "Damn, that woman is bull-headed."

"And so is her son. I think the visit will be good for both of you, Addy. She really misses you; we both do."

"How's Mom holding up since she graduated rehab?"

"Remarkably well, I think. She's much more focused and less scattered. I can sit with her and converse normally without her drifting off like she used to."

"Let's hope she stays clean, Ben. JJ will book two rooms for you in the Nobu Tower, where he and I are staying. JJ will arrange for a Caesar's Limo to pick you up at the airport. Nothing but first class, my friend."

"I'll email you our flight info. Looking forward to seeing you, kiddo."

Chapter 17

Tuesday, opening night at the Colosseum. For the first time since the Hollywood Bowl, Addison was feeling apprehensive. This was Las Vegas, the entertainment capital where major stars regularly performed at the hotels and resorts. Would he, could he, measure up?

Addison went to JJ's suite and expressed his uneasiness. JJ gave him a bit of tongue-lashing.

"Mr. Stone, stop already. You've proven yourself over and over again. Name two people who rose to international fame as fast as you have? Go ahead, name two or even one."

"I can't help it, JJ. The insecurities I grew up with haven't magically disappeared. They haunt me like I'm being punished like a fraud who doesn't deserve to be here or have."

"That's absolutely crazy."

"I know it is, but I can't get past it."

"Mr. Stone, you're successful beyond belief and beloved by fans worldwide. If that isn't enough to bolster your self-confidence, nothing ever will. It's time to live in the moment and bury the past once and for all. It's old news—stale news."

"I know, JJ, I know."

"Then, what's the problem?"

Addison shook his head from side to side. "I wish I knew."

"Have you considered therapy, Mr. Stone?"

"Over my dead body; ain't happening."

"There's nothing shameful about seeking help."

"Forget about it." Addison strolled to the door and left.

Whether Addison realized it or not, he took the same path as his mother when refusing help.

A comedian was to precede Addison's performance, but he never inquired who the comedian might be. He and JJ arrived at the Colosseum at 7:30 PM. A stage assistant led them to the star dressing room—he would follow the comedian at 8:30.

"Break a leg tonight, Mr. Stone."

"I still don't know what that means, JJ. And for God's sake, please stop calling me Sir and Mr. Stone."

JJ smiled. "Yes, sir, Mr. Stone. I'll be watching from the backstage lounge like always."

"You mean lurking."

The makeup man came, did his work, wished Addison luck, and left. Addison was too nervous to eat, so he decided to wait until after the show. He changed into the custom-made dark blue suit and pastel open-collar shirt he had made while they were in Rome.

His cell phone rang. It was Lacy.

"Mom, so good to hear your voice."

"I'm looking forward to seeing you, son. It's been too long."

"Thanks to my demanding schedule."

"Good luck on your opening night, son. I'm proud of you. See you next week."

"Thank you, Mom. Your call means a lot to me."

"Love you, Addy."

"Love you, Mom."

Lacy never once mentioned a visit to Hawaii.

At 8:00, the comedian came on and stood before the red stage curtain. It was none other than Billy Wonder, host of *Sing*

America Sing. Management had flown him in as a surprise to kick off.

Addison's first night. He had no idea it was Wonder until he was backstage and heard Wonder's introduction over the speaker.

"Billy Wonder? Wow, what a surprise! JJ, you knew about this?"

"I did indeed, Mr. Stone."

At 8:30, Billy began his introduction of Addison.

"Each week, I've had the honor of announcing a winner on *Sing American Sing*. Most everyone who watches the show will remember the night a nineteen-year-old young man from Addison, Alabama took our judges and the world by storm. His rise to fame from that night on has been nothing short of explosive. The next time he opens his mouth to sing, watch closely, songbirds flutter out. Remember how they preserved Albert Einstein's brain after he died? They plan to study Addison's voice box when he passes on."

The audience laughed and applauded.

From off-stage, Addison called out. "Are you going to bring me on or keep jabbering?"

The audience roared with laughter and more applause.

Billy raised his arms in a hopeless gesture. "You see how success has gone to this young man's head? Alright, enough from me. Ladies and gentlemen, please give a warm Caesars Palace welcome to the one and only Addison Stone."

The audience was on their feet, applauding.

Addison trotted onto the stage, embraced Billy, and whispered in his ear. "Great to see you, man. Thank you for doing this."

"My pleasure, Addison. This is a one-nighter for me. I'm flying back to New York in the morning. Now, knock 'em dead."

Billy handed the microphone to Addison. "Give it up for the one and only Billy Wonder."

Wonder waved and walked to the wings to thunderous

applause.

Addison turned to the curtain and raised his arms. "Open Sesame." The curtains parted from left to right, revealing a bright, vibrating, multicolored back wall behind the orchestra and Noble Street.

Addison strolled a few feet across the stage before turning to the audience. "That night on *Sing America Sing* was life-changing. Thanks to you, I've been on a magical rollercoaster ride through the clouds ever since, and for that, I've added you all to my will."

The audience applauded with scattered whistles, hoots, and hollers.

"Don't spend the fifty bucks all in one place." Addison turned to Noble Street and the orchestra. "Please welcome Ivey Wagner and the Noble Street Singers, our amazingly talented orchestra, and our esteemed conductor, Thomas Mann."

More enthusiastic applause.

Addison turned and half-bowed to the conductor. "Maestro, if you please, sir."

The orchestra began the intro to *You Love*, and the show was off and running.

After singing the three ABBA songs, Addison motioned to Noble Street. "Ladies and gentlemen, to continue our tribute to ABBA while I take a short pee break, give a round of applause for the lovely and talented Ivey Wagner and the Noble Street Singers."

As the group began to sing *Mamma Mia*, Addison exited stage left.

JJ was waiting and handed him a bottle of water. "It's going very well, sir."

"Yeah." Addison took a gulp of water and pointed to Noble Street. "Are they the greatest or what?"

"You are fortunate to have them, sir."

When Noble Street finished, Addison returned to the stage for the show's second half. When he had finished singing the last song, he took his bows, shook hands with the Conductor, and strolled off stage. The audience began chanting *Encore*!

"It appears they want you back, sir."

"They always do, JJ. No ego here."

Addison was pumped. Like a proud Peacock, he sauntered to center stage. He delivered his final songs with gusto. When he began singing *Time to Say Goodbye*, the audience was on their feet with a rousing standing ovation that seemed to go on forever. After taking several bows, Addison waved, blew a kiss, and left the stage.

Back in his dressing room, Addison greeted well-wishers. The last two were well-known and in-demand performers appearing at nearby Hotels. Addison was thrilled to have met them.

When they left, JJ returned.

"Did you see who those last two were?"

"I did indeed, Mr. Stone. Quite exciting."

"Anyone else?"

"No sir, they were the last."

"Great, I'm beat. I'll change clothes, go to my suite, and hit the sack. See you in the morning."

"Goodnight, sir."

As Addison began to change clothes, he heard the door open. Thinking it was JJ, he turned to find a tall, middle-aged man he did not recognize standing there.

"Yes, can I help you, ah…?"

"John."

"What can I do for you, John?"

"I wanted to compliment you on your performance."

"Thank you."

"I work here, so I sometimes get comp tickets for shows."

"Ah, good for you. Where do you work?"

"I'm one of the chefs at the Bacchanal Buffet."

"That's here on the property."

"Yes, it is."

"I'll have to check it out. Ah, John, sorry, but I was about to change and leave."

"Can we talk for a few minutes? Mind if I sit?"

Before Addison could say anything, John ambled to the sofa and sat. Trying to be cordial, Addison sat in a lounge chair across from him.

"This is a lovely dressing room. And the flowers, they're beautiful."

"Yes, they are. So, what can I do for you, John?"

John paused and looked away. He was acting a bit strange, making Addison a little uneasy.

"Is there something wrong, John?"

John looked away like he was admiring the room. "No, not really."

"Then what?

Without looking at Addison, John said low, "How's Lacy?"

"What?"

"Your mom, how is she?"

"How do you know, Lacy?"

John chuckled. "Well, before you were born, Lacy and I worked at Chick's."

"You're kidding. What a coincidence. Mom still works there." Addison stood, hoping John would leave. "I'll be sure to tell her I ran into you. Ah, you never told me your last name."

"Paloma, John Paloma." He stood and walked a few feet toward the door but stopped and slowly swiveled back, his eyes locking on Addison's. "I'm your father, Addison."

Addison's eyes widened—had he heard, right? "What did you say?"

"Has Lucy never told you?"

Addison pushed back in his chair. "Whoa, hold on. Is this a shakedown? Do you want something from me?"

"No, nothing, nothing at all."

"Then what? Why are you here?"

Paloma hesitated. "Um, I'm not really sure. Perhaps to apologize."

Addison's brow furrowed, and his eyes narrowed. He was getting more than a little uncomfortable. Was this guy for real?

"If you're telling me the truth, then—"

"I am, Addison. I am your father. I never intended to seek you out, but here we are at the same hotel, and—"

Addison cut him short. "What is this, some kind of soul-cleansing trip on your part? If it is, you should apologize to my mother, not me."

John lowered his head. "I could never face her now."

Addison popped to his feet. "Oh, but it's okay if you barge in here and face me? Give me a break."

"I'm sorry; I see now this was a mistake; I shouldn't have come."

"You have that right. All these years later, you dare to barge in here and claim to be my father."

"I'm not lying to you, Addison."

"I really don't care either way, Mr. Paloma."

"You're angry with me."

"How insightful of you, Mr. Paloma. Angry would be putting it mildly. Now, do yourself a favor. Go find a priest if it's forgiveness you're seeking? I'll pretend this unfortunate meeting ever took place."

"Addison, please, I—"

"No, nothing you say now will change anything. You abandoned my mother and me. The few times I pressed Lacy on who my father was, she blew up and told me never to ask again. I do recall she referred to you as a scumbag. I'm in no mood to entertain your *mea culpa's* now. Please leave before I call security!"

Paloma reached into his shirt pocket and pulled out a slip of paper. "This is my number if you ever want to talk." He dropped the slip of paper and a vase of flowers on the glass top-end table next to the lamp. "I wish you well, Addison."

"Gee, thanks. Don't let the door slam you in the ass on the way out."

John lowered his head. "I am sorry, Addison." And with that, Paloma left.

Addison plopped to the chair and placed his head in his

hands. "What the hell just happened?"

Bummed out over the meeting with John Paloma—furious would be more like it—Addison returned to his suite. He undressed and stood in the shower, letting the hot water rain down on his head. How was he going to face Lacy now? All these years later, why hadn't she told him the truth, and why did Paloma feel the need to seek him out now?

Questions and more questions he had no answers for.

Addison went to bed, but sleep would not come. Angrily, he tossed off the covers and took out his journal.

> *Did I or did I not just meet my biological father? How else would he know Lacy and Chick's Diner? He didn't ask anything of me, so I can only conclude he was telling me the truth and, in his lame way, seeking forgiveness. What was I supposed to do? Hug and kiss the fool and say, welcome, Daddy; it's great to finally meet you. Let's have lunch when Mom arrives in a few days. Mr. Paloma will forever remain a coward in my eyes. Now, how am I supposed to face Mom? Do I tell her the father of her son paid me a visit? That would lead nowhere but a guaranteed rift between Mom and me. I have no choice but to write it off as another of life's cruel moments and leave it at that.*

Chapter 18

Addison tossed and turned that night. At 6:45 AM, he gave up and dialed JJ's room. "I hope I didn't wake you."

"No, sir, I was up."

"Have breakfast with me in my suite."

"Is everything okay?"

"I'll fill you in when you get here. What do you want for breakfast?"

"Scrambled eggs, sausage, toast, and coffee."

"How about a whole roaster pig."

"For lunch, maybe, sir."

"I'll see you in an hour, JJ."

Addison ordered breakfast, then showered and dressed. He remained livid over the unfortunate meeting with Paloma.

Forty-five minutes later, JJ showed up.

Addison was sitting at the table. "Good morning, JJ; the food just arrived."

"Good morning, sir. Why the sullen look?"

"Sit down. I'll tell you while we eat."

Addison filled JJ in on John Paloma's visit. JJ looked stunned.

"He showed up at my dressing room door a few minutes after you left."

"My Goodness, Mr. Stone!"

"Who the hell does that son of a so-and-so think he is coming into my life twenty-one years later?"

"You had no idea, not even a clue?"

"None. It remained Mom's secret until that dirtbag walked in here last night. Now for the kicker: Paloma's a chef at Caesars Bacchanal Buffet. What are the odds of that?"

"I'm sorry, sir."

"What do I do now? Do I tell my mother?"

"Your mother must have had her reasons for not revealing who your father was, Mr. Stone. If you told her now, it could lead to a serious argument between you."

"Maybe what she and I need is a good argument."

"Do you love your mother, Mr. Stone?"

"Despite the crooked road she led me down growing up, yes, of course."

"Then protect your relationship with her; that's all that counts going forward."

"Easier said than done. I wish the fool had never shown up."

"Unless you intend to pursue a relationship with him, then —"

"No way, ain't gonna' happen. I'd sooner meet with the Devil."

"Then, sir, put him out of your mind."

"Easier said than done, JJ."

The next day, Lacy and Ben arrived. JJ had made dinner reservations at the Nobu Restaurant for 6:30.

"JJ, there's no way I can face her before I go on tonight. You take them to dinner. Tell her and Ben I had to be at the theater earlier than scheduled to review some last-minute changes. I'll see them in my dressing room after the show."

"Yes, perhaps that would be best, Mr. Stone."

"There is no best, JJ, just something in between."

JJ had reserved seats for Lacy and Ben in a box in the front row to the left of the stage.

During his performance, Addison was looser and more playful than usual; perhaps he was showing off for Lacy, who was seeing him live on stage for the first time.

After singing several songs, he said to the audience. "By now, the world knows I was named after my hometown of Addison, Alabama. With us tonight is the lady who bestowed that name on yours truly. Please welcome my mother, Lacy Stone, and our dear friend and neighbor, Ben Dickey. Mom, Ben, take a bow."

Lacy and Ben stood looking quite embarrassed as the audience gave them a round of applause.

"Okay, that's enough, or they'll catch the show biz bug and want their own act."

That brought a burst of laughter.

For the rest of the show, Addison moved about the stage effortlessly, joked with the audience, and told stories of growing up in Addison, Alabama.

Following the show, JJ escorted Lacy and Ben to Addison's dressing room before well-wishers arrived.

It was all Addison could do to force a smile. He hugged and kissed Lacy and Ben.

"It feels like a lifetime since I've seen you, Addison," Lacy said.

"For me too, Mom."

Ben patted Addison's shoulder, "Wonderful show, Addison. The audience loved you."

Lacy scanned the room. "My, my, look at all the beautiful flowers."

"Some are from Caesars, some from celebs appearing in town, and a few from people I don't know. Thank you for yours, Mom, they're beautiful. Make yourselves comfortable while I shake the hands of a few well-wishers."

Lacy sat on the right side of the sofa next to the end table, and Ben sat to her left.

Addison introduced Lacy and Ben to those who came to praise his performance. Lacy and Ben were excited to meet several well-known entertainers who stopped by.

When the last visitor had come and gone, Lacy asked. "Addy, why have you chosen to live in Hawaii?"

"It's stunningly beautiful there, Mom."

"But it's so far away."

"You and Ben will come and spend time there—maybe consider moving there."

"That's what I told her," Ben added.

"No, no, I can't leave Chick's."

"Oh, Mom. Why not?"

"Because I choose not to."

"Mom, that makes no sense. You don't have to work anymore. Come to Hawaii and enjoy the good life."

As she often did when she chose not to answer him, Lacy pursed her lips and looked away.

"Jesus, you're bullheaded," Addison snapped.

"It seems I passed it on to my son."

Addison's face tightened, and a wave of anger cursed through him. He locked eyes with Lacy. "As I recall, you passed on a lot of things to me, some not so helpful."

His tone inflamed Lacy. "Now, you listen to me; you don't get to talk to me that way, or I'll—

"Or you'll what, Mom?"

Ben was on his feet. "Hey, you two, this is supposed to be a fun reunion, remember? Let's act like it."

Addison's face turned red, and he stood. "Tell her that, Ben. Now, if you'll excuse me, I'm going to the restroom and throw up." Addison stomped off to the restroom, slamming the door behind him.

"What's going on here, Lacy?"

"Two very much alike people letting off steam."

"For God's sake, Lacy. This is neither the time nor place!"

JJ shifted uneasily in his chair. "If I may say—"

Lacy glared at JJ. "Whatever you're thinking, keep it to yourself."

Ben shook his head, sat beside JJ, and began a conversation.

"I thought the show was a smash, JJ. Boy, Addison has come a long way from the kid who sang in the church choir."

"He certainly has, Ben. From a front-row seat, I've watched how he matured into the seasoned performer you saw tonight. His audience demographics often change from venue to venue. Whether young or older, he knows how to play to each.

Lacy ignored them and turned to admire the vase of flowers on the glass end table to her right. Her spine stiffened, she gulped, and her face paled when she spotted a slip of paper lying against the base of the vase. The name Paloma and telephone number were scribbled on the paper. Lacy's eyes went to Ben and JJ; they were busy talking. She slowly reached for the note, crumpled it, and quickly stuffed it into her purse.

Addison returned from the restroom.

"Feel better?" Lacy said with an icy tone.

Addison did not answer.

"Gosh, I can't keep my eyes open. I'm ready for bed."

"You look a little flushed. Do you feel okay?"

"Yes, I'm fine, Ben. I'm tired, and we have a 9:00 AM flight home."

"I thought you were staying for a few days?"

"Addy, I can't leave Chick alone running plates to tables. I need to get back."

Addison shrugged as he always does. "I'll come down and see you off."

"No need, son. We're leaving for the airport at 7:30, and you need your rest."

Addison sighed. "No problem, I'll come to see you and Ben off. I'm sorry you're not staying longer."

"Then, my dearest son, make an honest effort to come home for a visit."

Addison let Lacy's snarky comment pass. "I might be able to work in a few days following this engagement, then it's back to

Hawaii."

Lacy hugged Addison, and Ben shook his hand, and they left.

Addison plopped down on the sofa. "JJ, knowing what I know now, that was painful."

"I understand, sir, but you handled it well."

"It won't solve anything to tell her I know about Paloma. It's twenty-one damn years too late."

At 7:20 the following morning, Addison went down to see Lacy and Ben off. Ben and Lacy were not there when he arrived, nor was the limo to take them to the airport. He approached the doorman.

"Good morning, Mr. Stone. Can I help you with anything?"

"My mother and her friend were to leave at 7:30 for the airport."

"Oh yes, I saw them. They left in the limo about five minutes ago."

"Ah. Okay, thanks."

Addison returned to his room and wrote in his journal.

> *Damn that woman, she's never, ever going to bury her demons. I prayed rehab would have helped not only with the drugs but also the pain of the past that continues to shadow her like a deadly storm. She needs professional help. I'm not confident she will seek it out. She's made it clear that she's in charge. Ben and I are just bystanders, knowing that it will come crashing down on her one day. I doubt she's even given it thought.*

"That's it, Mom," he said low. "I don't know what else to say or do."

On the final night of his gig at Caesars, Addison told JJ, "Praise the Lord, that's it. I'm tired. Let's get back to Hawaii before Lang books another engagement somewhere."

"You promised to visit your mother for a few days."

"I'm afraid I would confront her about Paloma, and it would end in another insult match, so I'm not going. Would you email Ben and tell him the Agency booked another performance in Hawaii, and I have to return."

"If that is your decision, sir."

"That's my decision, JJ."

"Are you planning anything special for your final night here?"

"Yes. I'll perform a striptease while Noble Street sings *Dancing Queen*."

Fortunately for everyone, Addison did not perform a striptease. Following a standing ovation at the end, he spoke to the audience.

"These weeks have been amazing for me, thanks to the wonderful Vegas audiences. I hope to return one day soon. Until then, stay out of trouble—if that's possible in this town. I wish you all well. Good night, and may you awake each morning to the sound of songbirds."

Addison received a standing ovation as he left the stage.

On the third day back in Honolulu, Andy called.

"Whatever it is, Andy, the answer is no."

"You don't know why I called, Addison."

"Let me guess, you want me to return to work. It's the only time you call. Okay, what's up?"

"First, congratulations on an amazing run at Caesars. They want you back whenever you want. Now, we have an offer from Stern Entertainment for a tour in Canada."

"I'm spending my time on a beautiful Honolulu beach. Why would I want to go to Canada? It's cold up there this time of year."

"Even if it's a month and a half away?"

"Andy, I have several million in the bank with more to come. I could stay here and spend the rest of my life sunning on the beach."

"You'd be bored to death and probably get sunburn."

"But I'd be happy. Okay, Sir Andy. How many stops?"

"Six beginning in Toronto in six weeks."

"Alright, book it. But then I'm coming home and hitting the beach again."

"Agreed."

"Yeah, sure, that's what you guys always say."

Andy laughed. "Hey, booking talent is how we make a living."

"And some fat living it is. Give my best to Lang."

When Addison turned twenty-two, he received a card and balloons from Lacy and Ben. JJ took him to dinner at a nearby restaurant.

"Do you feel any older Mr. Stone?"

"In today's world, I'm still considered a kid at twenty-two. We're known as the late generation. Nothing much happens before we hit thirty."

JJ laughed. "I think you broke the mold, sir."

"There are times I wished I had not."

Addison and JJ were in Toronto five weeks later to prepare for the Canadian tour. Canadian audiences couldn't get enough of him. Addison was doing two encores per show for the first time, and he seemed to love it. He reveled in the adulation and took advantage of it whenever an opportunity presented itself, especially when it came to the ladies. Addison was hitting home runs in that category more than he struck out. But it was Hanna he wanted to be with. She was never far from his thoughts.

Addison was becoming less and less tolerant of the public when they visited restaurants, which concerned JJ. Addison was becoming increasingly short with those who approached him for an autograph. He asked JJ to instruct the restaurant that his table was strictly off-limits and patrons were not to approach him.

It came to a head when a young man approached their table one evening seeking an autograph, and Addison refused.

"Mr. Stone, you and I have discussed this before. Your public is your bread and butter."

"Oh, no, JJ, not another lecture?"

"You embarrassed that young man. If that was to get out to press, it could turn many of your fans away."

"It's rude to bother anyone at dinner. I won't stand for it anymore."

"I understand your point, sir. But your fans want to believe you care about them, and autographs are one way to show you do."

"I do care about them, but I also care about my privacy. I will never understand this fan adulation crap anyway, JJ. It strikes me as childish. I'm just a singer, not a brain surgeon. What do they do with my signature, anyway? Childish, that's what it is."

But, sir—"

"End of lecture, JJ. Let's enjoy dinner."

Addison's fame and fortune grew beyond his wildest dreams for each of the next seven years. He was twenty-nine years old, remained in high demand, and continued performing worldwide. There were women in his life, but on-and-off relations never panned out. He had no compunction about using his celebrity to entice women to dinner and, hopefully, a roll in the sack later. But to him, there would never be another Hanna. His heart remained with her and always would. He never gave up trying to reach out to her over the years, but she never responded.

Hanna's career was on a role. She had more offers to produce and direct projects than she had time for. Awards for her production kept racking up. Addison began clipping and saving articles he came across about her booming career. He considered tracking her down and congratulating her in person. He backed off on that idea, fearing it would deepen the chasm between them if it did not go well.

In a melancholy mood one day, Addison called Ben.

"Hey, what a pleasant surprise. What's up, Addy?"

"I'm going to get right to the reason for my call, Ben."

"Hmm, that sounds ominous.

Addison hesitated. "You know who John Paloma is?"

Silence from Ben.

"Answer me, Ben."

"How do you know Paloma?"

"I ask you first."

"Addy, answer my question."

"Okay. A few days before you and Mom visited me in Vegas, He came to my dressing room after a show. Would you believe the son of a bitch works at one of Caesars' restaurants?

Ben whispered low, "Jesus!"

"I'm certain Mom knows that I know."

"How could she?"

"Before Paloma left that night, he wrote his phone number on a slip of paper in case I ever decided to contact him. He tossed it on the end table beside the sofa. I forgot about it, and it remained beside where Mom was sitting. It was only when you two left that I remembered it. But when I went to toss it out, the note from Paloma was gone."

"Damn it all to hell," Ben cursed.

"Why, Ben? Why did she keep it from me?"

Ben coughed and cleared his throat. "Your mother hated Paloma for abandoning her the way he did. He snuck off like the lowlife he turned out to be. Lacy vowed never to mention his name again and made me promise I never would."

"She had no right, Ben. If I had known, I might have had a relationship with him."

"I doubt that you would, Addy. John Paloma was all about John Paloma. I tried to warn your mother about his type, but she was charmed by him."

"Thank God you stepped in and filled the gap in my life."

"It filled a gap in both our lives, Addy."

"I don't plan on telling her about Paloma's visit. It won't

cure anything between us or bring back the missing years. Yes, what Paloma did was selfish and cowardly. But nothing can change the fact now that he is my father. Whether or not he was a good or bad man, everyone should have the right to know who gave them life; some history, however small, to cling to.

Chapter 19

The years passed quickly. Addison was in constant demand and continued performing across the globe. He celebrated his thirty-sixth birthday two days before his return to his Vegas home, Caesars Palace. This time, the engagement was for two months. His shows were sold out within the first two weeks of the announcement.

Besides staying in contact on the phone, Addison had not seen his mother or Ben since the unfortunate evening in Vegas when apparently Lacy found Paloma's note. Every time plans were made to meet up, Lacy found a convenient excuse why she had to postpone.

Deciding to reach out again, Addison sent Ben and Lacy an invitation to visit Vegas during his upcoming appearance at Caesars. "Your choice, whenever it's convenient," he wrote.

Ben wrote back. "Sorry, Addy, Lacy says she's not up to traveling right now."

"What's wrong with her now, Ben?"

"Same as always, Addy, only now it's getting worse."

"How so?"

"Lacy doesn't spend time with me like she used to; when she

does, she's passive and not very conversational. I don't know what to do to shake her out of it. Maybe you should come home for a few days."

"Ben, I can't. In two days, I begin a two-month stint in Vegas. Mom needs to see a doctor."

"I tried that, and she refused and insisted she was okay. All I can do is watch her and keep you posted. Happy thirty-eight birthday, kiddo."

"Thank you, Ben; I don't feel a day over seventy. I'll check with you when I can."

There were no birthday wishes from Lucy.

Addison's birthday party, hosted by Caesars, was invitation-only and hosted by Caesars Palace. A small band played Addison's favorite songs as the guests enjoyed a scrumptious dinner. The Noble Street Singers performed several numbers, after which Ivey Wagner spoke.

"We have been traveling with Addison since he was nineteen, right after he got out of diapers. He's been growing slowly, but we've brought him along as best we could."

The guests roared and applauded.

"Joking aside, performing with Addison Stone has been a wonderfully rewarding trip. So, from us to you, Addison, Happy Birthday. May you enjoy many more, and may they be with us at your side."

The audience applauded as Addison came to the microphone.

"Thank you, everyone, and thank you, Caesars Palace. It's good to be back. I love it here and might have to move to Vegas permanently."

Cheers and applause from the audience.

"I've been lucky in my career because of the fans who have supported me all these years. Without you, I would not be standing on this or any other stage. So, thank you from the bottom of my heart. Thank you, Ivey Wagner, Noble Street, the conductors and musicians who made me sound good, and my brilliant Englishman assistant, Jonathan James. I don't know how I would get through each day without him. JJ, you are my partner and friend, even though you insist on addressing me as *Mr. Stone* and *Sir* after all these years."

Sitting with several Caesars' managers, JJ looked embarrassed by the compliment.

"I've been asked to sing a few songs. I've chosen to sing my opening and closing numbers —*Your Love* and *Time to Say Goodbye*. Although, don't count on this boy saying goodbye anytime soon."

When Addison finished *Time to Say Goodbye*, the gathering stood and sang Happy Birthday.

On the second day of the third week of his run at Caesars, Addison received a call from Ben.

"Hey, Uncle Ben, how's it going?"

Ben's voice was low and slow. "Addy... I have bad news."

"What is it, Ben?"

Ben paused for several beats. "Addison, your mom died in her sleep last night."

Addison sucked in a sudden breath. "Oh, My God! How?"

"There was a half-empty bottle of white pills by her bed."

Addison's eyes teared up. "Damn it, Ben, I thought this time she had gotten clean."

"So did I, Addy. We had planned to have breakfast together before she was off to Chicks. I knocked on her door, but there was no answer. I tried the door—it was unlocked. The house was dark. I went to her bedroom—there she was in bed—I assumed she was still sleeping. When I attempted to wake her, she was unresponsive."

"Oh, dear God, Ben."

"In a panic, I called 911. The medics arrived within ten minutes. They tried to revive her but to no avail. They think she'd been dead for several hours."

"Damn it, damn it all to hell! What was she taking?"

"The medics said it was Fentanyl. At the Cullum Regional emergency room, a doctor confirmed that it was Fentanyl and signed off on the cause of death as an overdose. I asked that her remains be moved to the funeral home on Highway 278 West. They said they would as soon as authorization was received from you. I gave them JJ's cell phone number and his email. He should be receiving the paperwork anytime now. Follow the link and sign off on moving her to the funeral home."

Addison was silent, his eyes dripping with tears.

"Addison?"

"I don't know how to react or what to say, Ben."

"I know, Addy, I know."

"I'll catch the first flight out in the morning."

"Let me know your arrival time, and I'll pick you up in Birmingham."

"No, Ben, JJ will arrange a private jet to Southwest Regional Airport in Muscle Shoals. It's closer. I'll rent a car or catch an Uber home."

"Travel safe, Addy."

Addison hung up, dropped his head to his hands, and wept uncontrollably. "Damn you, Lacy," he shouted, "Damn you all to hell!"

He called JJ's room and filled him in.".

"Mr. Stone, I can't express how sorry I am for your loss."

"Thank you, JJ. Call FXAIR at the airport and book me a private jet to Southwest Regional in Muscle Shoals for first thing in the morning. Call Caesar's management and tell them I will perform tonight as scheduled but leave in the morning and will return in four days. Tell them to extend my engagement by four days to honor those holding tickets."

"Do you want me to go with you, sir?"

"It would be better if you hold down the fort here."

Addison was on an FXAIR jet to Alabama early the following morning. When he arrived, an Uber driver took him home. It was 2:00 PM when he arrived at the house. He went directly to Lacy's room and stood silently staring. He sat on the edge of the bed, placed his head in his hands, and wept.

Ten minutes later, he knocked on Ben's door. When Ben answered, neither said a word—they embraced.

Addison stepped inside and sat on the sofa. "What are the arrangements, Ben?"

"The hospital received your authorization for Lacy's remains will be transferred to the funeral home today. Cremation is set for the day after tomorrow. Is that too soon?"

"No."

"I knew you'd want a small ceremony, so I booked one at the funeral home at one that afternoon."

Addison punched his left palm with his fisted right. "Why, why did she do this, Ben?"

"Why does anyone do anything, Addy? We both know Lacy struggled to control her demons. Unfortunately, the same demons passed on to you as you were growing up. Only you went on; she never did."

"It was because you took me to choir practice one Saturday morning and changed my life."

"That only added to the baggage Lacy was already carrying."

"How?"

"Lacy never came to grips with your success. She often told me she had lost you."

"To what? I was never beyond her reach, Ben. All she had to do was reach out to me, and I would have been there for her." Addison lowered his head and spoke just above a whisper. "Maybe I was the one who should have reached out to her."

"Addy, this is not the time for self-recriminations; don't even go there. Lacy required professional help. The last time I brought it up, she bit my head off and told me to mind my own damn business, then didn't speak to me for two days."

Addison washed a hand over his face and stood. "I'm worn out, Ben. I'm going to bed."

"Maybe you should spend the night here with me, Addy?"

"No, Ben, I'll be fine."

"Try to get some sleep, son. Come over in the morning, and I'll fix us breakfast."

"Okay."

Back at the house, Addison ambled slowly through each room. The memories of growing up in this little house came flooding back: vivid scenes and recriminations, things that should have been said, and much that should not have.

When he reached Lacy's bedroom, he crossed his arms over his chest and stood silently staring at her bed. "Happy now, Mom?" he said aloud. "Is this how you planned to end the pain, or was it the only way you knew how to stop the pain?"

Before retiring, Addison made a short entry in his journal.

> *Maybe I did fail Mom... maybe I failed both of us. I will forever struggle to find the answer. I love you, Mom, and I forgive you. Now, I have to find a way to forgive myself.*

Addison and Ben had breakfast together, then went to the funeral home. They followed the funeral director down a long hallway to the preparation room. A chemical odor filled the air. Lacy's body, covered by a white sheet, lay on one of the prep tables.

When Addison was ready, he nodded to the funeral director, who rolled the sheet back to just below Lacy's neck. Addison took a deep breath and, with slow steps, approached the table. Lacy's eyes were closed. She looked like she was peacefully sleeping. Addison reached under the sheet and took Lacy's right hand in his; her hand was cold. He bent down and kissed Lacy's forehead. That's when he lost it. He released his hand from hers, placed his right arm across her body, lay his head next to Lacy's, and wept uncontrollably. "Goodbye, Mom; I will miss you with all my heart and wish it had been different for both of us."

Ben wiped a tear away, strolled to Addison's side, and placed his arm around Addison's shoulder.

"Her pain is gone, Ben, this time for good. May she rest in peace for the first time in her adult life."

Addison, Ben, Chick, his new waitress, his cook, a couple of church choir members, Millie Andrews, and several other townspeople who knew Lacy gathered at the funeral home that afternoon. There were flower arrangements from Addison, Ben, and Chick. Ben had arranged for Bruce Langford, the pastor of his church, to say a few parting words.

Following the service, and to Addison's dismay, TV news and a crowd had gathered outside the funeral home to get a glimpse of him. Onlookers took cell phone photos that would find their way to the Internet. One of the news reporters attempted to ask Addison a question, but Addison brushed him off.

"Ben, they have no respect for my privacy at a time like this."

Ben frowned. "Apparently not."

"Let's get out here before I start cursing the fools."

On the drive back to the house, Addison asked Ben if he would contact the landlord and settle the lease. "There's nothing in there I want, Ben. Donate everything of any worth to a local charity."

"Consider it done, Addy."

Ben drove Addison to Southwest Regional Airport in Muscle Shoals for his return flight to Vegas.

"Ben, nothing is keeping you here. You and I are all that's left of our little family. I would relish having you there with me in Hawaii."

"I'll sleep on it, Kiddo."

Addison laughed. "Don't sleep on it too long, old man. You're not getting any younger."

"Huh, tell me about it."

At the airport, the two men hugged goodbye.

"Be well, Ben. And, please, consider a permanent move to beautiful Hawaii."

"That's a tempting offer, son. It would be a significant move, so let me wrap my head around it."

"Okay, old man."

Once seated on the aircraft, Addison made an entry into his journal.

> *If Mom struggled so much with her demons, why didn't she reach out to me? Why? Either she didn't know how, or if she did, she chose not to. Then that snake Paloma entered the picture, and the distance between Mom and me grew wider. I failed to see, or chose to ignore, that it wasn't about me but her. She didn't live long enough to defeat her demons. My life is no longer whole; A part of me is lost to the darkness forever.*

JJ was at the airport to greet Addison. Addison looked tired; his face had a dark expression.

"Words are not enough, Mr. Stone, to express how sorry I am."

"Thank you, JJ. It was hard for Ben and me, but we got through it."

That night, Addison was back on stage at Caesars. Although it was all over the news that Addison Stone's mother passed away, he did not mention it during his performance.

Chapter 20

Following his engagement at Caesars, plus the four extended days, Addison and JJ flew home to Honolulu. Aria greeted them at the door, holding a rust-colored Retriever puppy in her arms.

"Mr. Stone, no words can express how saddened I am for your loss."

"Thank you, Aria." Addison eyed the puppy. "What's that you're holding?"

"Looks like a six-or-seven-month-old dog to me, Mr. Stone."

"What is it doing here, Aria?"

"Two days ago, I heard whining at the door. I found a big box with a note taped to the top that said, *Sorry for your loss*. It was signed simply: *From an admirer*. Imagine the look on my face when I carefully opened the box and found this cute little thing inside."

"Why would a stranger give me a dog?"

"Someone with compassion for your recent loss, sir."

JJ patted the puppy's head. "I think he's cute."

"Do you now, JJ?"

"Look at that smiling face, sir."

"That's a myth; dogs don't smile," Addison grumbled. "How

big will that thing get?"

"Some of these *things* get to be sixty to seventy pounds," Aria replied.

"Really? Give it to some kid. When it gets big enough, they can ride it like a pony. Can I go into my house now?"

Aria stepped aside. "Of course."

Addison shot her a stern look. "And that *thing* better not crap on the floor."

"Aria and I will look after it, sir."

"Damn right, you will, JJ." And with that, Addison marched into the house.

At dinner, with the puppy lying nearby, Addison announced that if they kept the dog, he would call it *Windy* after the cool ocean breezes.

"What do you mean *if* we keep the dog?" JJ asked.

"I'm still mulling it over."

"At least the name is appropriate, sir."

"Glad you approve, *Sir JJ*. Aria?"

Aria came to the kitchen door. "Yes, sir?"

"You want to add your two cents to this conversation?"

"About what?"

"To keep the dog or to not keep the dog?"

"He was a gift to you; you decide." Aria turned and left.

Addison raised an eyebrow. "As I expected, she could care less."

In the days that followed, wherever Addison went, Windy followed. "JJ, why does he follow me around? Why not you or Aria?"

"Must be chemistry, sir."

"Or my aftershave. He better stop flowing me or find himself at the nearest dog shelter."

"May I make a suggestion, sir?"

"Only if you stop calling me sir."

JJ ignored him. "Instead of Aria walking Windy, why don't

you give it a shot, *sir*?"

"What will that accomplish?"

"Just give it a try and see."

"So now you're the *Dog Whisperer*?"

"Try it for one week."

The following morning, Addison relented and walked Windy down to the water's edge. Addison sat on a large rock; Windy settled on the ground next to him. To his surprise, in the days that followed, Addison found that he was enjoying his morning walks with Windy.

"I'm not sure where you got your good manners," Addison said to Windy, "but you're still here because you keep your trap shut and don't soil the floors. For that, you should be very, very grateful. You didn't understand a word I said, did you, Windy?"

Windy looked up and whined softly.

Addison grinned. "Hmm, maybe you did."

The daily walks continued. Addison and Windy would sit by the water's edge while Addison talked away as if Windy understood his ramblings. Soon, man and dog became inseparable, just as JJ knew they would.

Addison sent Ben an email reminding him he had yet to decide on a move to Honolulu.

Ben responded, "Hold your horses, Tonto, I'm ready, I'm coming. Give me a month to button up things here, then I'm all yours. Let's hope you don't regret your generous offer. As you know, I can be a real pain in the ass at times." He signed off with, "More later, alligator."

A week later, Addison sat watching television alone in his study when he experienced a sharp pain in his right temple. It had happened several times before, but this time it was different. This time, it was more intense. He brushed it off as a stress migraine.

During dinner that evening, the phone in Addison's study rang.

"I'll get it," Aria called from the kitchen. A few moments

later, she returned. "It's for you, Mr. Stone."

"Who is it, Aria?"

"He said his name was Dr. Hunter. He said he needed to speak with you urgently."

"Want me to get it, sir?"

"No, JJ, finish your dinner. I'll see what he wants."

Addison went to his study and picked up the phone. "Hello?"

"Mr. Stone?"

"Yes."

"*The* Addison Stone?"

"Afraid so. What can I do for you, Doctor?"

"My name is Doctor William Hunter with Cullum Memorial Hospital. Do you know Benjamin Dickey?"

"Yes, of course."

"I'm afraid I have bad news. Mr. Dickey has died."

Addison collapsed to his chair. "What? How?"

"A semi-truck ran a red light and smashed into the driver's door of Mr. Dickey's vehicle just outside Cullum. He arrived at the hospital with massive trauma to his upper body and legs and was barely alive. We did all we could, Mr. Stone, but the damages to Mr. Dickey's body were beyond repair."

Addison swallowed hard. "Oh, dear God."

"I'm sorry. Are you and Mr. Dickey related?"

"Ben had no family I was ever aware of, but he was like a blood relative to my mother and me."

"The reason I ask—and I have no idea where he found the strength in his condition—but he requested a pad and pen. With a shaking hand and barely able to write, he scribbled your name and this number and added the word ***Kin*** in capital letters."

Addison closed his eyes and swallowed. "Thank goodness he did. Doctor, since Ben has no living relatives, is it possible for me to claim his remains?"

"Yes, you can, but there's paperwork involved."

"Take down my Fax number and send me the papers. I'll sign them and Fax them back immediately."

Addison gave Dr. Hunter the Fax number.

"Perfect, Mr. Stone. You'll need to have your signature notarized."

"Yes, of course. I'm in Hawaii."

"Yes, I know, Mr. Stone."

"I'll fly in the day after tomorrow to take care of the arrangements. You'll have the paperwork before the day is out."

"Mr. Stone, considering the purpose of my call, I hope this is not inappropriate. My wife and I attended one of your concerts while vacationing in Las Vegas; it was a wonderful experience. Your talent brings much joy to the lives of many."

"That's kind of you to say, Doctor, thank you."

Addison hung up and pushed back in his chair. "Dear God, Ben, not you, too." He held back tears when he told JJ and Aria Ben had been killed in a traffic accident. "I must return to the mainland immediately to take care of the funeral arrangements. JJ, plan on going with me."

"Of course, sir."

"Call Nichols Funeral Home in Addison, explain what happened, and that I'm assuming responsibility for the arrangements and cost of Ben's funeral. I need to sign some papers and get them notarized."

"There's a notary at the nearby UPS store, Mr. Stone."

"Great. Let's run down there when the paperwork arrives via our Fax. Book a flight to Birmingham and reserve two rooms at La Quinta Hotel in Cullum."

"I'm on it, sir."

When Addison and JJ arrived in Birmingham, they rented a vehicle and drove straight to the funeral home in Addison. At the sight of Ben's severely damaged body, Addison teared up; Ben's face was unrecognizable. Addison took Ben's hand and held it. "Following the cremation, I'd like to hold a small gathering in your chapel,"

"Yes, Mr. Stone, I'll arrange that."

On the day of Ben's cremation, Pastor Bruce Langford presided over a short service, as he had done for Lacy. The church choir was in attendance, as was Millie Andrews, several of Ben's local friends, and Lang and Andy, who had flown in for the day.

Addison stood and spoke. "There are special people in this world who come into one's life and make a lasting impression. In my life, that was Ben Dickey. He was there when I was born. He was the father I never knew, the guiding hand who helped me get to where I am today. To my mother and me, Ben was family. He was a kind, gentle, soft-spoken giving man. It is painful to imagine my life going forward without him.

As people were leaving, a man Addison did not know approached him.

"Mr. Stone, I'm attorney Steven Myerson. I drew up Ben's will a couple of years back. He listed you as the executor of his estate and left all his assets to you."

"Hmm, I didn't know that."

"How would you like to proceed?"

"Begin by giving whatever is in Ben's bank account, less the cost of the hospital charges and cremation, to a local charity. I'll cover the difference and your fee if there aren't sufficient funds. Can you arrange that?"

"Of course."

"His personal belongings should be donated to charity."

"Very good."

"Do you do any corporate work, Mr. Myerson?"

"I do."

"Can you have A. J. Stone Enterprises address changed to reflect the one my assistant will provide you?"

"Yes, of course."

Addison shook the man's hand. "Thank you."

Addison, JJ, Lang, and Andy snuck out the rear to avoid any reporters or crowd that might have gotten wind that he was there.

When they settled at a nearby restaurant, Lang said, "We were about to call you when JJ alerted us to Ben's death. Normally, I wouldn't discuss business at a time like this, but—"

"Then don't," Addison snapped.

"We're flying back to New York later today, Addison, and this is important."

"Okay, okay, Lang, what is it."

"An entertainment group in Branson, Missouri, is constructing a new theater there."

"Three cheers for them. What's that got to do with me."

Lang looked at Andy. "Tell him."

"Addison," Andy began, "They want to go into business with you. They want to name the theater the Addison Stone Entertainment Center."

"Why would they want to do that, Andy?"

"It would be your theater, Addison. You would entertain there year-round and share ownership 60/40 with the developers until they recoup their initial investment, then it's 50/50. Think of it: no more traveling and living out of a suitcase."

"Lang, I'm not moving anywhere, least of all to Branson, Missouri. I reside in Hawaii, end of story." Addison smirked and glanced at JJ. "These two have been smoking funny cigarettes again, JJ."

JJ stifled a laugh.

"At least hear us out, Addison."

"There's nothing to consider, Lang, over and out."

Lang sighed and sat back in his chair. "Are you sure you don't want to consider this before I turn them down?"

"One hundred percent sure, Lang. But be sure to tell them I appreciate the offer. Now, if there's nothing else, this is a day of mourning for me. I appreciate your coming. Have a safe flight home. JJ and I are off to Hawaii in the morning."

That evening, alone in his hotel room, Addison wrote in his journal.

> *There is a dark, hollow, and painful hole in my gut. I will now travel my journey alone. It pains me to think how it could have been different if Hanna and I had married and had children.*

Not a day goes by that I don't think of her, nor has my love for her waned—it never will. She's never married. Why? As far as I know, she's not involved in a serious relationship. Again, why? Until I learn that she is, I will never stop pursuing her.

Upon their return to Honolulu, the reception was always the same: Windy, tail waggling like crazy, came scampering out. He'd run to Addison, circled him, and growl, then to JJ, back to Addison, and back to JJ. This went on for several minutes before Windy calmed down.

Chapter 21

When Addison turned thirty-seven, he remained in as much demand as in his early years. He traveled the country and the world regularly; the public never got enough of his mesmerizing, magical voice. By then, Addison had recorded five albums, each becoming a best seller.

But Addison was growing weary of it all.

He lived on a beautiful estate by the sea in Honolulu and had more money than he could ever spend. But he was weary of the constant traveling, the public role-playing, and the lack of privacy when out in public. The Branson deal may have solved some of those problems, but that wasn't in the cards for him. He seriously considered leaving it all behind and retiring.

As Addison and Windy walked down to the water's edge one morning, Addison was struck by a sharp, stinging pain in his right temple, similar to what had occurred before. This time, however, the pain did not stop; he felt faint and quickly sat on his rock. "What the hell is going on?"

Windy whined as if he sensed Addison was in pain.

"Jeez, Windy, I thought I would pass out there for a minute.

Whew, that was close!"

Addison remained sitting until his head cleared and felt he could return safely to the house.

Late one afternoon, Addison, JJ, and Windy sat quietly on the patio, watching the golden Sun continue its dissent over the horizon.

"JJ, you've never talked to me about your life or why you chose this profession. Everyone has a story; I'm interested in yours."

"I'm afraid mine is mundane."

"No one's story is mundane, JJ. Try me."

"Hmm. Okay, if you wish."

"I wish."

I was the only child born to a lower-middle-class family in Bristol, England. Like many families at the time, my parents struggled to make ends meet. Dad worked two jobs, so we didn't see him much, and Mom took in other folks washing to help out. During summer school breaks, I found odd jobs to help out. That's about it; that's all there was to my early life."

"And this profession, what led you to it?"

"Ah, that. Back then, college was never mentioned because of the lack of money. The goal of parents was to get their children through high school and help them find a job."

"Sounds familiar, JJ. High school was the end of my education."

"I had no specific skills, nor did I know what I wanted to do with my life."

"Ditto again."

"I stumbled across an article in a magazine about the International Butler Academy in Simpelveld in the south of The Netherlands. I thought, hey, that sounds interesting, I could do that."

"A butler?"

"Yeah. I could wear nice clothes, live on some wealthy family's estate, eat well, and get paid for it. When I told my parents, they offered to take a small loan on our five-room row house to get me started. I would have to find a job to cover the rest. So, I went to Simpelveld for two days looking for work. I got lucky and was hired by the South Limbuyr Railway, selling tickets at the station from four in the afternoon to one in the morning. With finances secured, I signed up for the ten-week training program at the Butler School. I learned the essential duties of a butler, personal assistant, valet, house, and estate manager. I got lucky again when a wealthy family on the outskirts of Simpelveld hired me right out of school."

"Wow, you were pretty fortunate, JJ."

"Josh Amerson, an industrialist from Chicago, and his wife were friends with my employers, and they came to visit. Mr. Amberson was so impressed with my work that he offered to sponsor and hire me if I ever wanted to move to America. When I learned that I could make more money in America doing the same work, I took Mr. Amerson up on his offer six months later. He took me under his wing and encouraged me to take on additional responsibilities. I did, and in time, I became his executive assistant and manager of the estate."

"Bravo, JJ, Bravo."

"I met my wife, Elenore, there. She oversaw the kitchen staff and was an excellent cook herself." JJ wavered and lowered his head. "Elenore suffered from a rare blood disease. Two years after we were married, she was struck with sepsis and died."

"I'm so sorry, JJ."

"There have been relationships since, but none panned out. Elenore was the only one for me; no one could replace her. In time, I rose to the position of majordomo and have been gainfully employed ever since."

"You had the determination, drive, and intelligence to do something with your life."

They fell silent and watched the Sun dip over the horizon.

Addison waved. "See you in the morning, Mr. Sun." He reached down and patted Windy, then said to JJ. "I've been seriously considering retirement, JJ."

That took JJ by complete surprise. "Retirement? At thirty-seven?"

"I have commitments for the next year. After that, been there, done that, and I'm considering hanging it up."

"Seriously, Mr. Stone, what would you do with yourself?"

"Learn to play chess and get you to stop calling me sir and Mr. Stone."

"Ain't gonna happen, sir."

"I didn't think so."

"You're blessed with a talent others would kill for. Why would you hang it up now?"

"It's not love for me that audiences have, JJ; it's more like smothering. Everyone wants a piece of me. You've seen it; I can't venture out in public without being fawned over. The Paparazzi follow me everywhere. Reporters and TV—both local and the networks—want me to sit for endless interviews. I'm tired of it all. You give and give until there's little left for yourself. I no longer have pieces of me to give away. It's not like I found a cure for anything; I'm just a singer. I say screw it all."

"You don't mean that."

"I damn well do, JJ. I was never meant for this to begin with. Voice or no voice, my life has been an illusion, dare I say, a lie. I was too insecure to make my own decisions. I let others decide for me, beginning with Millie Andrews, Lang, Andy, and even Ben. Then came the success, the money, the women, and my ego took front and center, which caused me to lose the woman I loved. I was swept up in the excitement, the public adulation, and, of course, the money. I became someone I wasn't."

"Those that helped you meant well, sir. Without them, you would not be sitting in this magnificent house in beautiful Hawaii," JJ pointed to the ocean view, "overlooking that."

"I know that."

"So, what then, Mr. Stone?"

Addison folded his hands, set them in his lap, and sat quietly for a long moment. He had never spoken to anyone about his past and lifelong insecurities. But now, he wanted JJ to know.

"And then there was my mother. I never really knew her well. I know that sounds nuts, but when it came to our relationship, I came in second because Lacy could not move beyond her troubled past. It haunted and consumed her and affected me in ways I would rather it had not."

"How so, sir?"

"Lacy was raised by her father's parents after her parents, who were drug addicts, overdosed on heroin when Lacy was two."

"Oh, my."

"As if that wasn't enough, her grandparents were alcoholics who often got into raging arguments when they drank. Sometimes, in their alcoholic stupor, they took out their rage on Lacy, and she'd lock herself in her room to escape them. She was left with emotional scars that have plagued her ever since. Growing up, I was confused and consumed by her turbulent mood swings, and I unwittingly became her clone."

Addison stood, walked to the patio's edge, and stared at the distance for several moments. "I've never spoken to you about Hanna."

"No, I don't believe you have. Who is she?"

"Hanna… Hanna Potts. She's the daughter of the producers of *Sing America Sing*. We met at the reception following the show, and almost immediately, sparks flew. We met again in Los Angeles, where she was going to film school, then again in San Francisco, and then in Denver for a weekend. Over that weekend, we declared our love for one another and even went so far as to discuss marriage."

"After four visits, sir?"

"It was love at first sight: that beautiful face, those piercing eyes, her smile; she spoke in a soft, welcoming voice, and I was hooked. Hanna told me she felt the same about me, that if we hadn't met in New York, we would have met somehow, somewhere. She said it was Kismet."

"So, what happened, sir?"

Addison's eyes drifted. He took a deep breath and exhaled. "I made a mess of things, and she ended our relationship. That's another story for another time. I've attempted to contact her numerous times, but she refuses to return any of my calls."

"Perhaps by now she's married, sir."

"No, she's not. She graduated film school and has a successful documentary film company based in New York City."

"Forgive my bluntness, Mr. Stone, but you can't spend the rest of your life feeling sorry for what did not happen. Or is this a cathartic moment?"

Addison chuckled. "Yeah, maybe; we'll call it *the purging of the demons in the life and times of Addison Stone*." Addison strolled back to his chair and sat. "This business has been more than generous to me. Now, I'm asking myself, what do I do with all that money that could make a difference?" He chuckled. "I considered having it stuffed in my coffin, but sure as hell, someone would dig me up for the booty. As for cremation, they tell me the ink interferes with the cremation process."

JJ laughed. "Neither of which I believe is true, sir."

"The truth is, I've given serious thought to becoming a philanthropist."

"An admirable choice, Mr. Stone. It will guarantee you a special place in Heaven."

"Assuming there is such a place." Addison stood. "Okay, enough soul cleansing. Come on, let's see what The General has rustled up for dinner."

At six-thirty, Addison and JJ were enjoying Aria's Hawaiian Chicken Kebabs.

"JJ, now that Ben is gone, would you consider taking over his position as Chief Operating Officer of the company?"

JJ looked surprised. "Um, I, ah—"

"If you're interested, I'll add another fifty grand a year to your salary."

"I, ah, I am very flattered, sir."

"Good, then take the job. The accounting firm does all the work; you only have to sign checks. We'll engage an attorney here in Honolulu to look after corporate stuff. *Easy Peasy*!"

"Thank you for your confidence in me."

"Then you'll take the job?"

"Yes, sir, of course."

"Excellent. Now, no more calling me *sir* or *Mr. Stone*."

JJ grinned. "Don't count on it, Mr. Stone."

The phone in Addison's study rang.

"I'll get it," Aria called from the kitchen. A few minutes later, she entered the dining room. "It's for you, Mr. James."

"I'm in the middle of dinner, Aria; who is it?"

"He said his name was Matthew Dupont, Chairman of the new American Centrist Political Party."

"I know who he is," Addison said. "No doubt he wants my endorsement for one of his candidates for the next election. Take the call, JJ, and tell him I said no."

Ten minutes went by before JJ returned.

"Well, what did Mr. DuPont want?"

"He would not elaborate. He requested a meeting with you here in Honolulu. I told him I would speak with you and get back to him."

"He wants to travel here? He must be desperate for my endorsement. When does he want this meeting?"

"Three days from now."

Addison sat back in his chair and rubbed his chin. "Hmm. Okay, JJ, it's his nickel. Set up the meeting. But I'm not endorsing any damn candidate for any political party."

Chapter 22

Three days later, Matthew Dupont arrived along with another man.

Aria greeted them and escorted them to the study, where Addison and JJ waited.

"Mr. Stone, your guests have arrived."

"Thank you, Aria."

Aria snapped her fingers. "Come on, Windy, you're not needed here."

Windy scampered along behind her.

When the two men entered, Addison smiled. "Welcome to Honolulu, gentlemen."

The slightly heavy-set one introduced himself. "Mr. Stone, Mr. James, I'm Matthew DuPont, Chairman of—"

"Yes, I know who you are." Addison shook DuPont's hand.

"This gentleman with me is party Vice Chairman Steven Hill."

JJ motioned to two chairs in front of the desk where Addison now sat. "Please make yourselves comfortable. Coffee, tea, cold drinks?"

"Not for me," DuPont said.

"I'm good, thank you," Hill replied.

"Your career remains red hot," DuPont said. "How do you keep up with it?"

"One day at a time." Addison chuckled, "Some days, not at all. So, why have the chairman and Vice-chairman of the American Centrist Party flown all this way to speak with me?"

"Well, Mr. Stone—"

"Let's get on a first-name basis."

"Fine, Addison. November of next year's election will be our party's first time out of the gate."

"I wish you luck, but surely, you're aware most Americans are fed up with the two parties we have? I'm not sure they're ready for a third."

"A fair observation, Addison. Polls have consistently shown that sixty percent or more of voters would encourage a third party to discourage the endless polarization between the two existing parties."

Addison smirked. "Good luck with that."

"The ACP has two significant mountains to climb. First, shut down the extremists' spreading lies, misinformation, and senseless conspiracy theories; it's ruining our country. Too many are willing to believe the lies; others don't know what to believe anymore. Second, we need to expose the wealthy and powerful individuals and corporations who have exploited the masses for too many years. They have highjacked our economy with the support of many elected officials in exchange for supporting their re-elections with good old American dollars."

Hill picked it up. "Americans are more than ready to support a qualified individual from outside politics, someone known to the general public for their strong morals and integrity. Most importantly, someone genuinely concerned for the well-being of all citizens and not just their own."

"Someone like that, Steven," Addison said with a grin, "will be too smart to let themselves get mired in the Washington swamp as it's lovingly called."

"Addison, are you familiar with our party's platform?"

DuPont asked.

"No, I don't pay much attention to politics."

"Our platform is aligned with what the people want: age and term limits, election finance reform, and equality that applies to everyone regardless of color, creed, or religious beliefs."

"All of which has been tried before and failed, Matthew."

"If we win, Addison, I promise these challenges will be met head-on. They'll be strong blowback from big money. But, if the voters understand they hold the power given to them in the Constitution, they will vote for our agenda."

Addison glanced at JJ with a sly grin before turning to DuPont. "And you want my endorsement for your candidates?"

"No, we don't."

"Then what?"

Dupont paused just long enough to pique Addison's and JJ's interest. "We've come to ask if you would consider becoming our candidate for president of the United States."

The room went dead silent.

With a quizzical expression, Addison responded, "Would you repeat that?"

"We're asking if you will consider becoming our party's first presidential candidate."

"That's what I thought I heard." Addison's head bobbed back. He slapped his chest with an open hand and laughed. "Are you two on drugs? JJ, did you hear that?"

JJ smiled. "Yes, sir, I did."

"I assure you, Mr. Stone," Hill continued, "we are quite serious. You are a true Icon beloved the world over and—"

Addison waved him off. "What makes you believe that I, Addison Stone, have the slightest knowledge, let alone the interest, to run a country? Look, gentlemen, I've always been a registered independent. I do my duty as a citizen and vote for whomever I deem qualified without regard to party affiliation. Sometimes, I pick a winner, sometimes a royal dud. I'm a singer, an entertainer, not a politician, nor am I interested in becoming one. I have a super big ego, gentlemen, but not that big."

"You are one of the most beloved entertainers on the planet."

"Yeah, Matthew, that and five bucks will get you a cup of coffee at Starbucks. I know nothing about politics or governing. I disdain ambitious men and women seeking public office as a career that will advance their public image, boost their ego, and enrich them financially. The answer to the problem, gentlemen, is simple: seek out and vote for candidates capable of seeing the big picture and who will work to solve problems affecting all citizens. Too many voters, having not done their due diligence when picking a candidate, simply vote for whatever party they're affiliated with—most likely the same one their parents were—which doesn't get the job done. I'm flattered that you think I'm qualified for the job but trust me, I'm not."

"You graduated high school with the highest academic scores of your class and delivered the valedictorian speech."

Addison couldn't hold back a hearty laugh. "That speech, such as it was, was roundly criticized as the worst ever for that school."

"I read your speech," DuPont said. "You made your point without beating it into the ground."

"Yeah, but I was criticized for not saying more. Valedictorian speeches are usually filled with BS about how great the future will be, as if we had a clue. At that age, we're still learning not to put our underwear on backward. Look, gentlemen, I'd be a fool not to know you're looking to trade on my popularity."

"I'd be lying to you if I said we were not," DuPont said. "But I can look you in the eye and tell you that's only part of it. Your fan base alone could send you to the White House. That and the fact that we believe you could do the job is why we are here. Look what you have accomplished. You grew a God-given talent into a highly successful entity."

"Thanks, but others had something to do with it, too," Addison said. "Maybe more so than me."

"Your humility is admirable, but you do yourself an injustice. How many fan clubs do you have now?"

"Twelve clubs at last count with twelve million fans and counting," JJ confirmed.

"How many successful tours and record albums?"

"All of them," JJ responded.

"You make my point, JJ."

"I thank you for the offer and for coming all this way, but I doubt I'll change my mind. The entertainment business can be quite nasty. I can only imagine what it's like in politics."

"Please, Addison, sleep on it; consider our offer seriously. Whatever your decision, we will honor it. Give it a few days before you give us your final decision."

"Okay, Matthew, I'll get my brain's algorithms to work on it immediately."

DuPont and Hill stood. "I will leave you with this thought," Matthew said. "The ACP was formed and is financially backed by influential men and women whose goal is to ensure that democracy and equality continue for all citizens, not just the elite, who presently hold the keys to the door of democracy."

"You know, Matthew, I've often thought it strange that most people believe they must be a conservative or progressive; they can't be both. That's a big myth. Depending on the issue, one may lean conservative; on others, they may lean progressive. That fact cannot be denied; it's common sense. So, how can anyone be loyal to one political party or way of thinking?

"You're right, but try convincing the voting public that. Thank you again for meeting with us, Addison. We look forward to hearing from you."

"Safe flight, gentlemen, and good luck with the election."

JJ escorted the two men out. When Addison was sure they were out of ear range, he pushed back in his chair, slapped his chest, and laughed.

When JJ returned, Addison snickered. "Have you ever heard anything more bizarre?"

"It's clear, sir, they wish to trade on your popularity."

"Huh! Ya' think?"

"However, they did make their point."

"Oh, no, don't tell me you agree with them, JJ?"

"The country does require a third party. It will be up to the American people whether or not it succeeds or if it even gets off the ground. As for your becoming their candidate, that is a separate issue only you can decide, yea or nay. I suggest you sleep on it."

"I have enough trouble sleeping now, JJ. If I think about this seriously, I'll wake up with nightmares."

"Then, sir, the subject is dead upon arrival."

"Amen, and praise the anti-political party gods."

When JJ left, Addison wrote in his journal.

> *I've had many strange things happen, but none this wacky—not even close. DuPont and Hill must be smoking funny cigarettes to think I could be sitting in the Oval Office one day making life-and-death decisions that affect the lives of our citizens and others around the world. Maybe I could put on a Batman costume and pretend. Not funny, Addison. Now, put this wacky idea out of your thoughts.*

Nothing more was said about DuPont and Hill's visit for the next three days. Early in the morning of the fourth day, Addison was drinking his morning coffee on the patio with Windy by his side. A pain struck his right temple, causing him to jerk forward and spill some of his coffee on his right leg. "What the hell in heaven!" He moaned and rubbed at his temple. The pain lasted less than ten seconds, but this one was more severe than the last and left him feeling dizzy. He placed his coffee on the side table and waited until the dizziness subsided. "I spent an uneasy night considering DuPont's offer, and I'm—wait for it—seriously considering it. Windy, if there was ever a time you wanted to bite me, now would be that time."

"Did you say something, sir?"

JJ was standing by the door holding a cup of coffee.

"I said; What a beautiful morning it is. Come, sit with me."

JJ took a seat next to Addison.

It was indeed a glorious morning. The sun was bright and warm, and a slight breeze blew across the patio.

"Have you and Windy been for your walk yet?"

"Not until I finish my coffee, JJ."

"Did you sleep well, Mr. Stone?"

"Not really. I spent much of the last three nights pondering."

"About what, sir?"

Addison hesitated. "DuPont's offer."

JJ's spine went straight. "You aren't serious?"

"Have you ever known me not to be?"

"Often, Mr. Stone, often."

"Be careful, JJ; if I were to run and win, I'd make you my Chief of Staff."

JJ's brow rose. "Heaven forbids. And if you were to lose?"

"I'd retire as planned."

"What is of most concern, sir, is, if you were to win, would you call the shots, or would they?"

"Yeah, I've given thought to that. You know me well enough. I have no intention of becoming anyone's lackey figurehead. If I were to run and win, I'd insist on governing with the full weight and authority of the presidency. Once they get that message, they'll regret choosing me as their candidate. But then, that'll be their problem, not mine."

"Then you *are* considering their offer?"

"Let's just say I'm semi-serious until I—until you and me— negotiate with DuPont. We're scheduled to play Chicago soon?"

"It's your third stop."

"Call DuPont and arrange a luncheon the day after we arrive. Let's have lunch in my suite so we can talk freely without the great unwashed public watching. Set DuPont and Hill up with comp tickets for the show."

JJ blew a breath. "You never cease to surprise me; you've certainly done that in spade this morning."

"I try every morning, JJ. Sometimes I succeed, sometimes not. Okay, Windy, let's go for our walk."

When they returned, Addison went to his study and made an entry in his journal.

Either I'm arrogant enough to believe I could pull this off, or I'm the biggest fool currently trekking across the planet—more like both. On the other hand, given the likes of some who have been elected, I'm probably just as qualified, which isn't saying much when I think about it. Let's hope this is not my ego pursuing this. American politics and all the crap that accompanies it is an animal yet to be tamed, which begs the question, why would I put myself through this? Why indeed.

Chapter 23

Addison and JJ were on the road again, with stops in Denver, Kansas City, Chicago, and New York. In Chicago, the venue would be Lincoln Hall. On the scheduled day, Dupont and Hill arrived five minutes before noon. The front desk called and informed JJ they were on their way up.

JJ greeted them. "Gentlemen, good to see you again. Please, come in."

Addison smiled and shook hands with both men. "I hope you two have stayed out of trouble."

"We do our best, Mr. Stone," Hill replied. "We don't always succeed."

"Please, first names only, remember?"

JJ motioned to the living room. "Lunch will be up shortly; make yourselves comfortable."

Once seated, Matthew got right to the point. "I assume we're here because you're interested, Addison, or you would have called it in."

"Let's say I'm semi-interested."

"Hmm, okay."

"I've had a wonderful career, Matthew. No man could wish

for more. But as JJ will tell you, I've considered retiring and setting up a foundation to help needy children and adult drug addiction."

"Certainly, a worthy goal," Matthew said. "What motivated you to go in that direction?"

"I was moved by a quote I read by Author Pearl S. Buck, recipient of the Pulitzer and Noble Prizes for her best-selling book *The Good Earth*. Ms. Buck wrote… *If our American way of life fails the child, it fails us all.* Let me add to that: if we fail the child, we will have a troubled adult to deal with.

"Nothing could be truer," Mathew said. "You indicated you were semi-serious about accepting our offer. What exactly did you mean?"

"JJ will explain."

"Yes, well, If Mr. Stone were to accept your offer, he would want assurances that he can fulfill his existing performance commitments."

"Certainly."

"As Mr. Stone indicated, he plans to go forward with the foundation, although he will not oversee it personally or be involved with day-to-day activities."

"Not a problem," Matthew said. "The election is eighteen months away. Our convention will be held after the Republican and Democratic conventions. No announcements will be made before then."

"What about a primary?"

"They'll be none," Steven explained. "The committee to choose a candidate will announce their decision at our convention.

Addison chuckled low. "Isn't that risky? It seems to me its game is over if the public disagrees with your choice."

"Yes, we're aware of that," Matthew replied. "But it's more of a risk that a primary might leave us with a weak candidate. If that were to happen, we'd get swallowed up by the other two parties before we left the gate, and the ACP is dead."

"So," JJ said pointedly, "Addison is the bait. You're banking on his celebrity."

Hill opened his mouth to reply, but Addison cut him off.

"Before you answer that, Steven, you need to understand that my public persona is, as they say, lipstick on a dressed-up pig. People only see what they see, not what's behind the curtain. And I assure you, there isn't anyone in my business that doesn't have certain things made public.

"Everyone has a few skeletons in our closet. They wouldn't be human if they didn't."

"Because of my celebrity, there will be more than the usual mud-slinging. I—we—would have to convince the public I can do more than stand on a stage and sing pretty songs."

"We're prepared for that," Steven Hill injected.

"And, here's the Biggy. If I were to win, I would insist on governing as *President*, not as a *figurehead* following orders."

"Addison," Matthew began, "no one elected president comes to office with a degree in running a country. Hopefully, they bring with them integrity, honesty, a bit of wisdom, and a goal to move the country forward. As for using your celebrity, there is no way in hell we would have approached you if we did not have the utmost confidence that you can do the job."

Addison sat back, flipped one leg over the other, joined his hands, and set them in his lap. He shot a look at JJ, then to DuPont and Hill. "So, gentlemen, how do we get this train into the tunnel and out the other side?"

Steven smiled. "We'll begin by quietly producing a documentary on your life. We'll send a crew here to shoot background footage and interview you. The film will be shown on the night of the convention when your candidacy is announced."

Addison thought for several beats. "Let's hope I know what I'm doing." He took a breath, glanced briefly at JJ, and said, "Okay, gentlemen, I'm in."

"Wonderful," Dupont said.

There was a knock at the door.

JJ stood. "Ah, that would be lunch."

Two waiters wheeled in two food carts.

"The only thing missing," Steven Hill said, "is a bottle of champagne to celebrate. Oh, by the way, thank you for the tickets to the show."

"Our pleasure," JJ said.

After they shared a pleasant lunch, they all shook hands, and DuPont and Hill left.

"I hope you've made the right decision, sir."

"JJ, one must crack a few eggs to make an omelet."

"I believe, Mr. Stone, you just cracked a dozen or more."

"Since we can't predict what tomorrow will bring, my friend, one must roll the dice and hope for the best."

"Any more bon mots you want to share, sir?"

"That's it, that's all I have."

Chapter 24

When Addison completed his current tour, he and JJ returned home to Honolulu. JJ received a call from Steven Hill. If it is convenient for Addison, they would like to send the film crew in four days from now to get the footage and interview needed for the documentary.

"That sounds fine, Steven. I'll inform Mr. Stone."

"Great. If you or Addison have any questions between now and then, be sure to call."

When JJ told Addison, Addison rolled his eyes. "As if I haven't done enough repetitive interviews already."

"I would think this one will be quite different."

"How so?"

"This time, it is about your entire life, sir."

Addison frowned. "Which, I remind you, isn't over yet."

"I meant the questions will be more personal, more revealing."

"How much lying can I get away with?"

"Zero. Remember, the truth shall set you free, sir."

"JJ, we should take this act on the road."

"If we did, Mr. Stone, I would insist on top billing."

"Hold your breath on that one, Englishman."

Mid-morning on the fourth day, the video crew arrived. Aria greeted the producer at the door. After a brief introduction, Aria led the producer to the living room.

"Make yourself comfortable. Mr. Stone will join you shortly. May I get you anything?"

"Yes, thank you—Coffee, black."

Aria returned a few minutes later with coffee."

"Thank you," the producer said.

With her usual passive expression, *The General* turned and left with no further comment.

Moments later, Addison entered the room. He stopped cold and did a double take. Hanna was sitting there. She was the last person he expected to see sitting on the sofa drinking coffee in his living room. Her reddish-blond hair was trimmed shorter than he remembered. Her blue eyes still sparkled like diamonds. Hanna was as stunningly beautiful as when he first met her; she still took his breath away again.

Hanna smiled. "Hello, Addison. Some fancy digs you have here."

"Hanna! *I-I*-I don't know what to say."

"Try, hello, Hanna; how are you?"

"Yes, of course; how are you?"

"Fine, Addison, fine. And you?"

A speechless Addison walked several steps closer to her. "*W-w*, what are you doing here?"

"You do recall what I do for a living?"

"*Ah-ah*, of course."

"A New York PR firm hired Hanna Productions to produce your film. I assume they had no idea you and I had a history, or they wouldn't have hired my company." Hanna waited for Addison to say something, but he just stood staring at her.

"Are you just going to stand there and stare?"

"*I-t*, it's been eighteen years, Hanna. Give me a minute to compose myself."

Hanna glanced at her watch. "Time's up."

"I don't know what to say, Hanna. I've attempted to contact you many times over the years, but you chose not to respond."

"Yeah, well, I'm sorry, Addison. There were times I wanted to."

"Then why didn't you?"

Hanna wavered. "Fear."

"Fear? Of what?"

Hanna's eyes strayed across the room.

"Say what you mean, and mean what you say, Hanna."

"I wish it were that easy, Addison." She paused and looked away again.

"Come on, it can't be that hard."

"It is, but for better or worse, here's goes. Working with my parents on their productions during my early years, I was blessed to receive the best education this business could offer."

"Yes, you were very fortunate."

"During those years, I witnessed up close and personal what happens to some when fame comes too quickly. Some handle it well, others not so much. Suddenly, the public and the press treated them like royalty and fawned over them. Fan adulation followed them everywhere they went, and they were making mega bucks to boot. Their egos kicked in. The temptation to use their celebrity indiscriminately took center stage: the booze, wild parties, drugs, and women were there for the taking, and not necessarily in that order.

Addison knew precisely what she was saying. Except for the booze and drugs, he was guilty of the evening he spent with those two women. He had betrayed Hanna.

"Hanna, I made a mistake, and—"

Hanna raised a hand, "Let me finish, Addison. I vowed that if I was ever involved romantically with a celebrity, I would never allow myself to be a victim—yes, a victim—of such behavior. Can you understand that?"

Addison nodded. "Hanna, I know what I did was wrong, and I paid the price by losing you. I'm not proud of what I did, but I can't take it back, can I?

"To put it mildly, I was emotionally crushed when I saw that video of you and those two women. You had betrayed my trust, especially after we had spent the weekend in Denver professing our love for one another and planning our future. I wanted to punish you, Addison. I still loved you but could no longer be *with* you. Can you understand that?"

Addison lowered his gaze to the floor.

"I should have returned your call and told you this back then. I was wrong not to. You deserved your day in court, and I denied you that."

"Hanna, don't; I'm the one who needs to apologize." Addison shoved his hands in his pockets, walked to the window, and stared out. "What I did and what it cost me continues to haunt me. You slammed the door shut on our relationship, and I deserved it."

After several beats of awkward silence, Hanna stood, moved to Addison's side, and placed a hand on his shoulder. "Hurt as I was, I wanted to return your calls, I really did. But I was hurt; I was crushed. Stupid human pride kept me from returning your calls." Tears came to her eyes. "If my coming here now was a mistake, forgive me."

"Why did you come now? You could have sent one of your staff?"

"Believe me, I thought long and hard before accepting this assignment. But… if there was a ghost of a chance of us getting back together and trying again, this was it."

Addison did a slow turn and looked deep into Hanna's eyes. "I never stopped loving you, Hanna."

"Nor did I stop loving you." Hanna wiped a tear from her cheek. "It is too late for us after all these years?"

Addison took Hanna in his arms and smiled. "Never. When two people profess their love for one another as deeply as we once did, it's never too late."

Hanna smiled. "It was and remains, Kismet; the love gods sprinkled us with Kismet dust."

"Shame on us if we screw this up a second time. Can we start again from where we left off?"

Hanna giggled. "As the saying goes, in for a penny, in for a pound. Eighteen years ago, we were planning our future together. Still interested?

Addison put his mouth next to Hanna's left ear and softly began singing *Your Love*.

Hanna giggled. "Ever the performer."

"The answer, Love, is yes, yes, and yes again."

Hanna wiped at her eyes, took Addison's hand, and led him to the sofa, and they sat.

Aria entered with Windy following on a leash. "I'm taking the Big Shot for his walk, sir."

"Okay, Aria."

Hanna waited until Aria left. She grinned and said low. "So, you kept the dog."

"What?"

"The dog; you kept him."

"It was you?"

"I was so sorry when I learned of your mother's passing. I considered reaching out to express my condolences, but I feared that would open old wounds, so I sent you a gift instead."

"Anonymously."

"Silly me, why I thought a dog appropriate remains a mystery."

"You'll be happy to know Windy has become the much-loved ruling member of this household."

"Well, that's good to know."

"Now, how long are you here for?"

"We hope to have everything we need except for your interview, which we'll do once the crew tells me they have all the B-roll we need. Then we return to New York."

"Can you stay a few days longer?"

"Um, yes, I suppose I could."

"Good. Move in here for a few days."

Hanna smiled wide. "Okay, but my guys are not aware of our

past. I'll have to explain why I'm staying. While they're shooting exteriors, I'll run to the hotel and check out. I'll have to rebook my flight."

"My assistant, JJ, will take care of that when you return."

"Great. Give me a few minutes with my crew, and then I'll introduce you."

Hanna headed for the door. "Hanna."

"Yes, Addison?"

"Did we do what I think we just did?"

Hanna blew him a kiss. "Unless this was just a dream, we certainly did."

Hanna joined her crew outside and explained the past relationship between her and Addison.

"Wow," Henry said. "That's as powerful a love story as I've ever heard."

Patrick gave Hanna a quick hug. "Congratulations to you both."

Addison joined them, and Hanna introduced him. "This is lighting cameraman Henry Clovis and soundman Patrick Graves."

Henry looked around at the magnificent house and grounds. "You have a stunning place here, Mr. Stone."

"Thank you, Henry; I built it myself."

Hanna clapped her hands. "Okay, enough with the jokes. You two get to work shooting exteriors. Addison, do they have free rein to shoot around the property while I'm gone?"

"Of course. I'll have JJ show them around."

Hanna and Addison returned to the house, and Addison introduced her to JJ.

"JJ, this charming lady, is the producer and director of my documentary. Say hello to Ms. Hanna Potts."

JJ shot an inquisitive look at Addison.

"Yes, JJ, it's that, Hanna."

"Ah, Mr. Stone has spoken of you, Ms. Potts. May I say you are as lovely as he said."

"Why, thank you, JJ. My hats off to you. It can't be easy

taking care of this spoiled human."

JJ playfully rolled his eyes. "I prefer not to comment."

"Hanna and I are back together again. We plan to do what we set out to do eighteen years ago but didn't."

"What is that, sir?"

"When we return to New York—" Addison turned to Hanna. "We will make plans to be married."

A surprised JJ's brow went up. "You're doing what, sir?"

"Getting married."

"Ah, yes, sir, that's what I thought you said. Congratulations are in order."

"I'd be honored if you would be my best man, JJ."

"Well…ah, yes, of course, Mr. Stone. The honor would be mine."

"Excellent. You can now officially stop calling me sir and Mr. Stone."

JJ grinned. "Yes, of course, *Mr. Stone, sir.*"

"As you can see, Hanna, JJ is a bit of a smartass."

"I like him already, Addison."

Aria stuck her head in the door. "Did I hear one of you boys is getting hitched?"

"I am," Addison replied, "to this beautiful young lady."

Aria's eyes grew big, and she raised an eyebrow.

"It's a long story. I'll tell you about it one day.

"Congratulations." Aria glanced at Hanna. "You're gonna' have your hands full with that one." She turned and left.

"As you can see, Hanna, the sense of humor in this house requires some fine-tuning."

As soon as Hanna left for the hotel, JJ, looking slightly confused, said, "Mr. Stone, what am I missing here?"

"The reunion of two souls who never stopped loving one another."

"All these many years later, sir?"

"Fate, kismet, JJ, that's what it is."

Addison went to his study, opened his journal, and wrote:

"Today, what I believed would never happen did; after all these years, fate has brought Hanna and me together again. Considering that I've lost track of the number of women who have come in and out of my life—many were one-night stands with women looking to get intimate with a celebrity—what just happened with Hanna is a minor miracle. Never once was I emotionally involved with any of those other women. True emotional intimacy is reserved for the one you choose to spend your life with, which for me has always been Hanna. For as long as I live, I will now count every moment with Hanna as a gift to be cherished.

Chapter 25

That evening, Addison, Hanna, and JJ dined together. Aria was in and out of the dining room and showed little interest in Hanna, remaining the same stoic Aria as always.

Hanna waved her fork in Addison's direction. "Okay, dear boy, truth or dare."

"Neither," Addison answered.

"When I accepted this project, I was handed a completed script and told the documentary was for a planned network special of your phenomenal rise to stardom. I wasn't told which network or when the documentary would air. We were instructed not to discuss the project or share with anyone that the project was in the works."

"So?"

"Why all the secrecy?"

"I've been cast as the next James Bond, and they don't want it leaked."

"JJ, can I get a straight answer from you?"

"Afraid not, Ms. Potts; this is Mr. Stone's question to answer."

Hanna raised an eyebrow. "The ball's back in your court, Mr.

Stone."

Addison downed the rest of his wine and sat back.

Hanna gave him the evil eye. "Come on, truth or dare."

"Truth." Adddison stood, walked across the room, and paused momentarily before turning back. "I've agreed to be the presidential candidate for the American Centrist Party."

Hanna sighed. "Addison, can you please be serious for one minute? JJ?"

"He's telling you the truth, Ms. Potts."

Hanna gave JJ a stern look. "I hope you two are having fun at my expense."

"It's true, Hanna. The ACP asked me to be their candidate. I gave it serious thought and accepted."

With a stunned expression, Hanna crossed her arms. "Are you out of your mind? What do you know about politics?"

"I accepted because I know I can do the job just as well as anyone. Given who some were in the past, hopefully better."

Hanna slapped an open hand on the table. "Addison, they're using you for your celebrity, and you're allowing your ego to interfere with your common sense."

Addison glanced at JJ. "So, I've been told."

"The ACP knows damn well you'd have an excellent chance of winning because of who you are. God knows why, but people grovel at the feet of their celebrities, and there's no bigger one than you. You can't let them do this to you."

"You mean I can't let *me* do this to *me*." Addison abruptly stood. "I don't want to argue about this. Hanna. I've committed, and I'm going through with it."

"Addison, please, listen to me."

"I'm going to bed. You coming?"

"It's 7:15, Addison."

With shoulders slumped Addison strolled out of the room.

When he was out of range, Hanna whispered to JJ. "You have to talk some sense into him."

"Although I agree that he's making a mistake, Ms. Potts, I do not make these decisions for Mr. Stone."

"He can't be thinking clearly, JJ."

JJ shrugged.

Hanna stood. "I'm going to talk to him."

"Goodnight, Ms. Potts, and good luck."

"Please, call me Hanna."

"One thought before you go. After all these years, you've found one another again. Don't let this issue destroy what you have regained."

"Good night, JJ."

When Hanna entered the bedroom, Addison lay with the blanket pulled over his head. Hanna paused at the foot of the bed. "Can I say something?"

"Turn off the light and come to bed."

"Yes, sir, Sargeant Major Stone!"

Hanna undressed, slipped into bed, and nestled her head against Addison's back. "I only want what's best for you."

"Thank you."

"If you honestly believe this is what you want, I will stand with you, but—"

"No buts, Hanna. Let me sleep."

"Is this how we spend our first night together in eighteen years?"

Addison pulled the covers tighter.

"Okay, sulk. I'm going to your study and watch television."

She began to roll off the bed, but Addison turned and grabbed her arm. "Wait." He rolled over and embraced Hanna. "I'm sorry, I'm acting like a petulant little boy."

"You said it; I didn't."

"I considered my decision to accept carefully. My celebrity status aside, I believe if I were to win, I have a pretty good idea of the change this country desperately needs."

"And you think you're the one to do it."

"Hanna, I don't think I *believe*."

"You alone will not bring about change unless whoever controls Congress saddles up with you. They all have agendas; I'm sorry to say many of their agendas have little or nothing to do with the good of the country. What are the chances of you circling all of them around the same wagon? Little or none. It would be four years of frustration in your life. Who needs that?"

Addison playfully spanked Hanna's rear. "There must be something more interesting to do than lying here having this discussion."

Hanna laughed. "Go ahead, name three things real fast."

"*Shhhh*, be quiet, I'm thinking. Ah, I got it." Addison pulled her to him and kissed her. "I love you, Hanna."

"I love you more, Addison. And you're changing the subject."

On the final day of the shoot, Henry and Patrick were busy setting up lights before the fireplace in Addison's study."

"Just be yourself, Addison."

"Hanna, love, I've done this a few hundred times before."

"Not like this. We were given a specific list of questions, some quite personal."

"And if I chose not to answer one or more?"

"That would be your decision. And remember what I told you. When we edit, my voice will be removed, so answer the questions as if you are telling the story and not responding to me."

"Got it. Let's do this."

Surprisingly, Addison spoke quite openly about himself, his career, how it came about, and how he rose to international stardom quickly. He answered every question honestly and without hesitation, including Lacy's abuse by her grandparents Wilbur and Thelma, her subsequent mental and drug issues, and how his mother's irrational behavior affected him. When Hanna asked about Ben, Addison spoke lovingly of him, referring to Ben as his moral anchor.

Hanna's final question was about Addison's decision to accept the ACP offer as their presidential candidate.

"It was a difficult decision, to say the least. I asked myself a dozen times why I would take on the demanding responsibility of governing since I had never been actively involved with politics or politicians. I always followed the rule that people must do their due diligence about their preferred candidates without being influenced by me or anyone else. Unfortunately, that is not always the case. Many faithfully follow the Pied Piper, and all they get in return is a fall over a cliff."

"And you're going to change that?"

"First, we wait and see if the country even wants me. If not, so be it." Addison grinned. "I can always go back to singing for my supper."

Henry and Patrick packed their stuff when the interview ended and bid goodbye to Addison and Hanna.

"Hanna, we'll see you back in New York. And congratulations to you both. Hollywood should make a move of your story. People love happy endings."

"Thank you, Henry. Travel safe."

Hanna remained for two extra days. She wanted badly to discuss Addison's run for the presidency further. Still, she knew it would only lead to more quibbling between them, so she dropped it.

Like mischievous kids planning to raid the cookie jar, Addison and Hanna spent their short time walking hand in hand along the sun-drenched beach, gleefully making plans for their wedding.

"Where should this world-shattering event take place?" Hanna asked.

"Wherever you like, dear lady."

"How about the far side of the Moon?"

"Done, I'll have JJ make the arrangements with NASA."

When it came time for Hanna to return to New York, Addison drove her to the Airport. Reluctantly, he signed two autographs as they entered the terminal. Once Hanna was checked in, they walked to her departure gate and sat until

Hanna's flight was called for boarding.

"I don't want to leave, Addison."

"Great, stay."

"If I only could,"

Hanna's flight was called for boarding.

"Well, time's up," Hanna said with a sigh. "Time to fly."

They embraced and kissed. Several people nearby applauded.

Addison forced a smile and nodded to them. "Why can't I ever get away from it," he growled.

"Being a celebrity is bitch," Hanna whispered. "It's never gonna stop as long as you're alive and breathing."

"Thank you for the reminder. Safe flight, Love. See you after my Newark show."

Then, like a whisp of wind, Hanna was gone again.

When Addison returned home, he wrote in his journal.

> *Hanna and I are back together after eighteen years apart; we will be married, and I will be running for president of the United States. Say that fast five times. I would not have believed either was possible, especially having Hanna back again. But then, all good things come to good people who wait. There is no ego here... well, maybe a little.*

The last two stops on Addison's next tour were Symphony Hall in Newark, New Jersey, and Carnegie Hall in New York City. Following his performance in Jersey, he texted Hanna— *I'm on my way in the morning, beautiful.*

Ten minutes later, Hanna sent him a text. *Well, hurry up already, Big Boy!*

Addison and JJ arrived in New York the following day. JJ checked into the Hyatt Grand Central Hotel. Addison was going to stay with Hanna at her apartment.

"Okay, JJ. Hanna left her apartment unlocked for me. I'm going to catch a cab there. Call me if you need me."

His phone rang: it was Lang Sherman.

"How's our Megastar doing?"

"Tired, Lang; can't wait to return to Hawaii."

"After New York, you have a month off, then it's Vegas for a month."

"Whoopee, lucky me."

"You're going to kill them in New York."

"They love me in the Big Apple, Lang."

"I kill them everywhere, Tonto."

Lang laughed. "Say, can you break away for dinner tonight?"

"Yes, of course. How about The Carriage House on West 10th at seven?"

"See you there, *Kemosabe*."

While JJ held down the fort at the hotel, Addison caught a cab to Hanna's apartment. She arrived home late afternoon.

She flew into Addison's arms. "Finally!"

Addison kissed her forehead, eyes, cheeks, and then locked lips.

"Wow, Big Boy, that tastes delicious."

"Speaking of that, I'm having dinner with Lang; want to come?"

"Love to, but I have an eight o'clock conference call regarding another film we're working on."

"Anything interesting?"

"Not unless you get excited about the insecticides we spray on crops."

Chapter 26

At 6:55 PM, Addison and JJ arrived at the Carriage House. As they entered the restaurant, Addison rubbed vigorously at his right temple."

"Headache again, sir?"

"Yeah."

"You've had them more frequently lately. Maybe you should consult with a doctor and have that checked."

"Nah, the shit is about to hit the fan with Lang, and it's giving me a migraine."

"It's your life, sir, your decision on how you will live it, not Lang's or anyone else's."

"Tell that to Lang and Andy."

They were escorted to Lang's table; Andy was also there.

"It's great to see you both," Lang said.

There were handshakes all around. The waiter arrived with a bottle of champagne.

"What are we celebrating?" Addison asked.

Lang smiled wide. "Your incredible continued success."

Addison responded unsmilingly, "Okay, I can drink to that."

When everyone's glass was poured, Lang raised his.

"To Addison Stone, an extraordinary entertainer and the most successful client we've ever represented."

"Here, here," Andy said.

"Thank you, thank you," Addison smiled broadly. "I could not have done it without you two and your great team."

"Your talent fueled the ship, Addison. We simply steered it in the right direction."

"And," Addison added, "handsomely filled both our coffers along the way."

"That we did, Addison, that we did."

"Ah, gentlemen, if I may?" JJ raised his class. "To Mr. Stone's impending marriage."

"What?"

"Yes, it's true, Lang, I'm finally getting hitched."

"That's terrific news, Addison. Who's the lucky lady?"

"Hanna Potts."

Lang and Andy reacted with surprise.

"Um, would that be Hanna Potts, daughter of Stan and Sally Potts?"

"The very same, Andy."

"Wow. What, when, and how?"

"We met eighteen years ago at the reception following *Sing America Sing*. We got together several times after. I won't bore you with the details other than it took eighteen years to finally get our act together."

Andy whistled low. "Well, I'll be damned," He raised his class. "To Addison and Hanna, may they live a long and happy life."

During dinner, they chatted about Addison's extraordinary career, how the entertainment industry was changing, and not always for the good, and Addison and Hanna's wedding plans.

"Addison, can we talk business for a moment?"

Addison raised an eyebrow. "What an unusual request, Andy."

"We're getting a lot of offers following your month at Caesar Palace. I have the list with me." Andy reached into his suit jacket and pulled out a folded sheet of paper.

"I'm not accepting any new gigs, Andy."

"For how long?"

Addison looked to JJ—JJ shrugged.

"For good. I'm retiring from show biz."

Addison's statement struck Andy and Lang like a hard blow to the stomach.

"What are you talking about?"

"I'm finished, Lang, caput; I'm moving on."

"To what?"

"To the rest of my life. First, I plan on creating *The Lacy Stone Foundation* in honor of my late mother. The Foundation will provide financial assistance to organizations helping needy children and supporting drug rehabilitation programs. There's more." Addison turned to JJ. "Fill them in."

JJ cleared his throat. "Mr. Stone met with Chairman Matthew DuPont and Vice Chairman Steven Hill of the American Centrist Party."

"I know Matthew," Lang said. "He nuts if he thinks a third party has a ghost of a chance. Where did you meet up with him?"

"At my place in Honolulu." Then, as if they were discussing another performance venue, Addison said casually. "They asked if I would consider becoming their presidential candidate."

Lang glanced at Andy. There was a moment of silence, then both men laughed.

"For a second there, we almost believed you," Andy said.

"Running for president is no joke, gentlemen. I considered it very seriously before accepting."

The silence at the table became deafening. Neither Lang nor Andy knew how to respond.

"Mr. Stone will honor the Caesars' engagement," JJ added, "then begin work on the foundation and prepare for the election."

Lang blew a breath. "This is for real, Addison?"

"As real as real gets, Lang."

Lang's forehead furrowed. "For God's sake, Addison,

they're a brand-new, unproven political party desperate for a win. They offered this to you because of your celebrity and enormous following. Not a day goes by that your website, Facebook page, Twitter, and Instagram sites don't receive thousands of hits. You perform to sold-out audiences wherever you go, and—"

"Lang, hold on, I know all that. I'd be a fool if I didn't know my celebrity status was at play. DuPont readily admitted it. To have a chance at winning, they need a strong public figure with a following. More importantly, they believe I can govern as well as anyone, or they wouldn't have made the offer." Addison grinned. "Hell, remember Ronald Reagan?"

Lang's expression signaled his disapproval. That was different."

"How so, Lang? He was in show business, I'm in show business, and—"

"There's so damn much crap going on in the country and around the globe. If you became president, the world would look to you for answers. Are you really ready to take on that responsibility?"

"I wouldn't have accepted if I didn't believe I could. Besides, despite what people think, one man does not have all the answers. That's why they call it an administration; lots of brainy advisors hanging around the office with opinions."

"I don't know what else to say, Addison."

"There isn't anything more to say, Lang. I'm running for President, and that's that."

When Addison returned to Hanna's apartment that night, she was anxious to hear how his dinner had gone with Lang.

"Like a meteor striking the Pentagon. First, JJ broke the news about our impending wedding. Then he dropped the bomb that I was retiring and running for President. They weren't pleased about losing their top performer."

"I'll bet."

"Anyway, that's done. Onward Christian Soldiers."

"You'll be happy to hear, Addison; today, Caesars green-lit the taping of your final performance there. I told them it was for a planned network documentary, but they weren't to share that information. As long as we'll be in Vegas, how do you feel about getting married there?"

"Hanna, darling, I will marry you anywhere, even the far side of the Moon."

"I broke the news to Mom and Dad. You know they take more than a little credit for getting your career off the ground."

"As well, they should, Hanna. Did you spill the beans about my running for office?"

"Not a word. They'll hear about it with the rest of the world when it's announced. I want nothing to interfere with our wedding. Now, Dear Addison, it's either we watch one of the late-night shows *or*—"

"I go for *or.*"

"Good choice, young man; I'll meet you in the bedroom."

"Tomorrow, we go to Cartier to pick out your engagement ring."

"Ah, yes, bring your credit."

Following lunch, the next day, Addison and Hanna visited Cartier Jewelers. They chose a combination engagement and wedding ring for Hanna and a gold wedding band for Addison. The word *Forever* was etched on the inside of each ring.

Addison performed at Carnegie Hall to a rousing sold-out audience the following night. After the show, he did his usual meet and greet in his dressing room, signed autographs on his way out, and joined Hanna and her parents for dinner at Patsy's Italian Restaurant on West 56th Street.

"We are excited for both of you kids," Stan said.

"We're past being kids, Dad."

"What my dear Stanley is trying to say is, it's about time."

"Well, now," Addison said, "the proper way to kick this off is to seek your blessing to marry your beautiful daughter."

"Permission granted," Stan said without hesitation.

"I second that," Sally added.

"Addison and I talked it over, and Honolulu is to become our home base."

"What about your work, dear?"

"I can work from Honolulu most of the time, Mom. When I need to be in New York or on location, I'll fly back."

"That is when I let her," Addison joked.

The next day, Addison sat for an interview with Entertainment Tonight before dining out with Hanna and JJ.

"Addison, do you really have to return to Honolulu?"

"I need to unwind before taking on Vegas again, Hanna. Why don't you come to Honolulu with us?"

"I wish I could, honey, but your project is not the only one we're working on."

"Success is a bitch, isn't it, Love?"

"No one knows that better than you, *Megastar*."

On the way out of the restaurant, Addison felt light-headed, and he stumbled.

"Addison, what's wrong?"

He waved it off. "It's nothing, babe. I'm just tired from all the running around."

Addison and JJ exchanged glances.

When Addison and JJ returned to Honolulu, Aria and Windy greeted them at the door. Windy's tail wagged wildly. He whined and circled Addison like a racing Greyhound, then to JJ and back to Addison.

Addison rubbed Windy's head. "Yeah, yeah, we're back. Aria, why don't you greet us like Windy does?"

"I can't run that fast, Mr. Stone."

Addison dropped his suitcase in the hall and sighed. "For the next three weeks, I'm staying in bed. Aria, I'll take all my meals there."

"Don't count on it, Mr. Stone."

"That's what I thought. I'm going to nap before dinner, so hasta la vista to one and all. Come on, Windy, you can nap with me."

Aria had dinner on the table at 6:45.

"Did you sleep well, Mr. Stone?"

"Like a newborn, Aria."

During dinner, JJ, who always had something to say, was unusually quiet.

"When you're like this, JJ, I know something's eating you. What is it?"

JJ hesitated a beat. "Following your wedding, I plan on moving to my own place."

"Don't be silly. This is your home, too."

"No, sir. You and Hanna are entitled to your privacy."

"Well, how about the guest house? You could move in there?"

"I thought we agreed that would become the Foundation's office?"

"Yeah, but—"

"No buts, Mr. Stone, my decision is final. Who knows, maybe I'll find a lady of my own."

"I wish you much luck in that department, JJ. So be it if you want to find your own place."

They fell silent and continued to eat when Addison's right hand began to shake, and the fork slipped from his hand onto his plate. He grimaced and rubbed at this right temple. "Damn, these migraines! Aria, can you bring me a couple of Aleve?"

"Yes, sir," she answered from the kitchen.

"Your headaches are becoming more frequent, sir. It's time you consulted with a doctor."

Addison waved JJ off. "I'm fine."

Aria came back with two Aleve. "Here, take these. If your headaches continue, do like JJ says and consult a doctor."

Addison waved her off. "Not you, too? It's just a migraine,

Aria. Everybody gets them. It's the pressure of being on the road so bloody often. It wears you down, and you get headaches."

Aria shot a look at JJ, but neither pursued it further.

Chapter 27

Caesars Palace treated Addison's return as if he were royalty. Addison and JJ stayed in the Nobu Tower suites they had previously occupied. As usual, Addison's shows were sold out.

One week before the end of Addison's run and his and Hanna's upcoming wedding, Hanna's parents arrived. JJ had made reservations for dinner at Nobu Restaurant. Hanna's crew —this time five strong—would come two days later to prepare to shoot Addison's final performance for the documentary.

As they took their seats at a table in a private dining area at Nobu, Stan patted Addison on the shoulder. "Looking forward to the show, Addison."

"Thank you, Stan, and thank you both for making all this possible."

"We just provided the platform," Sally said. "You and your golden voice won over the audience and the judges."

Addison was anxious to hear of the wedding plans that Hanna had yet to discuss with him. "Hanna, this is a good time to share with me what you have in mind for our wedding."

Hanna beamed. "I thought you'd never ask. The ceremony

will occur at the Graceland Wedding Chapel the morning following your last performance. Jennie Fields, my college roommate, who has worked with my company from day one, is flying in to be my bridesmaid. Following the wedding, Caesars has offered to host the reception. What do you think so far?"

Addison answered with a beaming smile. "Sounds like you have it all buttoned up. Stan, Sally?"

"Whatever my baby girl wants," Stan said.

Sally tapped Stan's shoulder. "My dear husband spoiled this child from the day she was born."

Stan raised his right hand. "Guilty as charged."

"Addison, my wedding dress was custom-made in New York. I can't wait for you to see me in it."

Addison pecked Hanna on the cheek. "As Lang would say, we're off to the races."

On opening night, the Coliseum Theater was packed. No mention was made of Addison's retirement or that he would be running for president. That was reserved for the ACP's convention and not before. He did, however, share the news of his retirement with the Noble Street Singers.

"That's not for public consumption," Addison cautioned.

With a stunned look, Ivey Wagner moaned. "Say it ain't so, Addison."

"It's time, Ivey."

"For what? You're young and still number one."

"That and five bucks still gets you a cup of coffee at Starbucks."

"But, Addison—"

"Ivey, times change, tastes change. Entertainers come and go; before you know it, they'll be a new number one."

"No, not like you, Boss, not like you. Thank you for everything. You will be missed."

For his final performance at Caesars', Addison was looser with the audience than usual. He appeared to enjoy himself, kidding the audience between songs and telling slightly off-color jokes.

Following one of his songs, he stopped center stage and paused briefly, then walked to his left, stopped, and turned to the audience. "Tomorrow, yours truly is tying the knot with the love of his life."

The audience responded with rousing applause.

"Huh, easy for you to say. It took us a few years to realize our lives were incomplete apart. As the saying goes, better late than never."

More applause and laughter.

"Who, you ask, is the lady brave enough to marry a spoiled entertainer? Her name is Hanna Potts." Addison pointed to where Hanna was sitting. "Hanna, love, please take a bow."

Hanna had no idea Addison planned to announce their wedding. Sheepishly, she stood and bowed her head slightly.

"Sitting next to Hanna is my soon-to-be in-laws, Stan and Sally Potts."

Stan and Sally stood.

"I'm ready to be married, but I'm not sure I'm ready for in-laws."

The audience laughed and applauded.

"Thank you, thank you all. Now, on with the music."

He sang what would have been his encore, ending with After *Time to Say Goodbye*. He shook hands with the conductor, waved, and headed to the wings. The audience began to chant, *One more, one more, one more*!

Addison returned to center stage. "Okay, okay, just one more."

He spoke briefly with the conductor, then to Ivey. He returned to center stage and began singing *Endless Love,* never taking his eyes off Hanna. She was sitting close enough that Addison could see she was crying.

When he finished, he blew Hanna a kiss. She stood and blew one back. The audience was on their feet, cheering. As Addison bowed, waved, and made his way to the wings, the orchestra played *Your Love*.

Lang and Andy greeted Addison in the lounge area and shook his hand.

Ivey Wagner came to Addison, her eyes filled with tears, and she hugged him. "It's been a hell of a run, Addison."

"You mean one hell of a foot race, Ivey."

"That too."

Addison hugged each member of Noble Street.

Hanna and her parents were the first to join Addison in his dressing room.

Hanna put her arms around him. "Thank you for the song. You had me in teas."

Stan patted Addison's shoulder. "Congratulations, that was one powerful and emotional performance."

"Ditto," Sally added.

"Thank you. Now, how about we have dinner?"

"Not tonight," Hanna said. "Call me a traditionalist, but you won't see me again until we meet at the Chapel tomorrow."

Addison grimaced. "Not even dinner?"

"Not even dinner. JJ, feed this man, then put him to bed."

"Ten-four, Hanna. I'm on it."

Before retiring that evening, Addison wrote in his journal.

> *Tomorrow, Hanna and I will join hands and begin an exciting new chapter in our lives, one I wish we had started many years earlier. If we had, the arc of our lives would have been far different. But that is behind us now. I am eternally grateful the circle is complete. I am one lucky man.*

At 9:45 in the morning, the Graceland Wedding Chapel was packed with guests. The Chapel provided a limo for Hanna, her parents, and her bridesmaid, Jennie Fields. Caesars provided a limo for Addison and JJ. A Justice of the Peace would perform the ceremony.

Lang, Andy, Ty, and Millie Andrews had flown in for the wedding.

Addison and JJ, dressed in tuxedos, waited in a small room to the chapel's right. Addison, looking nervous, paced.

"May I say, sir, we look like movie stars in our tuxedoes about to walk the Red Carpet to cameras and flashing lights."

"One of us does, JJ; one of us doesn't," Addison said with a straight face and continued to pace.

A lady on the Chapel staff entered. "Mr. Stone, Mr. James, we are ready for you."

"Well, here we go," Addison said with a deadpan expression. "It's now or never."

"It's forever, Mr. Stone. Say the words."

"It's forever, repeat, it's forever!"

As they approached the door, Addison was struck with an eruptive pain in his right temple that felt like an electrical shock. The sensation traveled down his right leg to his foot; he stumbled and stopped.

"Something wrong, sir?"

Addison put his left hand against the wall to steady himself, raised his right foot, and wiggled it. "These new shoes, JJ, they're too darn tight. Okay, zoom, zoom, here we go."

Addison and JJ entered the Chapel and took their positions. The music began: unknown to Addison, Hanna had requested a recording of Andrea Bocelli singing *Your Love*. The guests stood, and all eyes went to the back of the chapel. The double doors opened, and Hanna and her father started their walk.

Hanna looked stunning in her Alexandra Grecco-designed white *Calla Gown* silk crepe wedding dress with long embroidered sheer tulle sleeves and side panels. Her Bridesmaid, Jennie Fields, followed, dressed in a floor-length pastel blue down and carrying a bouquet of white lilies.

Addison's face lit up like a thousand-watt bulb.

Hanna and her father sauntered slowly down the aisle for three minutes to avoid reaching Addison's side before the song ended.

When they came to their position, Hanna turned to her father, hugged him, and kissed his cheek. "Love you, Dad."

"Love you, Hanna, you look stunning." He kissed her cheek. "Enjoy a long, happy life, sweetheart."

Hanna took Addison's hand and smiled. "Hello, Mr. Stone. It's been a while."

"Hello, Ms. Potts; eighteen years to be exact."

After exchanging vows and rings, the Justice of the Peace pronounced them man and wife. "You may kiss the bride."

Addison grinned. "With pleasure."

The gathering applauded as Addison embraced Hanna and kissed her before they turned and took a theatrical bow.

Outside, fans, photographers, and video crews shot away as Hanna and Addison exited the Chapel. As Addison scanned the crowd, he noticed a man leaning alone against a tree across the street. The man looked familiar. Addison's eyes narrowed when he realized it was none other than John Paloma. They made eye contact. Paloma smiled, nodded, raised his right hand to belt level, and timidly waved.

Addison averted his eyes. "You son of a bitch," he cursed under his breath.

Inside the limo, Addison wrapped his arms around Hanna and kissed her. "Hello, Mrs. Stone. You look like Cinderella."

"Hello, Mr. Stone; you look like a Greek God. Did I ever tell you what the word *Kismet* means in Islam?"

"I would have remembered if you did, Love."

"It means the *Arbitrary Will of Allah—divinely ordained fate in Islam?*"

"You actually looked that up?"

"I did."

"Amazing."

The reception at Caesars Palace was held in Cleopatra's Barge. The guest list included several family members on

Hanna's side, Lang, Andy, Ty, Ivey, Noble Street Singers, Millie Andrews, senior Caesars Palace executives, and other notable guests and entertainers working in various Vegas showrooms.

Following a scrumptious dinner, the guests danced as the orchestra played songs from Addison's repertoire.

JJ got up and offered a toast to the newlyweds. "How lucky is this mediocre singer to have found a stunningly beautiful lady like Hanna? Stan, Sally, how could you have allowed this?"

"It was Hanna's decision," Stan called out.

The crowd laughed and applauded.

"Let us raise our glasses to Hanna and Addison's good health, long lives, and happiness."

Stan, sitting to Addison's right, whispered. "Take good care of her, Addison. Remember, happy wife, happy life."

"I will cherish her, Stan, scout's honor."

In the morning, Caesars Palace provided a limo to take Addison, Hanna, and JJ to the airport. Several passersby recognized Addison as they made their way to their departure gate.

Addison took Hanna's hand. "Ignore them, smile, and keep walking."

In the first-class section, Hanna sat by the window, Addison and JJ in aisle seats across from one another.

Once they had reached altitude, Hanna excused herself to visit the restroom. JJ leaned across the aisle.

"Mr. Stone?"

"What is it, JJ?"

"As we discussed, I'm moving out when we return."

Addison's brow went up. "To where?"

"I purchased a lovely condo in nearby Honokeama Cove Condominiums and closed on it while we were in Vegas. Two is a love nest, three's a crowd."

"You are not a crowd; you are family."

"Thank you, sir. I feel the same about you."

"We're going to miss not having you around all the time."

"Since the guesthouse is our new corporate office, I'm a few garages away."

"The new offices, right? I forgot. You'll have your hands full running Stone Enterprises and the Lacy Foundation, so start looking for an assistant."

"Yes, that's on the top of my list."

They were treated to the usual exuberant Windy greeting when they reached the front door. Windy jumped and hopped and whined.

"Congratulations to you both, and welcome to your new home, Mrs. Stone."

"Thank you, Aria; I'm slowly getting used to my new last name. Aria, I shipped three big boxes of my things express from New York. They're scheduled to arrive tomorrow."

"Very good, Mrs. Stone. JJ, I have all your belongings packed as you requested."

"Great, thank you, Aria."

"I made a pot roast, so I hope you're all hungry."

"I don't know about them," Addison said, "but I am. Let's get to it."

Addison was walking on air. As troubled as his past had been, it had come to a happy ending. He was anxious to preserve his thoughts in his journal, which he did immediately after dinner.

> *Unbelievably, my life has come full circle, from being a kid who suffered a confusing childhood to being thrust into the limelight on the world stage at nineteen and achieving success beyond anything I could have dreamed. Along the way, I made mistakes which I now regret. I can't change what I did in the past, but hopefully, I've learned from it.*
>
> *With all my heart, I wish my mother and Ben*

were here with me. I miss them terribly despite the turmoil Lacy brought to both of our lives. Although she struggled and failed to express herself in ways we both could understand and deal with, I know she loved me, and I hope she knew how much I loved her.

And then there were two disturbing, dare I say painful moments following the wedding. As Hanna and I made our way to the waiting limo, I glanced back at the guests exiting the chapel. There were no family members, no blood relatives. Then, I saw Johnny Paloma standing alone and apart from the others. We made brief eye contact before I turned away. If, as he claimed, he was indeed my biological father. I will never acknowledge him. He will always be the coward who deserted us.

I remember slipping into the limo with Hanna on my arm. At that moment, I vowed to devote my life to making her happy. Like a promise, a vow is not a vow unless you honor it. I will.

Addison and Hanna spent their honeymoon walking the beaches around Honolulu, swimming in their pool, eating Aria's sumptuous meals, and having copious amounts of intimacy.

One late evening, Addison and Hanna were lying in bed watching a documentary on ancient Egypt, a subject that Hanna enjoyed watching for its rich history.

When a commercial came on, Hanna asked Addison, "When do you see Matthew Dupont again?"

"The plan is to meet in Washington, but they haven't told me when."

Hanna rolled to one side and fell silent.

"Okay, let's have it. What's going on in that pretty head?"

"Whatever you do, I'm one hundred percent behind you; you know that."

"But?"

"You have a life others would die for. Yet, you're willing to toss it all away in exchange for the monumental responsibility of the presidency. The question I keep asking is, why? Think of the four years of stress and madness you'd have to contend with. You'd be under scrutiny every minute of every day from the press and the political pundits who, guaranteed, will second guess your every word. It doesn't matter how good a president you might be."

"Will be," Addison corrected.

"Alright, will be. The next person might not be so good, and we're back to square one, and the stupid cycle begins all over again. What does any of it have to do with simply living, being happy, and enjoying what we have? With the short time we're given on this planet, why spend one minute of it allowing ourselves to be caught up in mindless, selfish, hateful rhetoric? Why?"

"Hanna, love, although your point is well made, that's not the human reality, is it? I wish it were. But the reality is the country is in a political mess, and it has to stop. I don't speak political rhetoric; that's a language all its own and often misleading for political gain or to misdirect the narrative. I talk in plain English. That's what people need now: not political talk but plain English that people can understand and relate to. Have you ever heard of a politician who was asked a question to which they gave a straight answer? Hell no. *Yes* and *no* is not part of their vocabulary. They talk around the question. By the time they finished, everyone's forgotten what the question was. They must hold classes for newly elected members of Congress on how to pull off that sleight of hand."

"Addison. I'm talking about life; you're talking about politics. Make me one promise. When you get with DuPont and Hill, grill them. If anything concerns you—no matter how small or trivial —you'll give this venture a second thought. Maybe I should go to that meeting with you."

"No, JJ will be there; he'll have my back. Now, let's change the subject. How's my documentary coming?"

"My New York jail mates tell me it's looking good. I promise you'll be the first to see it when finished." Hanna rolled on top of Addison and kissed him. "Enough talk about your saving the world. Let's get down to some human lust."

"Precisely. It is, after all, our honeymoon." Hanna reached for the TV remote and turned the TV off. "Egypt can wait."

The following morning, Addison helped JJ load his belongings into his car.

"Okay, that's all of it. As for the guest house, all that has to be done is to remove the beds and get a couple of desks and file cabinets, and we're set to go."

"Great. Want me to go with you to unload at your new place?"

"No, sir. I'd rather you see it after I have it all fancied up."

And with that, JJ was off to his new home.

When Addison entered the house, Hanna was cursing loudly in the kitchen.

"Damn, the bloody fools!" she yelled.

Addison entered the kitchen. "Hey, what's going on?"

Aria shook her head. "Her belongings were sent to the wrong city."

"Seattle," Hanna fumed. "Does Seattle sound like Honolulu? The world has been going to hell in a handbasket ever since we gave up our lives to technology. I want my bloody clothes!"

"Sorry, Babe. Come for a walk with Windy and me. It'll calm you."

Hanna tossed her arms up. "I don't want to be calm; I want to strangle the idiots that screwed up." She stormed out of the kitchen.

Addison rolled his eyes. "Keep her away from sharp knives, Aria."

"I'll do my best, Mr. Stone," Aria responded with her usual deadpan expression.

Addison and Windy went for a walk to the beach, and

Addison settled on his regular big rock; Windy lay beside him. Suddenly, his eyesight became blurry, and he and he began to see double. "What the hell?" He rubbed at his eyes, but the blurriness and double vision persisted. He covered them with his hands.

Windy sensed something was wrong. He stood, whined, and nudged Addison's leg with his nose.

Addison removed his hands and opened his eyes; the blurriness and double vision began to subside. "I'm good, Windy. I'm good." He patted Windy's head. "Give me a minute."

Addison sat there for another ten minutes until he felt stable enough to return to the house.

The walk back took longer than usual as Addison cautiously took each step.

Chapter 28

Addison did not tell Hanna or JJ about the incident on the beach. There was no need to concern them. If it occurred again, he would consult with a doctor.

Hanna and Addison spent the next three weeks enjoying their new life together. Each morning at 9:00 AM Hawaii time, Hanna spent a half hour speaking with her staff in New York, discussing progress on Addison's film and two network documentaries they were producing. Then, she would join Addison and Windy on their morning walks to the beach, where Addison had JJ set up two folding chairs. That was followed by a swim in the pool. A short nap was often on the afternoon schedule.

Since Addison had broken the news about his run for the presidency, contact between him, Lang, and Andy had dropped off, other than to confirm upcoming performances on his remaining schedule.

Addison had agreed to a single performance at the 18,387-seat PPG Paint Center in Pittsburg. Since Hanna was needed at her office in New York, she flew with Addison and JJ to Pittsburg and then caught a connecting flight to New York. They would meet again in Honolulu after Addison and JJ met with Matthew DuPont and Steven Hill in Washington.

When the show's first half at the PPG Center ended, Addison sat with JJ in the wings while Noble Street sang *Mama Mia, Chiquita,* and *Dancing Queen.*

Addison looked tired. He put his feet on the coffee table and downed a cold bottle of water.

"Everything okay, sir?"

"Yeah, JJ, why?"

"You seem a bit off tonight."

"A bit off, how?"

"Less energy?"

"Just tired, I guess."

They sat quietly until Noble Street was nearing the end of *Dancing Queen,* which was Addison's cue to get ready to return to the stage. Addison sat glassy-eyed with his feet up on the coffee table.

"Mr. Stone, that's your cue."

"What?"

"Your cue to return, sir."

Addison's feet came off the table, and he stood. "Oh, right, we're off to the races again."

Addison strolled slower than usual to the center of the stage as the Orchestra began the intro to *I Surrender*. He removed the microphone from its stand, stared glassy-eye at the vast audience, and missed his cue to begin singing.

JJ sensed something was wrong. He stood and made his way to the edge of the stage curtain.

The conductor turned to see why Addison had missed his cue. Addison swayed from left to right before collapsing to the stage floor.

A loud *Ohhh* went up from the audience.

Ivey Wagner was the first to reach Addison. She dropped to her knees and lifted his head. "Addison?"

There was no response.

JJ raced across the stage, knelt down, and gripped Addison's shoulders. "Addison, Addison?"

Addison lay motionless.

The stage manager rushed from the wings to assist.

"He's unconscious," JJ yelled. "Call 911! Close the damn curtains!"

Audience members were on their feet, snapping photos with their cellphones.

Minutes later, Addison lay unconscious in an ambulance as it raced to the UPMC hospital emergency room; JJ sat by Addison's side, holding his left hand in his. A team of doctors and nurses were waiting when they arrived at the emergency room entrance. They rushed Addison to an exam room.

In the waiting area, JJ pulled out his phone and called Hanna. The phone rang several times before she answered.

"I know, JJ. Mom woke me and told me. It's all over the news and the Internet, with photos of Addison lying unconscious on the stage. My God, what had happened?

"I don't know, but whatever it is, it's not good, Hanna. I won't know more until I meet with the doctors."

"I'll get the first available flight out and meet you at the hospital."

"No, they won't let us see him tonight. We have a meeting with the doctors in the morning. When you arrive, check into the Ommi Will Penn Hotel. I reserved a room for you on my floor. I'm in 405, and you're in 401. Hanna, it's going to be okay."

Hanna raced to the airport and luckily got a last-minute seat on Delta's 12:00 PM flight as it was preparing to leave. She arrived in Pittsburg an hour and a half later, caught a taxi to the hotel, checked in, left her bag in her room, and went straight to JJ's room.

When JJ opened the door, Hanna fell into JJ's arms, crying.

"How is he, JJ?"

"I don't know any more than what I told you on the phone, Hanna. The doctors are running extensive tests. They'll know more when we meet at eleven in the morning. He's going to be okay, Hanna, he will."

234

Chapter 29

Addison lay motionless in the emergency exam room, surrounded by a half-dozen medical staff. Monitoring equipment, including a breathing tube, hummed away. Two drip bags flowed into his arms, and a blood pressure cup was attached to his right arm.

Addison's eyelids fluttered and opened.

"Welcome back, Mr. Stone."

Addison's dry lips parted. "*W-w, where -am-I?*" He was barely audible.

"You're in the ICU at UMPC Hospital in Pittsburgh; I'm Doctor Wilson."

"*H-h, hospital?*"

"Do you remember passing out during your performance?"

Addison looked confused. "*N-n, no-don't-r-r, remember…* anything."

"We've run a series of tests, Mr. Stone. I'm waiting for the results. When we know more, I'll check back with you. Now, you just try to rest."

Addison closed his eyes; within seconds, he was sleeping again.

At 9:30 the following morning, Dr. Wilson entered Addison's room. The whole top of Addison's head was bandaged.

Dr. Wilson pulled up a chair and sat by Addison's bed. "Mr. Stone? It's Dr. Wilson."

Addison licked his lips, and his eyelids slowly peeled open.

"Mr. Stone, can you hear me?"

Addison nodded in the affirmative. With difficulty, he said. "*W-h*-what-what-happened?"

"You passed out during your performance at the PPG Center."

"*P-p*…passed out?"

"We did blood tests and an MRI of your brain."

"*M-m…brain?* Addison lifted his right arm slowly and touched the right side of his head. "*W-w*-what's this?"

"It's a bandage, Mr. Stone. We did an emergency biopsy of a mass on the right side of your brain. I'm still waiting for more results."

Addison felt a chill and winched.

Dr. Wilson already had the results, but in Addison's heavily sedated state, he thought it best to discuss them with Hanna and JJ first. "Okay, Mr. Stone, I'll be back. You rest."

Hanna and JJ arrived at 10:50.

"I'm supposed to let the desk know when we've arrived. Be right back."

As JJ walked away, Hanna's phone rang. It was Lang Sherman. She left it to voice mail as she had the previous eight calls.

Just as JJ returned, a nurse approached.

"Mrs. Stone, Mr. James, the doctors will see you now."

They followed the nurse to Dr. Wilson's office. There were two others with him.

JJ introduced Hanna.

"Pleased to meet you, Mrs. Stone. I'm Dr. Henry Wilson, Director of Emergency Room Services. My colleagues are

Oncologist Dr. Helen Morgan and Neurosurgeon Dr. Mark Epstein."

"A pleasure, Mrs. Stone," Dr. Morgan said.

Dr. Epstein smiled slightly and nodded.

Wilson motioned to the sofa. "Please, be comfortable. Can we get you anything?"

"No, thank you," Hanna said."

JJ shook his head. "No."

Once they were seated, Wilson began. "Last night, we did an MRI of Mr. Stone's brain."

Hanna's eyes grew big. "A stroke?"

"There were no signs of a stroke or bleeding." Wilson stood. "The best way to explain what we found is to show you."

Wilson walked to a wall-mounted TV screen and turned it on. An image appeared. "This is your husband's brain," He pointed to a dark oval spot on the right side. "If you look closely, you'll see a golf ball-sized growth just above Mr. Stone's right ear."

Hanna's hand went to her mouth. "Oh, dear God!"

"As soon as we saw the mass, I knew we had to move quickly. I called Dr. Morgan and Dr. Epstein around 1:00 a.m. and requested they come in immediately. Dr. Morgan?"

"A biopsy was performed," Morgan began, "by drilling a small hole in the right side of Mr. Stone's head. A needle was inserted, and a sample was taken and analyzed." Morgan hesitated. "Mrs. Stone, your husband has a Glioblastoma."

"I don't know what that is."

"Glioblastoma is a type of cancer that starts as a growth of cells in the brain or spinal cord."

Hanna sucked in a quick breath. JJ took her hand in his.

"A Glioblastoma can proliferate quickly and invade and destroy healthy tissue, forming astrocyte cells that support nerve cells. Symptoms include headaches, pain in the temple area, blurred or double vision, dizzy spells, and possible seizures. Are you aware of Mr. Stone experiencing any of those symptoms?"

"He complained about headaches in recent months," JJ

answered, "but he brushed them off as occasional migraines brought on by stress. If there was more to the headaches, he didn't share it with me."

Hanna's eyes widened. "JJ, I wasn't aware he was having these headaches."

JJ made no comment.

"Given the size and location of the tumor," Dr. Mogan continued, "I'm surprised he didn't experience more severe symptoms sooner. Dr. Epstein will explain what comes next."

Epstein pointed to the image on the TV screen. "First, we'll need to remove the growth. The sooner, the better his chances. Since Mr. Stone cannot speak for himself in his condition, we'll need your permission to proceed, Mrs. Stone."

"Yes, of course, Doctor."

"A Glioblastoma often grows into healthy brain tissue, so removing all cancer cells we can is critical."

"What happens following surgery?"

Dr. Morgan explained. "Post-surgery treatments. We won't know which option will be best for Mr. Stone until we remove the mass and conduct additional analysis. That will be done today. Surgery will proceed at ten in the morning." Morgan glanced briefly at Wilson and Epstein, then at Hanna and JJ. "Mrs. Stone, there is no known cure for Glioblastoma."

Hanna's eyes widened; she sucked in a breath and held it. JJ squeezed her hand.

"Treatments can slow the cancer growth and reduce symptoms," Epstein continued. "Life expectancy without surgery and further treatment is three months."

Hanna began to cry. "No! This isn't happening."

JJ squeezed Hanna's hand tighter.

"Before we get ahead ourselves, Mrs. Stone, with proper treatment, a person with glioblastoma has a median survival time of fifteen months, but a small percentage have survived for ten or more years. I have one patient who lived for twenty years following surgery and treatment. Having said that, recurrence of Glioblastoma is the rule rather than the exception. There are relatively few treatment options if the cancers return."

Hanna covered her face; JJ put his arm around her shoulder.

"Forgive me; perhaps I was too blunt, Mrs. Stone. Although we encourage the patient and his family to remain positive, it is best that you understand the battle Mr. Stone is facing."

Hanna folded her hands and laid them in her lap. "I understand, Doctor."

"There is another issue. The brain contains two hemispheres, and each performs several roles. The left hemisphere controls the muscles on the right side of the body, while the right hemisphere controls those on the left."

"What does that mean in lay terms?" JJ asked.

"The right hemisphere of the brain is responsible for creativity rhythm, holistic awareness, creative thinking, spatial awareness, and daydreaming."

"You're telling us that Addison might not function normally."

"We can't predict, but yes, Mrs. Stone, your husband may experience limitations in his thinking and performance of his daily activities."

Hanna took a deep breath and exhaled slowly. "Can I see my husband?"

"Yes, of course. He's under heavy sedation. If awake, he will be groggy and somewhat unresponsive."

Hanna stood. "It's in your hands now, Doctor Epstein."

Epstein nodded. "Please know we will all do all we can."

"That's all we can ask, Doctor."

Dr. Wilson led Hanna and JJ to Addison's room in the ICU.

"JJ, if you don't mind, I'd like to be alone with Addison."

"Of course, Hanna."

When Hanna entered Addison's room and saw all the medical equipment attached to his body and the bandage covering his skull, she felt a cold chill. She approached the bed slowly; Addison appeared to be sleeping. Hanna pulled a chair close to the bed, then gently rested her head on Addison's chest and took his right hand in hers.

Addison moved and moaned.

"Addison, it's Hanna."

For several seconds, there was no response. Then Addison's eyelids opened halfway. "H-a-n-n-a."

Hanna stood and leaned over him so he could see her face.

A slight smile crossed Addison's lip. "What–happened–to me?" his voice was weak and barely above a whisper.

Hanna tried to explain as best she could, but the proper medical terms eluded her. She made no mention of life expectancy. He would learn about that soon enough.

"We meet with the doctors again in the morning before surgery."

"*S-s-s*…surgery?"

"Yes, my love."

Addison's eyes closed, and he drifted off to sleep again.

Hanna kissed him gently on his lips. "I love you, Addison; I have from the day I set eyes on you, and I always will."

With tears in her eyes, Hanna stepped out of the room. "You can go in now, JJ. I'm sure you want to see him."

Chapter 30

When they returned to the hotel, JJ suggested Hanna try to get some rest.

"Huh, good luck with that, JJ. Nightmares would be more like it."

"How about I knock on your door around six-thirty? We'll have dinner."

"I don't know how hungry I'll be, but six-thirty will be fine."

JJ took her hand. "How are you holding up? Are you okay?"

"What's okay, JJ?"

"I don't know anymore, Hanna. I feel like we've been gut-punched."

"Whipped to shreds would be more like it."

Back in her room, Hanna placed a call to her mother.

"Honey, what can you tell us?"

Hanna filled Sally in with as much information as she understood. "Surgery will begin tomorrow morning at ten."

"Your father is standing next to me. He wants to know if you want us there."

"No, Mom, let's wait. The doctor said if it goes well, Addison could be released in four to five days and begin post-op treatments. If I know my husband, he'll insist the treatments be done in Honolulu."

"Right now, it's best Addison listens to the doctors, Honey."

"Huh, tell hard-headed Mr. Stone that, Mom."

"Your Dad and I are praying for you both. Call us as soon as Addison's out of surgery. Now, you get some rest."

"That's all I've heard from JJ and the doctors. Get rest, Mrs. Stone."

"Follow their advice, honey.

At seven, Hanna and JJ were having dinner in the hotel restaurant. Hanna's spirits were broken. She looked like she had not slept in days.

"I will lose him for the second time, JJ, only this time for good."

"Hanna, don't think like that. Doctor Epstein said some patients live for ten years or more."

"But we'll always know he's living on borrowed time, won't we?"

"All the more reason to make every minute of every hour of every day count."

Hanna took a deep breath and exhaled. Her eyes drifted across the room to a dark, blank wall just inside a hallway in the rear of the restaurant. At that moment, the wall represented the end. She could not visualize life without Addison at her side.

Because it happened on stage in front of thousands, word of Addison's hospitalization spread through the news and social media like wildfire. Local, national, and international news organizations descended on the hospital, awaiting any information on Addison's condition. What was being reported was speculation since no official release had been issued from the hospital, Hanna, or the Sherman Agency.

When Hanna and JJ arrived at 9:30 the following day, she informed the hospital administration that no updates on her husband's condition were to be issued without her written consent.

JJ's phone constantly rang with calls from Lang, Andy, Ivey Wagner, and others. He changed his voicemail recording; *no calls would be returned until further notice.*

Before surgery, Hanna and JJ met with Oncologist Dr. Morgan.

"Dr. Epstein and his team are the best, Mrs. Stone; your husband is in excellent hands. In removing the tumor, the preference, whenever possible, is neurosurgery, a minimally invasive surgical procedure in which the tumor is removed through small holes about the size of a dime through the mouth or nose. However, Dr. Epstein has chosen to perform a Craniotomy because of the tumor's size and location. It involves removing a small section of skull bone to access the tumor. Mr. Stone will be awake but under sedation. This allows the surgeon to stimulate parts of Mr. Stone's brain to identify critical areas that control essential functions. Mr. Stone will not experience any pain."

"How long will the surgery take?" JJ asked.

"From prep to when Mr. Stone is returned to ICU, about four hours, longer if there are complications. The press has been hounding us for any information like a pack of hungry jackals. At some point, we will have to update them to stop the speculation and misleading information," Morgan said. "One or more reporters might make it past security to the waiting area and attempt to question you. May I suggest you and Mr. James make yourselves comfortable in the doctor's lounge?"

JJ nodded. "Thanks, that's very kind of you."

They were taken to the doctor's lounge, where they settled in for what would feel like an eternity.

"Coffee, Mrs. Stone?"

"Yes, strong and black. And JJ, you are part of our family; families call each other by their first names. His is Addison, and mine is Hanna."

"The habit of addressing my employers respectfully was

driven into me in Butler school. It is part of my job and difficult to break, *Hanna*."

"There now, was that so difficult?"

JJ smiled. "Yes, it was."

Four hours and forty-five minutes later, Dr. Epstein and Dr. Morgan joined Hanna and JJ in the lounge.

Dr. Epstein was smiling. "The surgery went well."

Hanna lay her right hand flat against her torso. "Oh, thank goodness." With tears streaming down her face, she turned and hugged JJ.

"We were able to remove the entire tumor. Our post-op treatment recommendation is going to be radiation treatments. Mr. Stone will require thirty continuous Monday through Friday treatments, maybe more after we evaluate. Each treatment is quick and painless. We'll schedule them to begin in a couple of weeks."

"Um, Doctor, that may be a problem."

"Oh?"

"Once my husband learns his post-op treatments are to be radiation, he'll want—no, insist—treatments to take place in Honolulu. Does that present a problem?"

"My preference would be the treatment be done here. But, yes, they can be done in Honolulu if Mr. Stone prefers. I would recommend the Samuel Mahelona Memorial Hospital in Honolulu under the direction of Oncologist Dr. Marian Ormsby. She and the hospital have an excellent reputation."

"Perfect. The hospital is close to our home."

"I suggest you return to Hawaii in an air ambulance accompanied by a qualified nurse practitioner. We'll recommend one."

"How soon will he be able to travel, Doctor?"

"Let's see how Mr. Stone is doing in five or six days. If we determine he's up to the trip, his records will be transferred to Mahelona Memorial. I'll communicate with Dr. Ormsby personally.

"We better release an update to the press soon," Hanna said, "The rumors of Addison's condition are flying around like a swarm of locus. You have my permission to proceed with that before the media has Addison dead and buried. JJ and I would like to review it before it's released."

"Certainly, Mrs. Stone."

"JJ and I want to thank you and your staff, Doctor, for all you have done for Addison."

Dr. Morgan smiled. "It's what we do, Mrs. Stone. Stay positive."

Six days later, Dr. Morgan signed off on Addison's release. Addison, Hanna, JJ, and a nurse practitioner left for Hawaii on an air ambulance the next day. Addison looked tired, but his spirits were up.

"Well, ladies and gentlemen, boys and girls, I'm still here. Let's keep kicking ass!"

Hanna laughed. "You've been kicking ass for many years now, Love."

Addison's face slackened, and his tone turned dark. "I guess it's safe to say that part of my life is over and out."

Hanna took his hand in hers. "Hey, give it time, sweetheart, give it time."

"JJ, any thoughts?"

"Well, *Addison*, I—"

Addison's head jerked up. "Whoa, what did you just call me?"

"Addison."

"Well, now, will miracles never cease. It's about damn time, *Jonathan*."

"Hanna threatened me with bodily harm if I did not."

Hanna smiled. "It's true, Addison, I did."

"I have no doubt you did, Love."

Upon their return to the house, Aria greeted them at the door. Her eyes teared when she saw Addison's bandaged head. She went to him, put her arms around his waist, pulled him to her, and kissed him on the cheek. "Welcome home, Mr. Stone."

It was the first real emotion they had witnessed coming from *The General*.

"Thank you, Aria. Now, where's my blood brother?"

"In the study. I was afraid Windy might jump up on you."

"Well, let the bugger out here."

Windy could be heard whinnying and scratching at the door of the study. When Aria opened it, Windy scrambled past Aria and headed for Addison. When he entered the living room and saw Addison, he abruptly stopped, sat, and groaned.

'What's wrong?"

"Your head, Addison," Hanna said. "The bandages."

Addison snapped his fingers. "It's okay, Big Boy, it's still me."

Slowly, cautiously, Windy crossed the floor until he was inches from Addison. He nuzzled his master's leg with his nose, sat, and stared.

"It's okay, boy, really."

JJ shook his head. "I swear, inside that dog's head is a human-thinking brain."

Addison chuckled. "Maybe one smarter than all of ours."

"Okay, enough fun and games," Hanna said. "We need to get Mr. Megastar to bed. But first, he needs to be fed. Aria, what's for dinner?"

Aria placed a finger to her lips and pretended to be thinking. "How about some nice fresh fried farts and buttermilk?"

JJ laughed. "Good one, Aria. You see, Addison, Aria has a wicked sense of humor under her icy exterior."

Aria pouted. "Icy exterior?"

Addison's lips curled into a grin. "Under the circumstances, I welcome all the humor I can get. Aria, how about a nice plate of pasta with meatballs for dinner."

"Knowing how much you enjoy it, Mr. Stone, I have sauce and meatballs in the freezer. I'll thaw them out. Spaghetti or Linguini?"

"Spaghetti. Sounds better than fried farts and buttermilk, no matter how fresh."

Hanna informed Addison that she had made a critical decision. She would no longer travel to her office in New York but would work from home to care for him. Addison was relieved. The Grim Reaper was knocking at his door; there was no avoiding it. The only question remaining was when the final knock would come. He would do his best not to dwell on it. Whatever time he had left, it would be with Hanna by his side. For that, he would be forever grateful.

In a Zoom call, Hanna informed her staff of her decision. She promoted her friend Jennie Fields to oversee New York operations until further notice.

Chapter 31

At six-forty-five, Aria set a large bowl of pasta and meatballs on the table. JJ was off to his new condo, so it was just Addison and Hanna. Windy sat quietly on the floor next to Addison's feet.

"Aria, come sit with us, have some pasta."

Aria made a face. "Hmm. Me?"

"Yes, you. Come sit."

"I'll notify the hospital in the morning that we're back so they can set up your radiation schedule," Hanna said. "And I must begin returning calls to let everyone know you're home safe and sound. Mom called; she and Dad want to visit. I told them it would be better to wait until you've completed your radiation treatment."

"Lang confirmed in an email that all remaining performance dates have been canceled," JJ said.

With a melancholy expression, Addison said, "You think?" Addison wisecracked. "Any other good news, JJ?"

"Just Matthew DuPont. He knows it's game over."

Addison's eyebrow went up. "Ah, what gave him the first clue?"

Hanna shot Addison a look. "Enough with the jokes."

Aria took a seat at the table. "What's the occasion?"

"For what?" Addison asked.

"For inviting the help to have dinner with you?"

Addison snickered. "Would you rather we didn't?"

"You have a sharp tongue this evening, Mr. Stone."

Hanna raised an eyebrow. "When does he not, Aria?"

"You two know I'm sitting beside you and can hear your snarky comments."

Hanna and Aria laughed; Addison did not.

"By the way, Addison, I was—"

Addison cut Hanna off. "At thirty-seven years old, I'm on the shortlist. You know it, JJ knows it, Aria knows it, and I suspect Windy knows it, and soon the world will know it."

"Addison, don't talk like that."

"I speak the truth, love."

Hanna's face slackened. "Enough. I don't want to hear any more gloom and doom talk."

"Ah, excuse me," Aria stood. "I think I'm needed in the kitchen until this conversation is over." She stood and headed for the kitchen.

"Aria, sit down, please. I didn't mean to upset you."

With a stern look, Aria swiveled back. "It's not me you're upsetting, Mr. Stone; it's your wife. She's going through a difficult emotional period. Morbid flippant remarks do not help."

"But it's the truth, Aria."

"From the day we are born, we're all dying, Mr. Stone, but we never know when. We can only hope it's later than sooner. Whatever time you have left, sir, relish each day to the fullest. You have a loving wife, a home in paradise, and people who love you."

"Yes, you're right, Aria. I'm sorry."

"Ah, for once, score one for me."

"Come on, sit down, finish your dinner, it's delicious."

Aria sat and continued eating. "The worst day was when I lost my husband. Thank God for my son. I don't know how I would have gotten through that painful period without him.

Ultimately, Mr. Stone, it's all about family, those you love, and those who love and care for you. Love is a potent aphrodisiac."

"Yes, it is." Addison changed the subject. "By the way, I thought the buttermilk and fried farts joke was very funny. Have any other good ones?"

"You're changing the subject," Hanna scolded.

Addison ignored her. "Anyway, loved your fart joke. Tell us another one."

"Okay, one more. Who are you when your bladder is full and ready to bust between rushing to and entering the bathroom?"

"I have no idea."

"European… *Uuro-pe-an.*"

"Ah, good one, Aria, thank you. I needed a moment of levity before apologizing for putting my foot in my mouth."

Hanna reached out and made the sign of the cross in front of Addison's face. "Consider yourself forgiven. When you're finished eating, you may sit on the patio with Windy for one hour, and then it's off to bed."

"And if I'm not sleepy?"

"You'll go to bed anyway and watch TV."

Addison saluted. "Yes, Commander Hanna."

When dinner was over, Hanna helped Addison out to the patio. When she returned, Aria was cleaning the table. "We're going to have to be patient with him, Aria."

"Yes, Mrs. Stone—"

"Hanna."

"Yes, Hanna. What Mr. Stone is going through is a terrible tragedy."

One hour later, Hanna guided an unsteady Addison to bed. "Want the TV on?"

"Yes, Love."

When Hanna left, Addison slipped out of bed, entered his study, and retrieved his journal.

I have to get my emotions under control. I

can't let these melancholy moments come over me like that. It's not fair to them, nor me. So now what? Do I wait to learn the cancer has returned? The doctors minced no words when pointing out that the odds of it returning were against me. But here I am, and here I will stay until my last Earthly breath. I am blessed; I have Hanna at my side. If only I could find the words to express how much I love and appreciate her. And yet, words are never enough; actions speak louder. So, Addison, follow the lady's advice, stop the doom and gloom, and put on a happy face. There'll be no feeling sorry for yourself. Be grateful; you've had more than your share of the good life. Got it, Megastar? Yes, sir, got it, sir. And, oh, make sure you tell her you love her each and every day.

Addison was under the covers when Hanna came to bed. Believing he was sleeping, she quietly undressed, got into bed, and laid with her back to him.

Addison rolled over. "Hey."

"Oh, I didn't wake you, did I?"

"No. Am I in the dog house?"

"A little bit. Well, maybe a lot."

"I'm sorry, Love."

Hanna rolled over and faced him. "There'll be no more talk in this house about dying. We have enough to deal with without your reminding us of—"

"I'm sorry, you're right."

"Let's get you into radiation and get on with our lives, one step at a time, one day at a time, making each more memorable than the one before. Now, kiss me, let's get some sleep. And you are not to get up in the middle of the night to visit the bathroom without waking me."

Addison slipped his arms around her. "I was hoping you

would rub my aching back."

Hanna groaned. "Roll over, you spoiled brat."

"And damn proud of it, Madam Stone."

In the morning, Addison sat on the patio, bemoaning that he could not resume his walks with Windy. That job now fell to Hanna or Aria until he proved strong enough to walk down to the water and back on his own.

Hanna called the hospital to set up Addison's radiation treatment, then joined him on the patio. "We have an appointment at ten on Monday morning to meet the Oncologist and schedule your radiation treatments. They told me your treatments are quick, in and out in less than an hour. I'll be your UBER driver."

"And a pretty one you are."

"Oh, sure, you're sucking up because you want a back rub tonight."

"You know me well."

"Windy and I are off for a walk. If you need anything, Aria's just arrived, and JJ is in the guesthouse."

"You mean corporate headquarters."

"If that's what we're calling it now."

"We are."

Although Hanna loved Windy, up until then, there had been little interaction between them; Windy was Addison's dog. But as the days passed, that began to change. With each daily walk, Hanna's affection for Windy grew. Like Addison, she would talk to Windy while they sat on the beach.

JJ showed up one morning while Hanna was walking Windy. "Good morning, Boss." He looked to the beach. "Hanna has really taken to Windy."

"I love watching them together, JJ."

"Yes, it's an inspiring site. I came by to tell you I hired an assistant to work with me on the Lacy Stone Foundation. Her name is Kailani Alama. She's a native Hawaiian born here in Honolulu. Her last name means *arise* or *awakening,* so she tells me. She graduated with a bachelor of arts degree in Communications from the University of Hawaii at Manoa. She's proficient in writing, problem-solving, cultural awareness, and critical thinking, all specialties the Foundation requires. She begins next week. As for Stone Enterprises, I'll handle that with assistance from our accounting and legal firms. As Lang would say, we're off to the races. Speaking of Lang, he and Andy want to visit."

"Not yet, JJ, not yet. Maybe in a few weeks."

JJ patted Addison's shoulder and smiled. "Hang in there, Boss. I'll be in the office if you need me." JJ gazed down to the shore where Hanna and Windy sat, and he beamed. "Now, that's one beautiful picture."

On Kailani Alama's first day on the job, JJ took her to the house and introduced her to Addison. She was a pretty young lady with a slim figure, blond hair, light blue eyes, and a flashing smile.

"I love your music, Mr. Stone. I saw one of your concerts here in Hawaii."

"Thank you, Kailani, and welcome to the team."

"I'm looking forward to it, sir."

Chapter 32

On the appointed day, Addison and Hanna traveled to the hospital. They met with Oncologist Marian Ormsby, who was to oversee Addison's treatments, which were to begin the following week.

"The primary concern with this cancer is a reoccurrence of Glioblastoma," Ormsby explained. "There are relatively few effective treatment options if it does."

Addison responded with a frown. "Doctor Morgan was clear on the point."

"At the first sign that the cancer is returning, we'll begin Temozolomide chemotherapy and continue with the radiation treatments. But, let's cross that bridge if and when it was to occur and hope it does not."

Addison bent his head forward, eyes on the floor; he had heard enough.

"Let's not get ahead of ourselves, Mr. Stone. There is a fifty percent chance the cancer may never return."

Addison lifted himself from his chair. "You'll understand when I say I'm not crazy about those odds." He placed a hand on Hanna's shoulder. "Honey, I'm going to the restroom. I'll meet you in the lobby." He headed for the door.

"Addison?"

"I'll be in the lobby, Hanna."

Hanna waited until Addison was out of the room. "Sorry, Doctor."

"It's normal human behavior, Mrs. Stone. All we can do is try to keep his spirits up."

"Thank you, Doctor. If we're finished here, I better go to him."

"Of course. I'll see you next week for the first treatment."

Hanna caught up with Addison in the Lobby. He looked despondent.

"Hey, are you okay?"

"Hanna, love, please, let's not play games. My chances are slim, and none."

Hanna took a beat before she said, "I thought we agreed no more doom and gloom. I know this will sound callous, but I'm gonna say it anyway. Stop feeling sorry for yourself." Hanna placed a hand on his arm. "You can be thankful for the past, relish each new day, or withdraw into a dark hole. Your choice."

Hanna turned and walked off.

"Hanna!"

She did not answer. During the drive home, neither said a word.

At the beginning of the third week of radiation treatments, Addison was showing signs of depression and occasional bursts of anger and began withdrawing into himself.

One afternoon, while Addison napped, Hanna and JJ met on the patio to discuss Addison's deepening depression.

"The Boss has to understand his system needs his help. Along with the medical, a positive attitude plays a significant role."

"I don't know what to do about it, JJ. He hardly converses with me anymore. He sits out here staring at the Bay for hours or retreats to his study with Windy. Aria says he's hardly spoken to her in several days. And if she says something to him, he just grunts."

"What's the doctor say?"

"She says depression is, unfortunately, normal in these cases. She suggested we seek professional counseling. When I brought it up to Addison, he huffed and left the room. We must find a way to snap him out of his dark moods."

"I want to help, Hanna, but I don't know how."

"Just be there for him; be his friend, JJ. He trusts you; he listens to you."

"Past tense, Hanna, he not listening to any of us. I'll try to spend more time with him."

Following Addison's final radiation treatment, an MRI was taken. Their worst fears were realized; there were signs the cancer cells were returning along with an infection called Subdural Empyema. Dr. Ormsby ordered Temozolomide chemotherapy to begin immediately.

Addison's depression only got worse.

Within weeks of treatments, Addison began to experience dizziness, increased fatigue, mild nausea, headaches, memory loss, and loss of appetite. At times, he appeared confused and unaware of what was happening around him.

"I'm really enjoying the side effects, Hanna. Are there any we might have missed?"

"Well, it's good to see you still have your sense of humor."

Addison chuckled low. "Lose that, and the black hole deepens."

"Ah, so you do listen to me." Hanna took Addison's hand in hers. "This fight is not over, Addison. I know you're going through hell, but concentrate on the good things in your life, like your incredible career and the fans who idolize you."

"Idolize is a pretty strong word, Hanna. It was more like a cult following."

"No, silly, it was your God-given talent. You and your voice reached people's hearts and minds in extraordinary ways. The songs you sang had been sung thousands of times before, but never with the emotion and joy you brought to them. Yes, you have a unique voice, but it was you, the man behind the voice, who brought the heart and soul to each song in a way that audiences responded to."

"You say these nice things because you're married to me."

"Oh, dear, you caught me." Hanna laughed and hugged him. "Okay, I've got some work to do for the gang in New York." She stood and began to leave.

"Hanna."

"Yes, Addison."

"I love you." He blew her a kiss.

"I love you more, Addison."

"I'll wrestle you for the title."

A wry smile crossed her lips. "You'll lose."

Chapter 33

Still sitting and rocking on the patio, Addison continued to hum *Your Love*. His mind was back still trying to wrap his head around how he had made it from the floor of Chick's Diner to here. Like a continuous loop, it played over and over in his head. "Ah, who the hell cares."

He carefully picked up the Entertainer of the Year Award from the end table and placed it on his lap. "I damned well deserve you, and don't you ever forget it."

The end was near for Addison; he knew it; he could feel it. He glanced down to the beach to where Hanna was walking Windy. He dared not share these dark feelings with her.

A young lady appeared on the lawn to his right.

"Good morning, Mr. Stone."

It was JJ's assistant, Kailani Alama.

"Hi, Kailani. What are you up to?"

"JJ asked me to check on you."

"Did he now? Come, sit with me."

Kailani entered through the screen door and took a seat next to Addison. She pointed to the award in his lap. "Congratulations on winning that awesome award."

"Thank you. I've won a few, but this one is special." Addison pointed to Hanna and Windy on the beach. "Is that a beautiful sight or what?"

"Yes, sir, it is. I make a great dog walker if Mrs. Stone is too busy one day."

"That's kind of you, and please stop calling me Mr. Stone. It took me years to get JJ to stop. You know I was named after my hometown?"

"Yes."

"Growing up, my nickname was Addy. I preferred it, but no one calls me that anymore. Go ahead, say it."

"Okay, Addy."

"Good. Enjoying the job?"

"Oh, my, yes. I research organizations dealing with child abuse and adult drug addiction. Once I verify their qualifications, I pass the names on to JJ. He makes the final decisions and arranges for them to receive a donation from the Foundation. Knowing how well the Foundation is doing for so many is rewarding work."

"How old are you, Kailani?"

"The grand old age of twenty-six."

"Is there a man in your life? Sorry, I don't mean to get personal."

"Not at all. And yes, his name is Brad. He's a lawyer. We've been together for a year, and I think he's ready to propose."

"And your answer will be?"

"Yes. I love the man and want to spend my life with him."

"Good for you. I wish you both great happiness."

"Thank you, Mr.—I mean, *Addy*."

Addison fell silent and gazed down to the Bay where Hanna sat with Windy. He could see her talking to Windy like he used to when he and Windy sat in that same spot. Talking to Windy proved cathartic for Addison; his way of dealing with the memories of the past that still lingered.

"Mind if I give you a bit of advice, Kailani?"

"Fire away."

"Fame and fortune came to me fast and furious at a young age, and I was ill-prepared to deal with it. To tell you the truth, I was scared as hell. Money, fame, and fan adulation came faster and faster. People waited on me hand and foot. The fans and the press shadowed me everywhere. You can't imagine the effect that had on me at that age. As my popularity and bank account grew, I began to see and live my life through rose-colored glasses. I became fearless when before I lived in fear." Addison paused, his eyes drifting again to Hanna and Windy on the beach. "I'm not proud of many things I did, but I hope I've learned from them. Now, none of it matters. Have you thought about how you'll spend the time you're given?"

"Yes and no. I don't dwell on it as much as I should, I suppose."

Addison reflected for a beat. "At your age, it's all about living in the moment, day to day, anticipating the next. But, one day, when the Grim Reaper is licking at your heels, you—"

Kailani tossed her head back and laughed. "The Grim Reaper?"

"Yeah. That's when you begin reflecting on your life, especially those you shared it with. Ultimately, all that counts are those you loved and loved you back—even that dog out there."

"In today's world," Kailani said, "we're forced to live in the fast lane, building careers and seeking advancements that bring us more money and more stuff, none of which ensures happiness. I think people only care about whatever diverts their attention, especially technology. I'm sorry to say, at times, that includes me."

"Smart girl that you recognize that, Kailani. We've been sucked into fast-moving technology like it was a religion. So, to get back to my advice, when you marry Brad, cherish him, build your life around him, and if he's smart—"

"He is."

"Then he'll build his life around you. Bonded together, you'll decide what you really want out of this life. If you do, you will win and achieve the happiness we seek. One last thought.

Only one thing in life is truly free. Everything else comes with a cost." He tapped at his temple, "It's in here. We control it; no one else does or should try. The only question is how we will use it. Will we let others influence us, or will we stand fast as the sole master of our brain, making our own decisions and not those who try to change us against our will?"

"I agree.

"Do you know who Morgan Freeman is?"

"Yes, he's a wonderful actor."

"In all his wisdom, Mr. Freeman said… *There are only two days in the year that nothing can be done. One is called yesterday, and the other is called tomorrow, so today is the right day to love, believe, do, and mostly live.* Enough of my sanctimonious pontificating. I sound like a reformed addict.

"Are you?" Kailani asked.

Addison looked away and thought. "Let just say not from alcohol or drugs."

Kailani stood. "Well, unless you need anything, *Addy*, I better get to work."

Addison smiled and patted her hand. "Go give some of our money away. Feel free to visit anytime."

"Thank you. If you don't mind, I'll leave you with a poem I read recently titled *Hugs, Love, and Great Karma* by Cindy Smith. The last line goes like this. *You can look at your life as a challenge, a test, or an amusement park and pick the best rides.*"

"That's beautiful, Kailani."

"Google it. I think you'll enjoy reading the whole poem."

"Thank you, Kailani, I will."

Then, like a wisp of wind, Kailani was gone.

Addison rocked and watched Hanna and Windy climb the lawn back to the house. When Hanna opened the screen door, Windy went to Addison and nuzzled his right foot.

Addison patted him. "Been behaving yourself?"

Windy growled low.

"I'll take that as a yes."

"Addison, was that Kailani I saw leaving?"

"JJ-sent-her-to check-on me." With no warning, Addison began stammering and appeared to have trouble composing a sentence.

"Addison, love, are you okay?"

"Y-y-yeah, fine."

"You're—"

"Yes. It's my damn studder that comes back to haunt me once in a while."

"Aria and I are going grocery shopping. I'm leaving you in charge of Quasimodo here. JJ will come to check on you."

"Yeah, *o-o*, okay."

"If you decide to lie down, call JJ or Kailani to assist you. See you when we get back."

Hanna hugged and kissed him and left.

"Now, Mr. Quasimodo,' Addison said to Windy, "be nice and let me close my eyes for a while. You think you can do that?"

Windy whined low.

"I'll take that as a yes." Addison closed his eyes, slowly rocking back and forth, humming *Your Love* for several minutes before falling asleep.

He wasn't sure how much time had passed when he opened his eyes again. JJ was sitting next to him. *"H-h,* how long have you… how long have you been here?"

"About ten minutes."

"What time is it?

"Ten forty-five."

"Whoa, *I-I,* I slept for over… for over an hour."

Addison was now slurring; JJ was having trouble understanding him.

"You're slurring, Addison."

"Yeah, *I-I,* I am?"

"I'll assist you to your bedroom if you want to lie down."

"*N-n,* no. In the bedroom, *I-I* see four walls. Here, I see the world. Where's Hanna?"

"Hanna and Aria went shopping."

"Oh, yeah, I forgot. *I-I'*, I'll wait for them *h-h*, here."

"I'll stay with you."

"No need, JJ."

JJ heard a vehicle coming up the driveway. "That would be the ladies returning now. I'll help them with the packages. Be back in a flash."

Several minutes after JJ left, Addison was struck with a sharp pain where the surgery took place. His hand went to it. "Damn it, damn it all to hell!"

"Who are you damning now?"

Addison turned—Hanna was standing by the door. "Everyone and anything, *L-l*, Love."

When Hanna reached Addison's side, she noticed his face was grayish. "You look pale." She placed the back of her right hand on his forehead. "And you're warm. Are you in pain again?"

"Ah, a little *b-b*, bit."

Come on, Megastar, let's get you to bed."

"Stay here *w-w*, with me." He was barely audible.

"Okay, for a few minutes, then it's to bed for you."

Hanna sat next to him and took his hand. Addison squeezed it. "Shopping go *o-o*, okay?"

"We bought lots of food."

"*G-g*, good."

Hanna squeezed his hand. "Love you, Addison."

"*I-l*, love you *m-m* more, Hanna."

Hanna smiled. "And I love you forever. Does that count for more?"

Addison's lips curled into a grin. "*M-m-m*, maybe."

Addison closed his eyes. Hanna closed hers. A few minutes later, they had both dosed off.

They had been sleeping for about seven or eight minutes when Addison's spine stiffened, his head snapped back a couple of inches, and his eyes shot open wide. His breathing quickened for several seconds, then began to slow.

Windy's head came up, and his eyes went to his master. Addison sucked in a long hard breath through his nose and held it momentarily before it seeped out like a deflating balloon. His right hand, still wrapped in Hanna, went slack.

Windy stood, rubbed his nose on Addison's leg, and whined, waking Hanna. Windy whined and bumped Addison's leg forcefully with his head.

Hanna's eyes went from Windy to Addison's face. "Addison?"

Addison's eyes remained open, but he was motionless.

"Addison!" Hanna placed her hand on his chest; he wasn't breathing.

"Oh, dear God!" Hanna cried. Her hand went to his neck—she could not detect a pulse. "Addison! Addison!" She began to cry and flung her arms around him. "Addison, my sweet Addison, please don't, please don't leave me! You are my soul, my reason for living. She tightened her arms around Addison and kissed his face.

JJ appeared at the door. He smiled, thinking they were playing around. "Hey, you two, find a room," he joked. "I just came over to—"

Hanna's head spun to JJ. "Addison's stopped breathing!"

"What?" JJ raced across the patio and checked for Addison's pulse, first Addison's wrist, then his neck. "I can't detect a pulse!" He dug in his pocket for his phone. "I'll call for help. We'll lay him on the floor and give him CPR until the medics get here."

JJ began to dial 911. Hanna reached up and placed her hand over JJ's phone. "No, JJ, wait!".

"For what, Hanna? The sooner we get help, the better chance he has."

"No, JJ, no! Even if they did revive him, his living hell will continue."

"What are you saying, Hanna!

"He's suffered enough. Let him go; let him rest now."

"Hanna—"

"Please, JJ, it's over."

JJ hesitated; his eyes began to tear. "I pray we're doing the right thing, Hanna."

"We are, JJ, we are."

Addison's left hand was still wrapped around the award in his lap. JJ reached for it.

"No, leave it there."

Ten minutes later, an ambulance arrived. The commotion drew the attention of Aria and Lailani, who rushed to the patio and watched in horror as the paramedics performed CPR on Addison but were unable to revive him. They quickly loaded Addison in the ambulance and rushed him to the hospital ER, where he was pronounced dead. The cause of death was a massive heart attack.

At Hanna's request, the first call JJ made was to Stan and Sally. They said they would be there as soon as they could book a flight.

That night, the house was a place of mourning, spent with JJ and Aria comforting Hanna.

JJ waited until early morning to break the news to Lang. He authorized the agency to release to the media the news that Addison Stone had passed away. Within minutes, the news flashed across the world. Within an hour, Addison's social media sites crashed with fan condolences. In the following days, thousands of sympathy cards were received in Honolulu addressed simply to *Addison Stone*.

Chapter 34

It was early morning. The sun was up, and the sky was bright blue. It was a perfect day in Hawaii.

Hanna, JJ, and Windy were sitting on the patio. Aria brought out a fresh pot of coffee.

"Thank you, Aria. Please, join us."

"Thank you, Mrs. Stone. Don't mind if I do."

They sat quietly, staring out at the Bay for several moments.

Hanna finally said, "I have decisions to make, and I'm in no mental state to make them."

"Let us help, Hanna," JJ said.

"To begin with, Lang suggested a formal public funeral to celebrate Addison's life. He went so far as to suggest Addison be buried beneath a monument in a Hawaiian cemetery like some shrine people pilgrimage to. I'll have none of that. His public life is over. I want this to be simple, personal, and private."

"If that is what you want, Hanna," JJ said, "Then that's what you should do."

"I will have Addison cremated without fanfare. This is about us, his family, not his fans or celebrity. Am I being selfish?"

"Not at all, Mrs. Stone," Aria said.

"Thank you both for your devotion to Addison and me through this painful time."

"We're here for you, Hanna, JJ said.

"Thank you, Aria, thank you, JJ."

Three days later, before Addison's cremation, Hanna, JJ, Aria, Stan, Sally, and Kailani gathered in the funeral home chapel. Hanna had requested an open casket while they said their goodbyes.

She laid a hand on Addison's crossed hands.

"Goodbye, my love. You will be in my heart forever." Leaning into the casket, she kissed Addison's forehead.

Hanna instructed the funeral director to provide two small black boxes of Addison's ashes: one for JJ and one for Aria. Hanna's was in a gold urn.

In the days that followed, Hanna fell into a deep depression. She walked the house aimlessly, would sit on the bed crying and caressing Addison's pillow, sat on the beach with Windy for extended periods, and sat alone on the patio rocking in Addison's chair.

JJ and Aria tried to console her, but Hanna wanted to be left alone with her bereavement.

A month passed, and Hanna's depression deepened. JJ tried to help, but nothing worked; Hanna had to do this herself. That meant making decisions about the future.

One day, after her walk with Windy, she called and asked JJ to join her on the patio.

"Of all the beautiful places in this house, this was Addison's favorite spot, JJ."

"We always knew where to find him and Windy."

"JJ, I've decided to return to work in New York."

"Oh, for how long?"

"Permanently. I can't remain here; there are too many memories. Everywhere I go in the house, I feel Addison's presence."

"What about the estate?"

"That's what I called you to discuss. Addison's assets were left to me, with an addendum that you receive ten percent of the selling price if I sold the property."

"Hanna, that's not necessary."

"That was Addison's wish, and I will honor it. No one was closer to Addison than you, JJ. You were his older, wiser brother; no words can express my gratitude. Now to business. Instead of selling the property, I will donate it to the Lacy Jane Foundation to be an on-site drug addiction counseling center."

"I think that's a wonderful idea, Hanna. Count my ten percent in."

"That's what I thought you'd say. Now, we'll reconfigure the big meeting room on the second floor into more bedrooms, divide the living room into two meeting rooms, and remodel the guest house to accommodate additional Foundation staff. That is if you plan on staying on."

"Yes, I'm staying."

"Then you'll remain on as the Foundation's director?"

"If you'll have me, yes, of course. I think Kailani would make a great assistant director."

"I agree. Beyond that, I know nothing about running a rehabilitation center. That'll be your area."

"And Aria?"

"I hope she'll stay on."

"Then we have a plan, Hanna."

"I'll stay until everything is accomplished, then I'm moving back to New York to resume running my company. Plan on me visiting a couple of times a year."

"I'll hold you to that, Hanna."

"I think I'm ready now to clean out Addison's belongings. There are lots of clothes we can donate."

Hanna got busy cleaning Addison's closet and study. While cleaning out his desk, she found his journal hidden under some papers in the bottom right drawer. She had no idea Addison even kept a journal. She opened it and briefly read a couple of the entries before flipping through the pages quickly until she came to the last entry and began to read.

Today, it's all about random thoughts rattling through my brain. Like most, my life's confluence has sometimes caused me to walk barefoot over hot coals. Do I have regrets? Hell, yes. Since I can't go back and correct them, I live with their memories. Sometimes, when I was guilty of doing something I should not have, I would stare in the mirror, not recognizing the image staring back. That was the alarm; that was usually the wake-up call to get back on track.

Only now, with the time I have left, do I understand what a small role I played in the human experience. I loathe that history will define me by my celebrity—if I am remembered at all. It was about the journey—or should have been—not the fame, money, or fan adulation but the journey itself.

I spent many hours trying to understand the human condition during my early years. No doubt, my mother had a significant influence on me when it came to that subject. As a child, it was a challenge—dare I say confusing—trying to come to grips with her erratic, bizarre, sometimes borderline violent actions. It was a painful journey for her. She struggled and suffered. I should have been there for her more than I was.

Dare I say that some of us learn late in life that something besides ourselves has to be served, or our lives remain unfulfilled. That something is the true love we share with others and protect, a test I failed early on. The day Hanna showed up on my doorstep and reaffirmed her love for me was true, deep, personal love, not to be denied. Hanna made me whole again, and I pray I've done the same for her.

Strange as it may sound to some, if I could go back and change anything, I wouldn't because it was all about the journey, built upon the decision I alone made. Stand on one foot and repeat: That was my journey, and no one else but me is responsible if the journey traveled a crooked road from time to time. Uttering the words Would-a, Could-a, Should-a is a copout. It took this late bloomer a while to come to that admission.

Onward and upward, world. Think before acting, and enjoy the journey. It's been a great ride—most of the time, anyway. Okay, that's it, it's showtime, folks.

Hanna closed the journal and wept. She called JJ in his office next door and asked him to meet her on the patio. A few minutes later, he arrived.

"Good morning, Hanna."

"Good morning. Coffee?"

"No, thanks. I've had three cups. What's up?"

"Sit, be comfortable."

JJ sat in the chair next to her. She handed Addison's journal to him.

"What this?"

"Addison's journal."

"I didn't know he had one."

"Neither did I. I found it in his desk hidden under some papers. I want you to have it."

"Oh, no, Hanna, I couldn't."

"I spent the last hour reading the journal's contents. Much of it was written during the years you spent with Addison. I want you to have it."

"But, Hanna, I—"

"Really, JJ, consider this my gift to thank you for all the

years of loyalty and guidance to Addison."

"I don't know what to say besides thank you."

"Ah, there's a method to my madness. Would you consider turning it into a book, adding your thoughts and observations?"

"I wouldn't know where to begin, Hanna."

"You could hire a book editor to help you shape it."

"Hanna, whatever he wrote in his diary must be pretty personal."

"It is, and that's what makes it unique. If you decide to take it on, leave nothing out, warts and all."

"You're sure of that."

"There's a message in the book that I believe must be shared."

"Well, I'll give it some thought."

"That's all I asked, JJ."

JJ stood, took Hanna's hand, lifted her to her feet, put his arms around her, and held her close.

Three months later, with the house remodeling completed, the Addison Jordon Stone Rehabilitation Center was opened with great fanfare. Hanna commissioned a life-sized bronze statue of Addison with Windy by his side. It was erected on the lawn just beyond the pool, overlooking Addison's favorite spot on the beach. His arms were extended with his palms up in a welcoming gesture.

The inscription on the base read *Addison Jordon Stone, Entertainer and Humanitarian.*

The memory of Addison Jordon Stone, one of the most beloved entertainers of his time, would live on for all time.

On the official ribbon-cutting day, several hundred, mostly Honolulu residents, gathered on the lawn before Addison's statue. The town of Addison, Alabama, sent a large floral wreath that hung on an easel next to Addison's statue. Stan, Sally, Lang, Andy, Ty, Ivey, Millie Andrews, and the Noble Street Singers were in attendance. The Mayor of Honolulu hosted the event, which was covered live and broadcast worldwide.

On the day Hanna was to return to New York, she stood on the patio with JJ and Aria. JJ had assumed he would drive her to the airport, but Hanna declined, preferring to say goodbye at the house.

"Returning to New York will be good therapy for me. But I leave with a heavy heart and deep sadness; you are my family; I will miss seeing you every day." She glanced at Windy sitting nearby. "And that goes for you, too, Buster. You're not getting rid of me by any means. I'll be back for visits as often as I can get away. Between visits, we'll Zoom a couple of times a month."

"We'll hold you to that, Mrs. Stone," Aria said.

"Please, Aria, families call each other by their first names."

Aria smiled. "Yes, of course, Hanna."

"Kailani, in addition to your many daily duties, your job is to keep JJ out of trouble."

Kailani grinned. "I'll try, Hanna, but I make no promises. As you know, he can be a handful."

A car pulled up to the house, and the horn blew.

"That would be my ride. Let's hope my belongings make it to New York and not some city in Europe."

Hanna hugged, kissed them, walked to the door, and stopped. With a Cheshire grin, she turned back and said, "Please keep the pigeons off Addison's statue."

Then, like a wisp of wind, Hanna was gone.

Hanna's documentary of Addison's life was not destined to remain on a dusty shelf. Six months following Addison's death, PBS broadcast a one-hour tribute to his life, supplemented by on-camera interviews with Hanna, JJ, Aria, Lang, Andy, Kailani, and Millie Andrews.

In conjunction with the PBS broadcast, JJ, with the help of a professional book editor, published a semi-memoir based on Addison's journal titled. It was titled:

—*Well, I'll Be Damned!* —

The Life and Times of Addison Jordon Stone in his own words.

Commentary by Jonathan James.

The book included the guest interviews from the PBS documentary. As expected, **Well I'll be Damned** remained on the best-seller list for six months.

ABOUT THE AUTHOR

ROBERT J. EMERY
WRITER-PRODUCER-DIRECTOR-AUTHOR

Email: media8@verizon.net
website: www.robertjemeryauthor.com
Facebook: https://www.facebook.com/rjemery/
Twitter: @bobemery

Current member of:
The Directors Guild of America
The Authors Guild
The Alliance of Independent Authors

Other novels by Robert J. Emery under the pen name R.J. Eastwood
Midnight Black, a suspense/thriller Novel
The Autopsy of Planet Earth, a science fiction adventure
Mr. Emery has written nine books: three novels and six nonfiction.

Over his four-decade career, Robert J. Emery has written, produced, and directed projects ranging from local and national television commercials to corporate communications films, writing and directing feature motion pictures (eight in all), and numerous network television documentaries.

Mr. Emery's interest in production and entertainment began with the Armed Forces Radio and Television Air Force on Guam, where he was stationed. Upon discharge, he became an on-air personality and news reporter at WCLW Radio in Mansfield, Ohio. Deciding radio was not what he wanted to do, he opened an advertising agency in Canton, Ohio, which led to writing and directing local TV commercials. He created, produced, and directed a daily one-hour morning TV talk show hosted by former Miss USA Diana Batts and TV personality Carl Day. In 1965, he wrote and directed his first feature film, *The Bittersweet Night*, followed by *Willy & Scratch, Dare the Devil, Scream Bloody Murder, Sign of Aquarius, Ride in a Pink Car, The Florida Connection,* and his last, *Swimming Upstream* for the Lifetime Television Movie Channel. That film was awarded the *Sapphire Halo Award for Best Dramatic Motion Picture* at the Los Angeles Angel City Film Festival.

As writer, producer, and director, Mr. Emery's television productions include the MSNBC primetime documentary *"For God & Country: A Marine Snipers Story,"* hosted by NBC's Lester Holt. The program won the *National Headliner Award for Best Documentary or Series of Reports* and the *Special Jury Award* in the Professional News Division (CINE Golden Eagle Competitions) informational category. He created the Starz/Encore series *The Directors (91-hour episodes),* which also ran in re-runs on the Reelz Channel and over 75 countries worldwide. *The Directors* won the Silver Plaque Award in the 2002 Chicago International Television Competition and the Award of Excellence 2003 Accolade Awards. The episode featuring George Lucas won First Place at the Florida Motion Picture & Television Association Awards for best television series episode. That was followed by the four-hour PBS mini-series *The Genocide Factor,* hosted by Academy Award© winner Jon Voight. The production won the *Houston International Worldfest Gold Special Jury Award for Best Television & Cable TV Series/Documentary.* He produced and directed *KidHealth,"* a 13-episode PBS series on children's healthcare in America hosted by Olympic Gold Medalist Peggy Fleming. Produced and directed *Golden Saddles, Silver Spurs - the History of Western Cinema* for the Starz/Encore Western Channel.

Mr. Emery received top honors for nine years at the New York Film Festival for his numerous productions for Shriners Hospital for Children.

In 2006, Mr. Emery retired from active production. He began work on his first novel, *In the Realm of Eden,* published in January 2010. The Next Generation Indie Book Awards Competition selected the novel as one of the top five finalists.

Mr. Emery was born and raised in Bristol, Rhode Island. He currently resides with his wife and family in Florida. When not writing or working on a project around the house, Mr. Emery can be found in the kitchen fixing great Italian meals thanks to the teachings of his Italian mother and to the delight of his wife, children, grandchildren, and friends.